NO MAN'S LAND

NO

A NOVEL

MAN'S

JOHN VIGNA

LAND

ARSENAL PULP PRESS
VANCOUVER

NO MAN'S LAND
Copyright © 2021 by John Vigna

ARSENAL PULP PRESS
Suite 202 – 211 East Georgia St.
Vancouver, BC V6A 1Z6
Canada
arsenalpulp.com

The publisher gratefully acknowledges the support of the Canada Council for the Arts and the British Columbia Arts Council for its publishing program, and the Government of Canada, and the Government of British Columbia (through the Book Publishing Tax Credit Program), for its publishing activities.

Arsenal Pulp Press acknowledges the xʷməθkʷəy̓əm (Musqueam), Sḵwx̱wú7mesh (Squamish) and səl̓ilwətaʔɬ (Tsleil-Waututh) Nations, custodians of the traditional, ancestral and unceded territories where our office is located. We pay respect to their histories, traditions and continuous living cultures and commit to accountability, respectful relations and friendship.

This is a work of fiction. Any resemblance of characters to persons either living or deceased is purely coincidental.

Cover and text design by Jazmin Welch
Front cover photo by Takahiro Sakamoto via Unsplash
Back cover photo by Dane Deaner via Unsplash
Edited by Brian Lam
Copy edited by Linda Pruessen
Proofread by Alison Strobel

Printed and bound in Canada

Library and Archives Canada Cataloguing in Publication:
Title: No man's land : a novel / John Vigna.
Names: Vigna, John, 1965– author.
Identifiers: Canadiana (print) 20210212578 | Canadiana (ebook) 20210212586 |
    ISBN 9781551528663 (softcover) | ISBN 9781551528670 (HTML)
Classification: LCC PS8643.I3565 N62 2021 | DDC C813/.6—dc23

And I brought you into a plentiful country, to eat the fruit thereof and the goodness thereof; but when ye entered, ye defiled my land, and made mine heritage an abomination.
—JEREMIAH 2:7

He had a word, too. Love, he called it. But I had been used to words for a long time. I knew that that word was like those others: just a shape to fill a lack; that when the right time came, you wouldn't need a word for that anymore …
—WILLIAM FAULKNER, *AS I LAY DYING*

"Let your light shine before men; that they may see your good works and glorify your Father who is in heaven." He said it meant that when you did a good thing it should seem to come from God, not from you. It should not feel to other people like your goodness, and it should not feel that way to you either. Any good thing is less good the more any human lays claim.
—MARILYNNE ROBINSON, *LILA*

In memory of my brother Paul—an old soul

IN THE BEGINNING, a land without form.

One of those arctic fronts blasted down from the high north, the back of god almighty's hand, slapped the land low. Buckled and broke the frozen casing of the world, carved it into wild pieces flung into the shadows of nunataks. Great glaciers bulldozed enormous tracts of rock and rubble across the plate of the earth. The sinew of continents snapped and drifted apart. The Cordilleran Ice Sheet clenched the land with a tight fist and briny water seeped out, drowning all features until it receded, suturing terrane to cracked crust. It sliced deep river valleys and shady inlets, scooped out bottomless lakes, and lay heavy and immense on the coastal plains. Welded limestone, dolomite and shale into jagged peaks, where a convoluted artery of rivers spilled from the lakes, and here the River Stag sprung loose like a band of molten lead, sluicing a path across the desolate valley.

Fireballs hurtled across the dark sky. Perseids and Lyrids showered the earth in a dazzling display of light. Second coming of christ. Seasons pass, marked by the Leonids and Quadrantids, the Taurids and Andromedids, scraping and slashing the fabric of the world above, dumping smashed fragments and dust on the planet below. Aurora borealis. Tears of Saint Lawrence. Oh heavenly presence, lead us not into temptation, but deliver us from evil.

Mint, common cattail and white angelica burst forth from loamy soil along the riverbanks. As though in prayer, aspen, birch, cottonwood, brushy alder and willow leaned over the roaring water. Farther inland, brilliant spurts of sky-blue lupine, wild-pink geranium, charity, twinflower, pink pyrola and bunchberry. Kinnikinnick carpeted the dark woods and stony slopes; glacier lily clawed its way to the timberline. Yellow bell, pearly and rosy everlasting. Rocky Mountain grape burst into scraggy blotches. High in the alpine, snow willows, bluebell and cinquefoil eked out a hardscrabble existence.

Here come the ungulates, the cloven-footed beasts. Bison and elk, moose and deer, wolves and coyotes, black and brown bears, humpbacked silvertip grizzlies. Bighorn rams, pikas, rock rabbits, blue-ruffled Franklin's grouse. Spotted-tail hawks, golden eagles, magpies and whisky jacks circled the skies, lowered their beaks and cut ribbons into the wind. In the cold rivers, Yellowstone cutthroat, Dolly Varden, rainbow, Eastern brook, Rocky Mountain whitefish, burbot, squawfish, suckers, steelhead and salmon swam downstream in the spring, and lunged upstream in the fall, wasted, wimpled wrecks. The wonder of it all. As it was in the beginning and would be in the end.

Here come the First Peoples. The Clovis culture snatch granite, feldspar, quartz and flintstone from the rocky ground and craft them into simple, blunt weapons for hunting. The Old Cordilleran people carve spear points of obsidian and basalt while the Agate Basin trap animals. Weapons precede hostilities. The Mummy Cave culture settle on the plains and construct atlatls to sling rocks at their enemies. The McKean culture oust the original peoples but not the Mummy Cave people. Their ingenuity to create atlatls and adapt to life on the plains ensures their survival. The Pelican Lake people reach Crowsnest and establish summer hunting camps for sheep, deer, bison, elk. They build stone weirs, nets and fish traps, and trawl whitefish and suckers, trap beaver, rabbits, squirrels. Then the Besant advance and seize the plains, avoiding the shadows of the mountains until the Plains Natives come and then the Avonlea, who alter the rules of the land and bring the bow and arrow, pound out sharp stone tools.

The Ktunaxa travel back and forth between the plains and mountains. They fish in early spring and the women collect root vegetables; in mid-June the men journey onto the plains and track bison. Summers are spent hunting and berry picking and they go bison hunting again in September. The Blackfoot, direct descendants of the Besant, chase them all out of the foothills.

Here come the Europeans, sallow-skinned men from far-flung countries who kill, torture, rape, and enslave the First Peoples. They bring their strange tongues, weapons, tools, diseases, and ties to their homelands as they violently seize and occupy and plunder the new land, enforce assimilation, claim the land as their own, bend it to their will. They stake, settle, build, control.

Now, on the crest of Crowsnest Pass, a father and his son, explorers from England, wipe their frozen eyelashes and suck ice out of their tin cups, the skin from their lips torn and stuck on the rim, blow on their fingertips to keep warm, survey the valley below. Sawtoothed ridges. Forests with timber stands too dense to welcome sunshine. A jade-coloured lake, the origin of the Stag, as if a great tear had been shed by the maker themself. The wind roars in their ears, screaming a warning to return home and live out their days quietly, track the seasons, take only what they need to survive another year. A choice. This is how a lifetime might pass.

BOOK
ONE

1887

ONE

FOR THREE DAYS, an arctic northerner whipped the bison up from the shrubby plains over the Pass. The way through the mountains. They came wandering in frozen black clumps, their immense heads clotted with ice, hocks bloodied from punching the snow's hard crust, a trail of faint blood that would lead the hunters to them. The bison clustered around the lake, snorting steam from their clammy nostrils. Cold fog rose off the Stag, a thin ribbon that trickled west. The land blanched, smoking.

Will leaned over his horse and called to his father who lifted himself as if waking from a deep sleep. During the squall they had followed the river, hacking at primordial stalks of devil's club, the prickly spines impeding their passage. His father coughed and wheezed as sleet turned to snow. Tail end of day cinched taut. The old man reached into his breast pocket, unfolded a worn piece of parchment and studied the map. They were a few days away from the coalfields if they kept a westerly course and chased the Stag. He pointed toward an adjacent ridge, folded the map and tucked it back into his cape.

Will clucked into his horse's ear and rode on. The trail meandered between pine and fir trunks where bison hair clung in tufts, until the path vanished into the throat of the fog.

A black wolf loped along the path like an apparition and halted. Tall and lean, tilting its head as if trying to behold the contents of Will's soul. Will's horse jerked its long neck and Will spoke into its ear, ran his hand along its warm face and the horse quieted. The wolf cocked its head again, shifted its back leg. Will pulled a rifle from his scabbard. The wolf sniffed the air, lifted a leg and urinated before it turned and trotted into the woods.

Will jabbed a knuckle into the corner of his eyes, closed them tight and wiped his hand on his sleeve. He slid the gun back into the scabbard and squinted at his father slouched over his horse.

"Up ahead," Will said. "In that saddle."

He snapped the reins and kicked his horse up the slope.

———————————

Will stoked the fire. Wolves howled in the valley below. His father was a colonel by rank; his people were explorers and pioneers of the land but in truth, he was an indisposed company man, employed by Her Majesty's government, surveying his way west with Will after he deserted wife and homeland to find fortune in a land that was more foreign and unforgiving than advertised.

His father lay next to the fire shivering, wrestled with a buffalo hide, pulled it toward his chin and muttered, "Gimme yours."

Will shut his eyes. Thin screech of a raven, its feathers spread apart, scratched the low branches. Shower of snow. He snatched a fistful of dirt. There was a rage, a grief in it. A people, a land that was not his own, a father who was a tyrant and traitor. He dug his fingers into the dark soil and clawed at it, as if he might tear the world apart, lifted it to his nose, inhaled and flung it away where it lay black against the snow. He chewed the inside of his cheek. Tang of rust. Scraped a sleeve across his face. "I'll relieve you of that map now."

His father raised himself, let out a small groan and lumbered toward Will, weighted as if the snow tumbling on his shoulders sagged with the burden of all his years. He slumped down next to Will and coughed. "Son, you got too much hot blood pumping through you, like a frightened little weasel." He let out a long breath. "Cool yourself. Put another stick on the fire."

The old man followed the sound of his son in the dark woods, removed the map from his breast pocket, crumpled it and tossed it into the fire where it curled in the flames. Will returned with an armful of branches and a splintered log. He placed a branch on the flames; the damp wood hissed, smoke thickened. He faced his father. Firelight in his black eyes. His father let out a low sigh and seized Will's arm, pulled him closer, his fingers digging into Will's flesh. The old man's mouth smelled of rot and his grip was weak. He glanced at the chunk of wood in Will's hand and let go of him. "You'll carve a life of misery. No action stands on its own accord. It echoes across your path and the path of other men."

"The map," Will said.

His father coughed. Snow fell fat and wet. He wiped his face and cleared the phlegm from his throat, spat into the fire. "You don't know the decisions you make when you're making them. The world remembers all you've turned your back on."

"Like your family?"

"I did what was best for all of us."

"You did what was best for you."

"I did what was best for all of us, son."

Will picked up a log and held it against his palm.

"I'm asking for the last time. The map."

The old man studied his son.

"What?" Will said. "You at least owe me that."

His father stared off into the darkness, closed his eyes and when he opened them he looked at his son. "You're fulfilling your fate. It just makes me sad is all."

"What fate?"

The old man gestured to the log Will gripped. He let out a long breath. "When you were born, not yet an hour old, my father pointed at your hands and said, 'Watch this boy, he's got the hands of a thief.'"

Will shifted the log in his hand and spat. "What in god's name are you saying?"

The old man coughed. He cleared his throat and spat. "He condemned you."

"That ain't right. I was only alive for an hour."

His father nodded.

"Why didn't you stand up for me?" Will said.

"What do you think I've been doing all these years? Why do you think I brought you here?"

Will shifted the log in his hand. "You're lying."

"You were broken from the beginning. My father saw it." The old man paused and shook his head sadly. "Your mother saw it. And I saw it."

Will clenched his jaw. "You haven't protected me. I've been fending for myself, alone."

His father shook his head, closed his eyes and mumbled, "Our Father, who art in heaven, hallowed be thy name—"

"I know about what you did. Back at the Pass, with all of those travellers," Will said.

"You know what?"

"I saw you. I saw you with them and I heard what that old man said to you." Will cleared his throat and spat. "I wasn't broken. You broke me."

"You broke yourself."

Will clenched his teeth and let out a loud yell.

The fire popped behind them. His father opened his eyes and met Will's stare. "The map's gone, son."

"Stop lying for once."

Will smashed the log down on his father's head. There was a dull crack and then silence. His father's mouth tightened into a grimace but there was something else at the corner of it. Resignation, as if he had always known this was his fate. The old man gasped, struggled to raise himself and staggered toward his horse. He fell to his knees.

Will began to weep. "Where are you going?"

His father did not reply.

"Where in god's name are you going?" Will blubbered, sucking air as he punched out the words.

His father wheezed. He held up a hand to his head, swept a shock of hair from his forehead, studied the blood on his palm, folded over himself and sank to the ground.

Snow shrieked beneath Will's feet. His father lay on his side, labouring in long uneven breaths; blood welled around his head and seeped into the snow. He opened his mouth slowly as if each moment cost him his entire life's effort.

"You don't know what you're doing." His father's words came out in a weak whisper. He swallowed, his Adam's apple slid under his skin, shiny with sweat and blood. He gazed out over the land below them. The Stag lay in the dark, coiled like a rope chasing the valley bottom, twisting and meandering west before it flushed open on the west coast, a month's ride away. The wind had picked up and snow funnelled in whorls around them.

The horses stirred at the edge of camp. His father clutched at the dirt and snow, a trickle of blood ran down over his eyes. He leaned on his elbow to raise himself. His eyes shot open and his face went slack. Dirt dribbled out of his hand onto the ground. He slumped over and lay on his side.

Will bent down and placed a hand on his father's head; his eyes stared at the dirt.

Wolves cried down valley. Will dug into his father's pockets. Ripped off his father's cape and turned out the pockets and ransacked his wool pants and rifled through them again. He turned his father over with his boot, examined his limp body and the ground nearby.

"That map was my birthright." He slapped his father's body and swore.

Snow blew horizontally, slanting in hard, sharp bits. Will wrapped his father's cape around him, piled more wood on the fire, scaffolded it in layers until it burned bright and hot, an obscene extravagance from the land itself. He dragged his father to the fire, lifted and dumped him over the flames. The logs collapsed beneath the weight of the man. A rash of embers sputtered in the air. His father's garments smoked and burst into flames and then his skin rippled and burned, sizzling in the flames.

Will muttered, "In the sweat of thy face shalt thou eat bread, till thou return unto the ground; for out of it wast thou taken: for dust thou art, and unto dust shalt thou return."

The smoke stung his eyes, and he coughed. A terrible force lifted up and pushed him back. Like his father's body might shift, put weight on an elbow and prop himself, brush off the ashes and slap him. The old man's arms contracted over his chest, fists balled like he was prepared to fight. His body jerked and twisted.

Will tossed a blanket over the old man and sat upwind from the flames to avoid the stench. Turned to the valley below, lands unknown and unmapped. Wolves bawled. Something scurried in the brush, sticks crunched and cracked. A faint voice trailed off on the breeze. Footsteps rasped on the snow, a branch cracked. Will peered into the darkness. The fire snapped behind him. To the left of the horses two large trees tipped against one another. He squirmed his body into the narrow space between them, pulled the cape over his head, alert for sounds. He wept again and spent the night shivering in the hollow of the tree.

The snow ceased when first light broke in the east. Will snatched a fistful of snow, squeezed it to a pulp and wiped his hands on his trousers.

He seized another fistful and scoured his face with it. The fire smoul-
dered low to the ground. Dirt and blood blotted the snow. He surveyed
the valley in the bluing light, studied the path down and lit up on his
horse. Wrapped his father's cape tight around his shoulders, clenched
it at his chest and descended the hummock, clucking to the old man's
horse, its hooves clopping, rising and falling, tracking behind him.

TWO

DAYS OF EXPLORATION AND HARDSHIP. Will, thin, ragged, incessantly hungry, pursued the Stag west. After the snow melted, he yanked wild raspberry shoots out of the ground and snapped the tips off. The outside skin, covered with fine needles, split when he peeled it. He devoured the flesh inside, ate it like candy. Tried the tiny buds on top of stinging nettles but his eyes watered once they hit his tongue. Browsed on wild rose petals, pigweed and lamb's quarters, wild peas, pea vine flowers. He ripped dandelion roots from the ground, brushed the dirt on his leg and gulped them down.

Come berry season he gorged on berries of every manner until his stomach throbbed: huckleberries, horse berries, Saskatoon berries, wild raspberries, strawberries, salmonberries, thimbleberries. He trapped squirrels and prairie dogs in an archaic contraption fashioned out of hawthorn twigs, tied together by long wisps of fescue.

He panned for gold in the river, stooped like a thin old man, the sun thrashing down on his back, his fingers shrivelled from hours in the cold water, tumbling rocks and the constant flow of the stream rolling on the only sound in his ear. Days and nights merged into one long static syllable.

Change of fortune. Summer, 1887. Thin sliver of the moon. Sky pinpricked like the inside of a tin cup punctured by a knife tip. So many stars, those that hung and winked and those that fell in arcs and those that came into being and flared bright and were swallowed by the night that had birthed them. A caravan of men, women and children trundled west, bivouacked along the river, cookfires smouldering low. They corralled their wagons together into a semicircle and lashed canvas sheets between them into a feeble shelter. They were fantastically filthy; the dust of the land crept into the creases of their eyes and foreheads.

Will offered the ferryman, a man named Galbraith, a sack of Oregon grapes and two squirrels for fare and was rafted across the river where fish swam silently, flashing like gemstones in the cold clear water. When he reached the other side and stepped off the crude raft, he dropped to his knees and groped at the mud on the banks, his stomach heaving beneath him. Will followed the smell of roasted meat to a cluster of solemn pilgrims that appeared out of the land itself, an outrageous presence in their polluted garments, gathered around a grave. The body of a man lay in the ground, a mound of dirt next to the hole. An old man with skin stretched like cured hide intoned: "Glory be to the father, to the son, and to the holy ghost; as it was in the beginning, is now, and ever shall be, world without end, amen."

The travellers mourned the loss of their own and perhaps this was why they took in Will, fed and offered him shelter. Will accepted their humble generosity and ate until he retched. He scooped palms of river water and leaned over his knees, studying the pilgrims, noting a woman they called Angeline. She moved in and out of the other caravan members quietly. A small black stone wrapped in rabbit sinew hung against her neck. On a day when the sun smashed the land like an anvil, he followed her to the river where she stared across the wide expanse of water moving past like a hammered band of forged steel. She stood tall and slender; unlike the other women in the caravan, she was not yet broken from the vicissitudes of travel, worn down and sculpted hard like the land itself. Her skin was soft and clear, her hair bound by two long braids. She lowered herself and sat on a boulder.

Will came up behind her and placed a palm on her braids and stroked them. She lifted her head. He tugged at the braids. Her shoulders lifted and tensed, her eyes moving back and forth until he released the braid and stroked it again. Her shoulders relaxed as she dropped her gaze. He unbraided her hair, laid it out across his hands, combed his fingers through the coarse threads. Grabbed her jaw and pulled her face toward him. She placed a hand on his wrist and removed his hand from her jaw. She stood and lowered her head over his, her hair falling over both of them, and they were both inside of it like night itself, her necklace swinging against his chin, pebbled skin fragrant and warm with sweat and woodsmoke. He pulled her face to his so their lips touched.

"You are mine." He handed her his handkerchief, made by his mother's hand, WF etched in the corner of the cloth.

Angeline took the cloth and studied it. Her fingers traced the lettering. She removed her clothes and laid them out on the shore and nodded at Will to do the same. He tore them off and placed his hands over his privates. She offered her hand. He took it and she led him into the silent river. The current tugged at his legs; he steadied himself and held on to her as they grappled for purchase over the slick rocks. She stopped when they were up to their waists, the current pulling at them, and laved water over his head, his face and shoulders, his chest and abdomen. With palmfuls of sand and small pebbles she scrubbed his chest, back, thighs and calves. Thin streaks of blood marked the trails where she had dragged a sharp pebble. After she rinsed him, his skin quivered.

They sunned on the rocks and dressed when the sun set in the west. She held his hand and traced his knuckles and fingertips and the lines on his palms. He pulled his hand away but she held him by the wrist, kissed the back of his hand and rested his palm against her belly. He followed her back to camp, his face glowing, his hair damp.

Each day Will moved quietly among the caravan. The women did not return his looks; the men exchanged few words with him. Angeline's mother never spoke his name, nor did any other man, woman or child. Angeline's father noted the heavy stoop of Will's shoulders, the weight of a hidden truth.

Will stayed with the caravan on the banks of the Stag for the season. He travelled with the men to hunt deer, elk, and bison. They climbed and descended the same pass as he had with his father. They chased the river and Will glanced upward at the hillside where he and his father had made their last camp together. Pikas cried out. Two ravens perched on a pine tree staring down at them. When Will turned to the men, Angeline's father was studying him.

———————

In the late September sunlight, among the winking aspens lining the riverbank, Angeline told him how far they had travelled, the disease and death that ravaged their numbers, the nights they sought out meaning in the stars as the men took turns reading passages from the bible.

Will tried to pull her toward him but she shook free of him and pushed his hand away.

"You must hear this," she said.

"It's just a story."

"It's who I am."

He laughed.

"You can't know me without knowing where I came from."

He laughed again.

She shook her head. "Tell me your story then."

He glared at her for a long time. "My history is of no concern to you. It bears no consequence on who I am. I am alone as any other."

"We are all part of the same story," she said. "From time imme-morial. It's still being acted out and will continue to be told when we are no longer alive, just as it was for those who preceded us; just as it will for those who proceed us. There are many destinies but these are defined by our individual gestures. The repetition of these gestures. A man with no people is a dangerous man. He has no witness, no reckoning by his own people. He has no place in the world and in his search for his place, he turns to the weakest vice: violence."

Will told her what his father's father had said about his hands. He laughed and told her it was a fool's tale. "I know this gesture for certain." He lay back and signalled for her to climb on top of him. "You are mine."

She yanked her hand away and laughed. "If you say you are alone like any other, that means I am alone. And yet you tell me I am yours."

"Has there been any doubt since I claimed you at the river?"

Angeline was quiet. Will stroked her shoulder. She shrugged him off. "Stop."

Will moved his hand down her back and caressed the top of her buttocks.

"I said stop."

He left his hand against her skin.

"What did your father say?" she said.

Will laughed and stroked her bottom.

"Stop."

"He said nothing."

Angeline studied him. "Are you telling me the truth?"

"Would it make you feel better?"

"Are you?"

"Yes."

She held his face. "You look like a marmot. Eyes darting around as if you're seeking escape."

He kissed her and pulled her down on top of him.

She rose and fell above him, clawed at the sand around his head, dropped clammy fistfuls of it on his chest; the taste of grit in his teeth, the musk of her sex and the tang of the river stung his eyes. They floated into the body of the river, stared up at the gold and yellow leaves falling from the blue sky, their hands intertwined, holding tight in the low current, the hush of the water plugging his ears, her hair splayed out behind her like a dark inkwell against the clear water, trout grazing their backs with their dorsal fins, a weightlessness that drowned all senses, one by one, suspended, held aloft by the heavy, breathing, cumbersome world that Angeline and her family represented in their stories of hardship. But he believed nothing in what she told him, no more than what his or her father recited from the bible. Tales that only the weak deceived themselves in. Every man was responsible for his own being, every man must make his own way and rely on no other, for to do so was to put your life in another's hands and no man, no woman, no god could handle, should handle that kind of moral responsibility.

His body sank against the shoals that rolled beneath him as he raised himself, the light cold and bright on his skin, his hand outstretched toward Angeline. Her eyes were closed, her small dark nipples pointed upward from the thrust of her breasts. Her necklace a black heart against her chest, the swell of her belly and the dark patch between her legs ready and still as if being carried into an afterlife that she believed in. He shuddered.

She opened her eyes, raised a palm over them and smiled. "You will learn to love the water."

He hauled her out of the river, wiped the hair from her face, rested his hand on her neck and stroked the lines of sinew, his thumb against her vein, the pulse beating deep, strong. She kissed him, pressed her body against his. He held the necklace up against the sunlight, turned it over and examined it. He rubbed the dense rock, put his tongue to it and tasted metallic dirt. He spat it out, scooped up a palmful of river water, rinsed his mouth and spat into the river.

"Where did you get this?"

She pointed behind him, to a rise of treed hillsides, shoulders of an immense granite range.

"Get dressed."

Angeline stretched out her legs and tilted her face back, closed her eyes against the sun as it slid behind the peaks.

"Now."

She opened her eyes.

"Just do as I say."

She stood and dressed slowly. When she turned to him she clenched her arms as if to embrace herself, small against the river and brush beyond.

"We'll go for a ride and have a look, that's it."

She shook her head. "My father said it's the black of the devil's soul, to let that land be."

He snatched her elbows and hauled her back to camp. Blue streaks of smoke lashed the air above the settlement. Voices murmured in tents, the hush of mealtime. They crossed camp. He climbed up on the horse and yanked Angeline up to sit behind him. He held her by the wrists with one hand on the reins as they rode out. Angeline lowered her head against his back and after riding for a while he released her wrists.

They rode hard and fast, the horse sweated and breathed violently beneath them, and some hours later he disembarked, studied the mountains that cropped up like marbled tombstones, striated with thick veins of black and brown sedimentary rock. The ground in all directions was black, as if scorched from an interminable fire. Along the riverbanks, clusters of lizards lazed on the rocks. Will ran in large circles in each direction, whooping and hollering.

He squatted, scooped a handful of marl, tasted it and spat it out. He unsheathed his bowie knife, cut into a chunk of anthracite. It flaked away and split open, dense and hard. He held it up in the moonlight, the gloss of bituminous coal against the smooth skin of the blade.

"I'm cold," Angeline said.

He turned, surprised by her presence. "Wait here." He scoured the area for pine branches and brought several armfuls back to a flat spot at the edge of a clearing. He grabbed all manner of rocks the size of his fist and built a small circle on the ground, ripped up loose moss, snapped small sticks, and stacked these with the moss beneath them to start a fire. As it began to gather life he added larger sticks and branches until it thrived on its own. The black ground and rocks beneath the fire glowed red. They sat listening to the crack of wood. A breeze bent and twisted the flames.

"This is my future." He stared into the darkness. "All of this. It's mine."

At dawn, the fire had gone out; the rocks that had glowed throughout the night blackened as they cooled. Will rose silently to avoid waking Angeline, brushed the ashes from his trousers and grabbed his axe. He outlined the perimeter and clobbered crudely chopped corner and line posts into the ground and marked the boundary lines by blazing trees and hacking at the underbrush. As the sun climbed, sweat leached through his garments and lifted off his body. His hands bled where blisters broke, slick with blood and serum. He stopped and peeled away the flesh from the small vesicles and larger bullae. The coalfields stretched as far as he could see in all directions, a dark shadow that leapt mountain ranges and sucked up river bottoms. He noted his claim thus far, dwarfed by the unstaked land around him, and tore strips from his shirttails and wrapped them around his palm to dress the blisters. Turned his shoulders and head to loosen the tightness in his neck and dug his fingers into his shoulders to work out the knots. He gazed out over the land and set to work again, increased his pace, groaned pneumatic grunts with each hammering down of a stake, the blood leaking through his dressings, stains darkening the handle of his axe. He worked without pause as the sun arched overhead, his body slick with sweat, his raw hands screaming. Stumbled over uneven ground that seemed to rise up on him, mocked him as he slammed stakes into it. The sun slid over the western horizon and a cobalt light fell over the land. Will appraised the lines staking his claim. In pitch darkness he staggered to where he'd left Angeline that morning and collapsed at her side.

"I'm hungry," she said.

"I'll get us something to eat tomorrow." He reached for her but she turned away.

"My father will come for me," she said.

"I'm not finished."

"Haven't you done enough?"

"No."

"He will come for me tomorrow. He won't let you finish this."

Will swore and propped himself up and held out his hand. He led her to the horse and heaved himself up first and then pulled her up behind him. They galloped through the cool of the night. Angeline's necklace dug into his back.

"Slow down," she said.

He stared ahead, squinting into the distance, leaned over the horse's mane and clucked in its ear, kicked its side with his heels to go faster. She held him tight, and they rode throughout the night. They were greeted at the camp by dogs barking and the scorch of pine resin from low burning fires. Their clothes and the undercarriage of the horse were caked in black dust. Will hopped off, limped to their tent and retrieved his saddle and blanket roll. Bridled Angeline's father's horse, a tall merle roan, with a rawhide hackamore and led it to a tree, leaned against the animal with his shoulder and flung the saddle over it, kicked it hard in the stomach and cinched the saddle tight. He led it across the camp, the horse shaking its head sideways as if deer flies buzzed in its ear.

Angeline rushed after him. "That's not yours."

He nodded toward his exhausted horse, its back glistening as it cropped grass. "I'll return it." He slipped his foot into the stirrup and swung up onto the saddle. She stood on her toes and held out her arms for him to lift her up onto the horse. He leaned down toward her. The dressings on his hands were tattered, blackened strips that dangled off his palms like a derelict's rags. He pulled the necklace off her and slipped it over his head where it hung off his neck. "I'll come back for you."

"We're striking out in a few days," she said.

He placed a hand on her head. "I give you my word." He chucked his horse forward. Angeline ran after him, calling out as he vanished into the grey timber. If he had looked back, he would have seen her holding her belly, dark in the last night of her youth, the grass rasping in the wake of her father's pony.

THREE

MONTHS OF TOIL AND LABOUR entered Will's life. He poured all of his reserves and resources into walled tents and wool blankets, shovels and pickaxes, lamps and explosives. He registered his claim, enlisted a few men from Cape Breton and set up camp, downriver from the land of charcoal rock.

The men worked shifts around the clock. They tunnelled in the perpetual dark wielding pickaxes, the damp air choked with fine black dust, dull and muffled sounds confirmation that they were not alone, that other men existed alongside of them. They dug deeper, staked stobs and carved caves out of the seams in the rock. Timber pillars propped up makeshift timber roofs and skeletal ponies staggered out dragging carts of coal. Piles of smoking slag dotted the camp.

It was a time of lugubrious labour plagued by death. Methane explosions, fires, and black damp; men crushed by the rocks of pillars and rooms collapsing around them, men who settled grievances with pickaxes. But the camp grew and Will no longer worked below ground but above, managing workers, transforming the camp into a hardscrabble village. He trusted no man, held his own counsel and kept debts on all men in his employ.

From this group, he commissioned Clay Cooley and a dozen delinquents and instructed them where to find Angeline and the caravan, made them repeat his orders, had each man describe for him what he had told them.

"It'll bring some cheer to see some lasses," Cooley said.

"She's my wife. Bring her back unharmed."

Cooley placed a finger against a nostril and snorted to the side. He did the same with the other nostril, pinched his nose and wiped his thumb and index finger on his sleeve.

Will held up his hand. "Do we have an understanding?"

"You want to do it yourself?"

Will studied Cooley and then the others. "Do we?"

Cooley glared at him, turned and the others fell in behind him. They mounted their horses and rode off.

Will spent a restless night listening to wolves yip in the darkness, turning over the conversation with Cooley. At daybreak, he assembled a few men to saddle their horses. They rode for most of the day chasing Cooley's tracks and in the late afternoon came upon a cluster of horses and wagons at the edge of Joseph's Prairie, a skiff of pale-blue smoke from cookfires hanging in the air.

They heard Cooley's men before they saw them. The report of gunfire echoed across the land, and then horses thundering over the clay-baked, scrubby ground, the drumbeat of their hooves rattling rocks loose, tumbling beneath the crust of the ancient ground, a dark void where they clanged, a sound so terrible that the earth shuddered up through Will's pony, up into Will's gut, and Cooley's men emerged like bearded phantoms, squinting into the dust, kicking their labouring horses, rifles and pistols raised above their shoulders. Some of his men were without horses, running with women under their arms, and other men laid women over their laps or held them upright, clenching them by the throat, as if they were leading the charge from their saddles and were forced to watch the horror unfold before them, and those women who were not on the mounts were lashed and dragged behind the galloping horses, the awful cries of their children screaming for them.

Everywhere dust battered and churned into the clouded air, mottled bits of broken land that smote down only to rise again alighting on man and pony, an incandescent biblical delirium.

Will slipped off his horse, tethered it to a tree and scuttled along the ground to look for Angeline. His men beat their way toward Cooley's men, their ponies hammering forward, his men rising in their stirrups and hoisting their rifles over the flattened ears and bulging eyes of their horses whose chattering teeth spit forth strings of drool.

Will lay flat on the ground, clasped his hands together and murmured, "Dear god, forgive me."

Will's men dropped from their mounts as grey gun smoke rose over the dust and they lifted their guns and pressed the triggers and their bullets discharged, ripping through the polluted air. Cooley's men and horses crumpled to the ground where they lay screaming and writhing in the dirt while the captive women fell from the horses, pried themselves free of the assassins and ran howling toward their children, and Cooley's men staggered around on the ground, sliding their hands over their wounds, one man roaring as he thrashed at his horse to roll off his leg, the horse screeching and writhing, its eyes crazed, teeth snapping at the turgid air. Nearby a man sat wheezing and gazed around him while blood poured from a bullet in his chest and another man crawled along the ground with his back punctured by bullets until he stopped mid crawl. Cooley's and Will's men scampered over the land seeking cover where there was none, some raised pistols to their own temples and pulled the trigger and buckled to the ground and those men not yet dead seemed confused by the pallor around them, blubbering gibberish, and other men rested their heads in their hands bawling brokenly.

Under the cover of gun smoke, Will crawled toward the corpse of a horse. Cooley rode out of the bedlam and pointed his pony toward him, kicking its sides wildly. Will drew his knife and cut into the horse, retching as its hot entrails spilled out steaming. He wiped away the innards and wormed into the hollowed husk of the horse, curled up among its viscera, hot smouldering flesh vacated by blood, the heavy smell feculent in his nostrils, his eyes watering, stinging and raw. He pulled on the slippery flaps of horseflesh, stretched the leathery skin around his body, slick with the blood and stench of the wasted pony, and he lay still, praying silently. He repeated "dear god dear god dear god" soundlessly, like one who is struck dumb by the horrors he has witnessed. Through a jagged pinhole in the corpse's long neck, he saw Cooley's horse gallop, rangy legs like sinewy trunks of an ancient tree, knobby and gnarled at the knees, mottled with spatters of blood and dirt, before it halted some yards away. Will held his breath and waited. The horse's leg cocked then straightened and then Cooley's legs and body and face appeared in front of Will, a long knife clenched in his fist.

Cooley sniffed the air, his nostrils whistling on the exhale, his jaw tight, pulsing. A horse lay on its side, thrashing its head back and forth. Cooley lifted his knife and punched it into the horse's neck and its shrieks faded into a low moan and then it was quiet. Will soiled himself; the stink of his excrement filled the cadaver. Cooley moved between the strewn bodies scattered around the battlefield, kicked them over onto their backs and worked his way to where Will lay concealed. Cooley stopped, his body stock-still, and faced the horse. Will lay inside, curled like a fetus, his eye steady, unblinking. Cooley stared at him; Will did not blink. Cooley raised his knife and drove it into the horse's neck. Will did not blink. Cooley yanked out the knife, cursed and drove it down again. Will returned Cooley's gaze with that of a dead man, playing the role with a fear he had never known. Cooley yanked out the knife one more time and thrust it down beside the horse's backside. Will chewed the insides of the horse's flesh to mask his fear, the thick taste of gamy blood clouded in his mouth; he clenched his jaw to prevent himself from gagging. Cooley strode to his horse, lifted his foot into the stirrup, climbed into the saddle and galloped back to where his men were fighting. The hollowed echo of hooves on the ground were the last thing Will heard before closing his eyes, the world black and stuffed with the ripe stench of viscera, the nearly dead howling and moaning all about him.

FOUR

THEY CAME IN PACKS like a pestilence, clusters of filthy ragtags, crouched over the corpses, plugging their noses against the stink of carrion and horse urine. Their garments flapped off their grimy arms, and some appeared tall as giants, others as if god's thumb had pushed them down into their own bodies. Musicians thumped snap drums and squeezed baleful tunes out of arm organs. Another slapped two femur bones together, beating a mute monotone. A silent clown.

Will closed and opened his eyes. A blue sky blazed above. He slid out of the cavity of the horse, waved off the flies that buzzed around him. A grubby hand pried into his pockets. Another hand covered in scars, raised above the grimy skin, angry pink and white strands, nails peeled back, dull red sores, grabbed at Will's necklace, snapped it free. The clown held up the coal. His hair was pointed in a cone on top of his head, his lips smeared with red greasepaint. Will seized his wrist.

"I ain't dead yet."

The clown dropped the necklace into Will's hands. He pointed to the dead men littering the landscape and moved his arm slowly across it and looked back at Will, lifted a hand to his face and mimed wiping tears.

Will sat up. He tied the necklace together and slipped it around his neck. He struggled to stand.

The clown placed his hands against his chest, tilted back and silently laughed, his throat pulsing, putrid. He picked up a stone and sawed at the foreleg of the horse. When he tore through the skin and sinew, he grabbed the foreleg with both hands, twisted it until it snapped loose.

He set to skinning the leg, peeling away the layers of muscle and flesh by sliding the stone downward, close to the bone. The flesh sloughed off in bloody sheets. He was skilled at it, it was impossible not to recognize that, and when he was done, he dropped the leg, turned toward the corpse of one of Will's men nearby and tore off his shirt. He picked up the leg and wrapped the top of it with the deerskin, tied it off; he held it out in front of him, admired his work, turned it around to view each angle. The clown placed the padded part of the leg under his armpit, crouched down and limped ahead, turned and shuffled back to Will.

Will took the leg and leaned on it, hopped without putting any weight on his foot. He nodded, but the clown was bent over, butchering the flanks and rump of the horse, sawing at it with his flint.

Will hobbled over the land littered with the dead, paused to rearrange his arms and hold on to the crutch. Flies settled on the blackened corpses, everywhere the ripe fetor of decay. Two dogs pulled at a man's intestines and gnawed on them. Crows circled above squawking. Some alighted on the ground waiting for the dogs to leave. Others pecked at the horseflesh but were waved off by the ragtags who crouched over the corpses, yanking off clothes, turning pockets inside out, ripping jewellery off their necks. They hacked out teeth and smashed the enamel to release bits of gold. They slashed off fingers and removed rings, tossing the digits to dogs skittering nearby.

The sect was presided over by a small man dressed in a black cassock that dragged along the ground. He wore a crown made of cedar twigs and green boughs, and black kinked hair rose up from his head like a nest. He squinted through the smoke as if peering into another world, grislier than the one surrounding him. Will nodded at him; the man broke out in a low laugh and turned away, calling out instructions to his people.

Will considered the corpses as he hopped past them. To his left, Angeline's father and a few men from the caravan laid twisted in the dirt. Angeline's mother curved over him as if in prayer. Bullet holes leaking blood pockmarked her back. Ahead of Will, a group of ragtags spoke quietly among themselves. They leaned over a body at the river-bank. A woman stood and held something close to her chest wrapped in a bloodied cloth. As she rushed past him with another woman, her large breast flopped free from her top and a small wrinkled hand reached out for it beneath the cloth. And then a bleating, a sharp pierc-ing wail, a sound so incongruous from the desolate land, so startling that Will's eyes teared up. The woman stopped and pushed her breast into the infant's mouth and glared back at Will. Her hair was wild and knotted as if made of the mud and sticks of the land itself. Will reached for his hat but his head was bare; he bowed.

She glanced down at the newborn suckling and then back at Will. "Savages," she hissed, "every one of you." She strode off, weaving in and out of the maimed and the dead, heading toward the treeline.

The man in black glared after her. "Bulah," he called.

She stopped.

"That which were born, not of blood," he said, "nor of the will of the flesh, nor of the will of man, but of God must be sacrificed in blood."

Bulah raced ahead into the treeline.

The cluster of ragtags on the riverbank had all dispersed to strip other bodies downstream. Will hobbled over to see the body Bulah had left.

Angeline lay naked, a wash of blood covered her belly and her legs were bent at odd angles. Will tried to straighten her legs but they were stiff and this took some work. He gathered her clothes; a sleeve was missing, a length of her braid had been cut off. He placed her garments over her body. He removed his shirt and covered her face with it and sat down choking and sucking air in sharp gasps.

The man in black called out, "Are you prepared to unburden yourself of all that weighs upon you?"

Will lifted his head. Many of the deceased were stripped and clumps of clothing were stacked in piles here and there. One of the ragtags dragged a naked man by his right boot until he reached a cluster of corpses and stopped. He pulled off the boot and tossed it onto a pile of clothing, but left the man's hat on his head, and walked away. The man's chest rose and fell slowly.

Will hobbled over and squatted next to him. He lifted the brim of the hat. Clay Cooley moaned. Will studied his face. "You betrayed me."

Cooley opened his mouth and rasped.

"Quiet." Will seized his jaw. He searched the ground, found a branch, snapped it over his knee and set the splintered end of the branch against Cooley's head, behind his earlobe. "Look at me."

Cooley shook his head.

"Look at what you've done to me, to my wife and her family." Will pushed the branch into the soft flesh where jaw and ear met. He gripped Cooley's face and pushed the stick in deeper. Cooley's eyes widened. Will raised himself to one knee and jammed the stick in and waited until Cooley stopped breathing.

Will brushed off his trousers and picked up his crutch. He called to the clown, asked him to bring a few others with him. The clown glanced at the man in black, who nodded. The man in black held a blanket and walked up to Will. He looked down at Cooley, handed Will the blanket, placed his hands on either side of his head and said in a low voice, "Confess and be free."

Will's shoulders trembled.

The man held Will's head firm and looked into his eyes. "Confess."

"Are you a holy man?" Will said.

"I am."

Will spoke of the land he had travelled from, his father and all that he had seen him do and all that Will had done to him, and when he had finished, the man in black kissed the top of his head and whispered, "You have a second chance to do right. Can you embrace it? Are you willing to earn your own forgiveness so god can forgive you?"

Will glared at the man. "There's nobody who can forgive me."

"What now?"

"What does anyone who is damned do?"

The man in black removed his hands from Will's head and gestured to the clown. The clown whistled; the ragtags loaded their horses with their looting. He whistled again and the sect rode off, trailing the man in black. From the forest, an infant's cry rose up as Bulah rushed to catch up with them, clutching Will and Angeline's daughter close to her chest.

The light faded and an immense silence settled over the land. Will went to Angeline and laid the blanket over her. He sat beside her through the night and when the day broke he lifted Angeline and mounted his pony, heeled it lightly and the pony began to walk. He held his wife against his shoulder and rode back to the fields of black rock.

BOOK
TWO

1902

FIVE

EARLY EVENING IN CROWSNEST. A bruised sky blasted with thunderheads. Barn swallows swirled in waves that undulated low to the ground. Burnt charcoal and toasted wood on the air. Children ran screaming and dogs barked after each other in the street, leaping through shadows cast by squat wooden buildings while two crows sat on the eaves peering down.

The grimy sect plundered into town, rambling down the dirt street. Davey pulled up the rear with Bobby. The children stopped playing and stood against the sides of buildings as the assemblage played strange tunes on decrepit banjos and mouth organs, papery accordions and pewter spoons. The crew passed the clanging of the blacksmith's, where a red glow flared in the pitch of the shop, and ambled past a girl standing in front of a doll shop, wearing a sun hat and white dress, clutching a wilted bunch of orange gerberas at her chest. Davey tipped her hat and smiled at her.

The crew arrived before a large walled tent, went through a flap held back by two boys and stepped over the boards, scuffed and worn by the boots of dozens of pilgrims who stood shoulder to shoulder under the canvas dome. Standing-room-only in the primitive theatre, ripe with the stench of damp wool and sour sweat. Paraffin lamps smoked at the front. Davey and Bobby stopped at the back while the rest of the faction crossed the length of the space plucking at their instruments before they halted to line up one two three four on the wooden pallets at the front of the tent. They turned around and faced the audience.

There was a murmur in the crowd. The crew continued to play as two women of their own lumbered about in the pale lamplight like filthy ghouls, faces smeared with dark greasepaint. One was dressed as a woman of society, her large bosom spilling out of her top; the other limped around the stage as a deformed hunchback, hissing. It was she who spoke first.

"I, that am curtail'd of this fair proportion, cheated of features by dissembling nature, deform'd, unfinished, sent before my time into this breathing world, scarce half made up, and that so lamely and unfashionable that dogs bark at me ..." The actor stumbled around the stage, and when the crowd heard dogs barking outside of the tent, they roared with laughter. The tent walls flashed with lightning. The other actor approached her, fluttering her eyelids, pushed her powdered bosom toward the hunchback and smiled grotesquely, her misshapen teeth stained like rancid lard. A clown wore tattered garments adorned with sickle moons and stars with jester faces and caps embroidered in colourful beadwork. He circled the stage in large, exaggerated strides with his arms out in front of him. Thunder rumbled in the hills beyond town.

"... And therefore since I cannot prove a lover, to entertain these fair well-spoken days, I am determined to prove a villain, and hate the idle pleasures of these days." The hunchback then made a fustian display of bludgeoning the woman with a knife and the woman cried out and dropped to the ground, her heavy breasts rising and falling. The crowd quieted as the hunchback turned to face the audience. Lightning flared up the tent walls. An immense clap of thunder followed. The clown covered his eyes, then his mouth and ears with his palms, and looked upward.

"Make peace with god, for you will all die, my friends. Eventually. Inevitably. Inescapably. Veritably." The hunchback pointed toward the woman breathing on the ground, her eyes open, and lewdly winked at the crowd. "It is the only certainty of your sad lives." The audience roared with laughter and quieted when the hunchback held one hand to her ear. "Have you that holy feeling in yourselves, to counsel me to make peace with god?" A few pilgrims nodded their heads. "And are you aware yet to your own souls so blind, that you will war with god by murdering me?"

The clown circled the hunchback, then stood behind him, miming the hunchback's actions. She spoke again. "Oft have I heard that grief softens the mind, and makes it fearful and degenerate; think therefore on revenge, and cease to weep."

A man standing near Davey shouted, "Revenge is the cure of all ills!" A grumbling purled through the tent as some of the crowd shifted from where they stood.

The hunchback held up a finger, placed it against her lips and looked at the actor on the ground and the clown did the same. "And God saw that the wickedness of man was great in the earth, and that every imagination of the thoughts of his heart was only evil continually. And it repented the Lord that he had made man on the earth, and it grieved him at his heart." She stopped and leaned forward with the clown. The hunchback whispered in a raspy voice, "Friends, death is a reality we all choose to ignore. It won't happen to us until it does and we are never prepared. Never. 'It's too early,' we cry out. 'I'm not ready,' we lament. And for those of you who believe that you are yourself alone, that there is no room for God in your life, I leave you with one question to ponder tonight: What is the trust or strength of a foolish man?"

A streak of lightning followed by a clap of thunder shuddered the tent walls. Rain began to drum overhead. The actor lifted herself up and held hands with the hunchback and the clown kicked up its heels to both sides. All three of them bowed. A scattering of confused applause. The hunchback and the woman lifted their hands together and motioned to the rear of the tent and the crowd turned. "Greet thee man of god," the hunchback said, "thy holiest, most honourable of all men, Reverend Brown."

A woman held back the tent flap and a man in a cedar crown and black cassock strode in, smiling. He stood with the others along the back wall and pressed their palms and clasped their shoulders. He paused in front of Davey and smiled before making his way to the front, nodding to the men and women he glided past and placing his hands on the heads of their children. To these pilgrims he was a man of commerce and jurisprudence, a miner and farmer, a husband and father. An everyman. A holy man. The actors bowed on stage when he arrived at the front. They exited holding hands stage right. He faced the crowd and removed his crown. Beneath it, kinked black hair rose above his head like an enormous root vegetable bulb resting on his collared neck. He surveyed the crowd with his arms outstretched as he commenced to speak.

"Friends. My good friends, my devoted family, my brothers and sisters. We are many but we are really just one when the devil himself seeks us out. He set up here in Crowsnest, the only home most of you have ever known. I saw him when I looked in that man's eyes and when I looked into that man's eyes. I saw him in the eyes of your children out in the street. He's out there in the dogs and up there in the birds and inside here in each and every one of you." He held up a finger, looked at it and turned to the congregation. "I inquired of the devil: Did you ask these good people if you could make a place for yourself here? And he said, No, I did not. I asked, Why? He replied, Did you ask the same of the son of god? I replied, Yes, the son of god has already asked each and every man, woman and child here. For this is their home.

"Well, he said. And I told him, brother, take all the time you need. I called him brother for all men, good and evil, are cast in god, our father's image. I said, brother, he is not to be trifled with for he is here now."

The reverend tilted his head back; his eyes travelled across the roof of the tent. He turned his gaze downward until his eyes rested on a child at the side of the congregation clinging to his mother's dress. "Open your eyes, brothers, and you will see that the lord is here now."

The congregation looked up at the tent dome, at the walls, into each other's eyes.

Reverend Brown smiled and held a hand to his ear. "Son of god: my brother, my truth and my maker, why thou so sad?" He nodded and faced the congregation. "He says there is a blackness that has stained our hearts, one that is through and through each and every one of us, coursing through our veins, and there ain't any goodness left. And he says he sheds no tears out of sadness, nor shall any man. He sheds no tears of joy, nor shall any man."

Reverend Brown turned toward the ceiling and said, "Then why?" He held his hand to his ear and nodded. "He tells me that he sheds tears to cleanse the souls of every man, for every man shall not pass through to salvation without removing first the stain of his sins. For sins are evidence of who a man might have been but not of who a man might purport to be."

A brute with a misshapen nose, long stringy hair and vicious eyes called out from the rear of the gallery. "Isn't spreading falsehood breaking one of the commandments?"

The reverend stopped his sermon; silence purled through the tent. He turned his small hands along the twigs of his crown, studied the man and pushed his way forward past the crate-board pulpit into the crowd that parted for him. He nodded for one of the women who had preceded him on the stage to approach and she did so, holding a tin cup in front of her, and the crowd moved aside so that she, too, could pass without obstruction. She stood next to Reverend Brown, who took the cup from her and said, "Much obliged, Bulah."

Reverend Brown turned to address the congregation. "My dear friends, my brothers and sisters, the man who raises this question is simply lost. He holds no malice. His only sin is that he is not yet the man he aspires to be, the same as any other man or woman or child gathered here. Why, you might ask? Fear."

There were yelps of surprise in the crowd. The brute grimaced and pointed at the reverend. "I ain't no coward."

Reverend Brown smiled. "This is true, brother. And no man makes that claim, least of all me or our god. You are a brave man prepared to confront yourself, who you are and who you might become. Would you like to find your way? Are you prepared to shed a fraudulent version of yourself? A man that places himself in the hands of god from this moment forward to life everlasting?"

The man stood with his arms crossed. He jabbed a finger in Reverend Brown's chest. "You don't look like no man of god to me."

"I am just a man like any other." Here, the reverend paused and lifted the tin cup above the brute's head with one hand and with the other placed the heel of his palm against the man's forehead, resting his short fingers on top of his head. "Art thou ready?"

The man scowled.

Reverend Brown poured the contents of the tin cup over the brute's head. "With this water, these tears of thy lord god, wash away this man's sins and bless him with thy presence in his life for time everlasting." He pushed back the man's forehead and the water ran down his face over his chin into his collar and shirt. Bulah offered the reverend a cloth and he washed the grime and gun smoke from the man's face, and when he was done, he made the sign of the cross in front of the man and the man's face shone in that faint light. Reverend Brown placed his hands on the man's shoulders and turned him to face the crowd. The brute shifted his weight from foot to foot, his eyes darting back and forth at the congregation. The reverend kept a hand on his shoulder. "All that was broken in you is now mended." The man no longer resembled a thug in appearance but a pious being that might be seen kneeling on a pew at morning mass. "You are cleansed of your filth, purified from desires that have led you astray. You have faced your fear and defeated it. My good brother, you are saved. Go in peace."

Someone clapped and the rest of the audience joined in. The man stared off at a point in the distance and when he blinked, he bowed his head and his shoulders shook. The tent was silent and when he stopped shaking, he wiped his eyes, lifted his face to the crowd. His eyes were red and damp and he clenched his mouth as if he might sob again. The congregation applauded and cheered.

Bulah took off her hat and gestured for Davey and Bobby to join her. Davey shook her head. Bobby made his way through the crowd with Bulah, and every man, woman and even child dropped coins and banknotes into the hat. Soon the crown of the hat sagged, and the other woman, the one they called Gussie, did the same with her hat. Some of the ragtags followed each woman, working the crowd to collect offerings that citizens were more than obliged to donate.

A man shouted out that he, too, wanted to be purified and soon another made this claim. Cries of piety rose in the tent, voices called out, some clapped, others stomped their boots on the hard dirt. Reverend Brown raised his hands to quiet the crowd. "Brothers and sisters, tomorrow morning I will meet and baptize each and every one of you at the Stag, the source of all life in this valley."

"I've been too long in the dark night!" a man shouted.

Reverend Brown smiled. "I admire your enthusiasm, sir. For those of you like this brave, earnest man, that cannot wait until morning, exit this tent and stand with your faces upturned in the rain that falls outside these very walls. Let god's tears wash over you with thy neighbour as thy witness."

The man who'd shouted ran past Davey, flipped open a canvas flap and went outside. Another man joined and then others, including children. They sprinted into the clearing and stood, a few dozen in number, faces upturned, the rain drumming over them and dimpling the ground. After a few minutes the rain ceased and they wandered into town, laughing in their damp clothes.

———————

Bulah and Bobby found Davey standing outside of the hotel saloon. Bulah glanced at Davey before entering the saloon. Davey shook her head, shifted her quiver on her shoulder and marched through the street clutching a bow in her left hand. Bobby trailed after her. A light breeze rose up from the west. The sky had cleared and it was nicked with stars. She stopped, sat against a wooden wall, looked up and pointed. "There's all kinds of things up there."

"Looks like a bunch of stars to me." Bobby sat next to her.

She traced a bear, a ladle, a boat.

They studied the sky and the outline of mountains around them. Piano played from the saloon. Two dogs loped past.

"It's like there's no other place to go," Davey said. "As if we're all surrounded by rock all around us. Rock and sky."

"We can't just sit here all night." Bobby stood and offered his hand.

"Why not?" She helped herself up.

The low voice of a man, a slap and then the whimper of a child. Then a girl's halting voice, singing a simple hymn. Davey followed the sound down the street, turned and came upon a wagon behind the livery. A wilted bunch of orange gerberas lay with its petals scattered in the dirt. A young boy and the girl they'd seen earlier wearing a white dress and sun hat now stood naked and shivering. They wept and shielded their privates with their small hands and turned their bodies sideways in a broken attempt at modesty in the filth of the street. Bobby held Davey's arm but she shrugged him off and stepped forward. A black robe was bunched up around Reverend Brown's shoulders and neck. He sat naked before the two children against a bale of hay, his legs splayed open and his hand outstretched. The girl's white dress lay on the ground next to the boy's garments, and the thug that had been baptized stood naked, clenching a dark bottle that he drank from deeply. Reverend Brown held up a banknote and the children moved toward him. "One more song," he said.

Davey notched an arrow, drew her bow and took aim on the reverend. He twisted around and smiled at Davey.

"Go on," Davey called out to the children. "Get dressed and go home."

"Now wait a minute," the thug said. "Wait a goddamn minute." He faced Reverend Brown. "What in the hell is going on here?"

Reverend Brown smiled. "Leave her be."

The thug took a drink from his bottle and emptied it. "You ain't no man of god. I knew it the moment I seen you and your pack of clowns."

"And yet, here you stand," the reverend said.

The thug raised his bottle by the neck.

"Brother, think on it for a moment longer." Reverend Brown picked up his rifle and laid it across his bare thighs. "It only takes the briefest of moments to change one's life irrevocably."

"Irre-irre- ... All your fancy talk don't hide the fact that you need saving yourself." The thug tossed the bottle into the dirt. He gathered his clothes and pulled them on. "We ain't brothers. Just so we're clear on that." He stumbled off into town.

"Go on," Davey said. "Go home."

The children scooped up their clothes and bolted.

"Bobby, what do you think?" Reverend Brown said.

"I don't hold the facts," Bobby said.

Reverend Brown laughed. "Indeed." He jutted his chin. "I'll see you in the saloon, my little brother."

Bobby turned to Davey.

"Git," Reverend Brown said. "This is between me and the lass."

Bobby walked away.

"Come closer, lass." Reverend Brown held up a banknote.

Davey pointed her arrow at him.

"That's all right, you put on a fine performance for me the other night. A real wolverine. We'll get another chance, right as rain."

"I didn't do anything I wanted to do," Davey said.

"Nothing is ever done to oneself that one does not accept."

"You held a knife to my throat. What choice did I have?"

"You chose to live," he said, "and so you participated in that act."

Davey shook her head. "You saying so doesn't make it true. I see you. I've always seen you."

She stepped aside as he stood and tugged his cassock down, slipped his arms through it and let the robe fall over his stomach and legs. He brushed the hay from his robe.

He grabbed a fistful of her hair. "I'm the only family you got, the only one who cares for you. Remember that."

"You ain't my family." Davey tried to free herself but he pulled her hair tighter and yanked her down in front of him.

"Look at me. Good lass. I'm your only family. Now nod for me and I'll let you go."

Davey clenched her teeth.

"Give me a nod. That's it, just like that." Reverend Brown tugged her hair to make her nod up and down. He smiled. Davey tried to turn away but he yanked her hair until she whimpered. "That's a good girl. That wasn't so difficult, was it?" He straightened his crown and smiled at her before striding toward the saloon.

Davey stood, lifted the bow and mimed drawing the string and releasing it at his back. When he entered the saloon she lowered her bow, slipped the arrow into the quiver on her back, wiped her face with her sleeve. She walked along the dirt street past the saloon to the outskirts of town where she sat against a tree and tipped her hat over her eyes. The rain started again and fell on the trees around her. In town, the voices of the men rang out as they drank and shouted until she fell into a half-sleep.

In the morning, the air tasted cool from the intermittent rain throughout the night. Birds chattered and metal clanged forth from the blacksmith's. Bulah stood bleary-eyed and unsteady before Davey and offered her hand. Davey took it, pulled herself up.

"You reek," Davey said.

Bulah shrugged her shoulders. "Can you give it a pause, at least for today?"

They walked through town in silence and crossed over to the river. A long lineup had formed on the riverbank and in due time Reverend Brown, Gussie, Bobby and the rest of the ragtags arrived in a procession of strange music that had no sense of rhythm or melody.

Davey stopped and remained at a distance as Bulah and Gussie moved down the line and encouraged each person to donate a sum by pushing a hat in front of them. The women smiled and moved on if they were satisfied with the donation. If they were not, they shook the hat in front of the person and glared at them.

The reverend stood at the edge of the river and addressed the crowd. "All power is given unto me in heaven and in earth. Go ye therefore and teach all peoples, baptizing them in the name of the father, and of the son, and of the holy ghost: teach them to observe all things whatsoever I have commanded you: and, lo, I am with you always, even unto the end of the word. Amen."

He held out his arms and turned his face to the sky, closed his eyes and smiled. A few of the citizens glanced among themselves and then to Gussie and Bulah. Reverend Brown opened his eyes and told the gathering this story:

"On a mountaintop, I once saw an old hunter command a sheep to fall dead. Then the old hunter raised the animal back from the dead and the animal darted off and leapt from the mountainside, fell instantly lifeless—as if it had died the moment its hooves parted from the land. This I saw with my own eyes. I ate of the animal afterward. It was unwounded, healthy and perfectly wild. It tasted of the land itself."

Davey turned away and regarded the river running west.

"He that believeth and is baptized shall be saved," Reverend Brown continued, crossing himself and looking upward. "But he that believeth not shall be damned."

He pulled his black cassock over his head and dropped it to the ground and stood naked in the cold morning light. His skin, save for patches of dark hair on his legs, privates, belly and chest, was pale, lily-white up to his neckline and face where the skin was sun-baked. His hands were tanned from the wrists. Some in the crowd gasped; most averted their eyes. He waded into the shallows and scooped up two palmfuls of water. "I have shed my cloak. Can you see me for who I am? I have washed my hands. Will you take mine in yours? As children, you were once naked in the sight of all, and were not ashamed. You once had hands that were untainted. You once bore the likeness of Adam, who was naked in the garden and was not ashamed."

He motioned to the crowd for them to do as he had done. "Shed thy cloaks, my fellow sinners. Come, be washed of thy sins and repent so thou might be cleansed."

The townsfolk shifted and glanced among themselves. Gussie and Bulah reached the back of the line and carried their hats, sagging with the donations, back to the reverend.

"Shed. Thy. Cloaks." He enunciated each word emphatically. No one gave any indication that they would remove their clothing. Gussie removed a pistol from beneath her coat and pointed it at selected individuals. The reverend repeated, "Shed thy cloaks." His voice quiet, flat. The men deliberately removed their clothes and dropped them to their feet. Gussie motioned for the first man to approach Reverend Brown and the man shuffled toward him with his hands cupped over his crotch, dragging his trousers at his ankles. He removed his boots and shook his trousers off, stepped into the river; the water reached his shins. Reverend Brown held his arms open in an exaggerated gesture of welcome. The man's skin was filthy above the collar line and the shirt cuff but otherwise white and bright as the day he was born.

"My good man, what is thy name?"

"Bleasdell. Tom Bleasdell."

"And now I ask thee, Mr Tom Bleasdell, dost thou desire to obtain eternal life through an unyielding faith in god?"

Bleasdell nodded.

"Mr Bleasdell, please affirm your intentions for all who bear witness to this momentous occasion."

"I affirm."

"God says, 'If thou desire life eternal, thou must be true and thou must shun all falsehoods.' Tom Bleasdell, do you accept this truth?"

"I do."

Reverend Brown exhaled on Bleasdell's head. "Cast away thy darkness, so thou might live in light for life everlasting."

Reverend Brown paused and addressed the crowd: "You are Tom Bleasdell's neighbours and witnesses. Do you forgive this man's sins?"

A few people nodded.

"Do you banish all darkness from your hearts and vow to protect his light as he has vowed to protect yours?"

More people nodded.

Reverend Brown made the sign of the cross over the forehead and breast of Tom Bleasdell. "I give you the sign of the holy cross, to remind you at all times that you have openly professed your faith in god and your fellow man. I mark your breast with the symbol of the holy cross, to remind you at all times that you must keep god and your neighbour in your heart always, through each daily test to your faith."

Reverend Brown stopped and lowered his voice: "And now I ask you, Tom Bleasdell, before I administer the sacrament of baptism, do you renounce the devil?"

"I do."

"Do you renounce the lusts of the flesh?"

"I do."

Davey turned to a commotion on the riverbank. The thug from the night before made his way to the front of the crowd. His hair was matted with mud, his face scarred with blackfly bites. The stench of feces rose off him. "Do you, Mister Holy Man, renounce the lusts of the flesh?"

A woman cried out. Another man laughed and announced that the drink was to blame.

"Do you, reverend?" the thug said. "Or whoever you are?"

The reverend cleared his throat. "We were never promised an easy life, my friend. Everyone must face their own challenges every moment of their days. You ask if I renounce the lusts of the flesh? I answer, I am a man like any other. I try, and like any other man, it is not easy. But I respect the man who tries instead of the man that accuses."

"You ain't ever tried."

Gussie and Keegan seized the man by both arms. He shouted, "Lies, all of it lies. He ain't no man of god."

They hauled him up the riverbank. Silence descended on the gathering. "Forgive him, my friends, for he knows not what he says." Reverend Brown smiled at Tom Bleasdell. He reached into the water and scooped a palmful and splashed it against Bleasdell's breast. "Do believe in providing to those in need?"

Bleasdell nodded.

"Please answer for all to hear," Reverend Brown said.

"I do."

Reverend Brown smiled. "Will you show your commitment to your beliefs here in front of your neighbours by making a generous donation?"

Tom Bleasdell nodded. "I will."

The reverend reached down into the river again and cupped two palmfuls of water and poured it over Bleasdell's head. "I baptize you in the name of god, all that he represents, all that you aspire to be, and in the name of your neighbours, thy witnesses and therefore your family from here on in."

Reverend Brown dug down into the mud of the river; it dripped from his hand as he drew a simple cross over Bleasdell's heart. He took Bleasdell by the shoulders and turned him to face the crowd on the riverbank. "Friends, I present your brother in truth. A man you have witnessed as being reborn, a man who will live his life according to the commandments and law of god, a man who has given you his word to hold and protect. A man you should be proud to call your neighbour. Mr Tom Bleasdell."

Everyone shouted, "Amen."

Bleasdell faced his people. The mud cross on his chest dripped down to his stomach. He looked as if he might weep, waded slowly through the water to the shore where he picked up his clothes and walked past the line where townsfolk nodded or touched him on the shoulder. He went into town clutching his clothes against his waist.

Bulah motioned for the next man to shed his clothes, and he did so without further encouragement. Davey made her way along the riverbank and then cut through the woods into town.

———————

In the evening, Davey sat with Bulah and Bobby across from the saloon where the rest of the ragtags drank. Shouts and music jangled from within.

"That was as much a pile of bunk that I've ever seen," Davey said.

"It's not my place to say whether it is or not," Bulah said.

"He'll say whatever he wants to say, whether it makes sense or not. Deceiving honest people out of their money and clothes."

"That may be so, girl. But there's no arguing the veracity that he makes believers out of those who do not believe."

"How's that?"

"Because they want to believe, and a man who wants to believe will see beyond his hesitations if he has the faith and support of another. He provides that."

"A man who wants to believe will see what he wants to see," Davey said. "Including falsehoods."

Two men stumbled out of the saloon and urinated into the street.

"He's keeping us all looked after," Bobby said.

"I can keep after myself," Davey said.

Bulah laughed. She stood and cupped Davey's shoulder. "A wise man knows when it's time to be helped by another and when it's time to help oneself." She let go of Davey's shoulder, crossed the street and turned back. "We all need someone to believe in. That's a fact." Bulah swung the saloon's doors open; laughter and music leaked out until the doors swung shut.

Davey and Bobby sat in silence a long while before they rose and entered the hotel. They climbed the stairs. The door to the room at the end of the hall was open. There were low voices, a small boy singing softly, women giggling and the thick smell of pipe tobacco. Reverend Brown sat at a table with three other men playing cards. A naked woman stood behind each man; two stood behind Reverend Brown. One of the women wore the reverend's cedar crown. The women rested their bosoms on his shoulders and ran their hands through the reverend's curly hair. He raised his eyes, shifted the pipe from one side of his mouth to the other, smiled at Davey and Bobby, and motioned for them to enter the room. Bobby stepped forward. Davey turned, descended the stairs and exited the hotel. When she reached the end of the street, she doglegged it into the woods where she found the large fir tree she had slept beneath the previous night. She laid her quiver beside her, the bow on her lap. Looked up at the stars through the trees above her for a long time before tipping her hat forward and closing her eyes.

Magpies chattered in the trees at sunrise. Davey opened her eyes and slid back her hat. Reverend Brown stood above her, smiling with his cassock bunched in his right fist. She sat up.

"I'm just admiring god's fine work."

Davey reached at her side and searched the ground around her.

"Looking for this?" The reverend held the bow.

Davey grabbed an arrow from her quiver and pointed it at his privates.

The reverend chuckled. "Put down thy arrow, girl."

She pushed it closer to him.

"Careful, girl. This moment was decided already. You have no choice but to play out what is predestined."

"I'll put an end to you whether it's been decided or not."

"You believe yourself to be brave, but you're just a rattle-brained child." Reverend Brown motioned to Davey's right. Gussie stood next to her. She pushed the muzzle of her pistol against Davey's temple.

"One fact in life that you have not yet learned: there's always more than you can see."

"I see you fine."

He nodded to Gussie. "Leave her be. She's still learning the ways of the world. She's trying things on, discarding some, keeping others. A path for which she is an agent, not the author."

Gussie lowered her gun.

"You've had your fun," Davey said. "Give me my bow."

Reverend Brown turned to where the others sat on their horses farther up the trail, the animals' tails twitching. He tossed her bow a few feet away, flapped out his cassock and pulled it over his head and down the length of his body and tied up the front while staring at Davey. "Let's get a move on."

The reverend and Gussie returned to the crew and climbed onto their horses. Davey got up, brushed the pine needles from her legs, picked up her bow and slid the arrow into the quiver. She made her way toward Bulah. Her horse trailed Bulah's pony. The rest of the party, led by Reverend Brown, had already moved on.

"What's this all about?" Bulah handed Davey the reins to her horse.

"Where were you?" Davey said.

"At the hotel."

"Sleeping one off?"

"What I do is my business."

Davey shook her head. "If I asked you to stop, would you?"

"Are you asking me now?"

Davey studied her for a moment. "It's not my burden to tell you what you should or shouldn't do." She climbed her horse and clucked it forward. Bulah followed closely, keeping pace.

SIX

THEY RODE OFF THE VALLEY BOTTOM up into the mountains and
threaded their way through stunted firs that rose like stern gnomes.
Their horses weaved in and out of bluebunch wheatgrass, trampling
over long threads of dried fir scattered on the ground. Pikas chirped.
The crew entered a wooded patch and cantered beneath stencilled
parasols of larch trees whose needles lay like threads of gold on the
dusty path. Reverend Brown led, followed by Keegan, Gussie, Bobby,
Bulah, Davey and a line of disciples and dogs, many walking or labouring as they dragged travois behind them. Late in the afternoon, they
crossed an alpine saddle where bluebottles and winged ants shot
upward, flitting in the light against a flawless sky. Bulah trotted past
Davey, Gussie and Keegan and rode up to Reverend Brown and took
the lead.

In the early evening, Bulah led them across a slope scarred with
shattered salmonberry, white pus foaming at the plants' broken joints,
the undercarriages of the ponies and dogs damp with slurried soot.
Her horse halted and snapped its head back and forth.

Davey clucked. Bulah turned around. Davey pointed to her left
and brought a finger to her mouth.

Two small brown-coated bear cubs clicked up a tree and when they
reached a height, they started mewling.

Bulah turned back to Davey and smiled.

"Let's get a move on," Keegan called out.

Bulah studied the woods and kicked her horse in the ribs, but the horse whinnied and shook its head. She whipped it across the rump; the horse stepped forward. She rode through smashed brush and stopped at the tree where the cubs cried above her. Davey joined her. Neither of them moved. The tree trunk was scored with fresh claw marks and the air was redolent of green pine resin and the thick musk of animal sweat. On the ground, chunks of red rot were scattered from the diggings; tufts of coarse brown fur hung from shrubs. Bulah pointed at the cubs.

"They're beautiful," Davey said. "So tiny and furry."

Bulah's eyes were damp. "Go on," she said, "I'll be right behind you."

Davey took one more look at the cubs and did as she was told.

Bulah kicked her horse and started back along the slender trail just as a large grizzly bear crashed through the brush. The bear stopped behind Bulah, stood on its rear legs and towered over her, huffing and clacking its teeth, the russet fabric of its oval face oscillating toward her, a glob of macerated berries swinging from its jaws.

Bulah's horse whinnied, jerking its head back and forth as it rose onto its hindquarters, bucking her from the saddle and slamming her down on the forest floor. She lay winded, gulping air in short gasps. The cubs squealed above them. One of the dogs leapt onto the grizzly bear from behind. It twisted around and the dog swung howling from the beast's backside. The bear growled and swatted at the dog, slicing its side open where it lay bleeding and whimpering against a small boulder. Bulah coughed and writhed on the ground. The bear swiped at her leg, clamped its teeth down on her shoulder and shook her like a plaything. Saliva drooled onto the back of Bulah's neck. Bulah screamed. Davey whipped her horse toward her. The grizzly hurled Bulah against the base of a tree and raised itself to face the crew. Davey inserted an arrow in the nock, drew the bowstring. The reverend leaned down from his saddle and grabbed Bulah's arm. One of the cubs screeched. The beast turned, its enormous paw swinging like a heavy pendulum in the air, and flung Reverend Brown off his horse. Davey rested the arrow above the riser, drew in a deep breath and released the arrow. The bear lifted its face and snarled. The reverend cried out. Davey's arrow tore through his shoulder and nailed him to the bear. A shot fired and then another, sound booming above them, and then two heavy thuds on the ground. Davey spun around. Keegan lowered his rifle. The cubs lay motionless on the forest floor. Gussie pointed her pistol at the bear's leg and shot it. The bear groaned on its hindquarters, striking the reverend with its paws and tossing him sideways, the arrow's fletching tearing through the reverend's shoulder. Reverend Brown lay on the ground groaning. Davey's arrow flopped back and forth in the bear's shoulder. The beast snatched at it and snapped the arrow, the nub still embedded in its flesh. It snarled, dropped to all fours and circled the cubs, snuffling and snorting their limp bodies. Gussie raised her pistol and let out another shot; the bullet whistled past the bear. The bear roared and limped into the woods, a trail of bloodied leaves and broken branches crushed in its wake.

Davey offered her hand to Bulah.

"I'm all right. Just a few scrapes," Bulah said.

Reverend Brown examined the gash in her shoulder. He pulled a cloth from his saddlebag, tore it in strips and wrapped the wound. Davey held Bulah's forearm while he finished dressing her wound.

"Are you all right?" Davey's voice broke.

Bulah winced, placed a hand on Davey's cheek, and nodded.

"Are you sure?"

"Yes." Bulah forced a smile. "I'll be fine."

Reverend Brown's cassock was torn and damp with blood. The clown dressed his wound with lichen. He tore both arms off his own shirt, folded one in half and placed it against the wound. With the other shirt sleeve, he wrapped the dressing and tied it tight. Reverend Brown grabbed the clown and pulled him so that their foreheads touched. They stared into each other's eyes. The reverend unsheathed his knife. "Wait here." He took off running into the woods.

His boots thumped down the path. The crew heard the reverend's breath come in punctured gasps, they heard his shouts, and they heard the bear growl. There was no sound save for the wind in the treetops.

Keegan flogged his horse and the ragtags followed him into the woods. They tracked blood on the dirt and leaves, rocks and exposed tree roots. The reverend appeared ahead of them, and then they lost him at a precipice he had descended. They eyed the direction he was heading, turned their horses up the trail and found a way down where they picked up his footprints. Here, pine needles and pale dirt were upturned and scattered in fresh piles, as if the bear had swept the area with its immense paws. They stopped at the edge of another small crag. Reverend Brown bolted behind the bear across a shallow gully, shouting. The crew rode up one edge of the cliff and went down through the gully but lost sight of them. They picked up a faint trace of trail across a dried creek bed, up a thick draw where the brush was smashed, but lost the tracks when they hit a scree slope at dusk. They traversed the slope and backtracked but none could find a sign of blood or beast or reverend. They crossed the slope and went back a third time, scanning the rocky terrain. Nothing but high alpine wind and the chittering of pikas. They peered down the gully and up the scree slope. It grew dark and faint stars began to appear. The wind relented and they made camp at the edge of the slope beneath the trees.

"You shot him," Gussie said.

"I saved Bulah," Davey said.

"I seen your intent."

"You saw nothing."

"What's that supposed to mean?"

Davey shook her head.

"Tell me, girl. What that's supposed to mean?"

Davey watched her for a long time.

"He seen you, too," Gussie said in a low voice. "He seen you like I did."

"Leave her be," Bulah said. "I owe her my life. Same could be said of him."

Davey pulled the blanket up and lay in the dark, the bow close to her body. She stared at the stars and listened to the silence that enveloped the camp.

They rose at daybreak. Bulah mounted her horse. Gussie and Davey followed with the rest of the crew. They rode across the slope scanning the ground for signs of the bear and the reverend. They encountered shreds of bloodied clothing, dark blood on the leaves of plants, enormous paw prints. They turned to where they had made camp and negotiated the slope again, rode for a while before Bulah raised a hand. She rode over to Gussie, climbed down from her horse, removed her hat and stood with her head bowed. Gussie did the same. One by one the crew disembarked from their horses and held their hats in their hands with their heads bowed. A man played a melancholic dirge on his fiddle. The clown sat on a rock and looked out over the country before lowering his head onto his arms.

Bulah instructed two men to build a fire. Bulah and Gussie removed the reverend's bags and saddle from his horse and laid them out beside the fire they had built. Not one lifted their head. Bulah tossed the reverend's saddle and bags onto the fire. Each man and woman gathered sticks and branches and small logs and took turns feeding the fire, spreading the girth of it. One man dug a trench around the perimeter of the fire; the flames thundered in the pit, rising above them all, the heat blistering. Gussie turned to the reverend's horse. She stroked the animal's side, spoke into its ear. She lifted her revolver from her belt and continued to caress the horse, placed the barrel against the underside of its jaw and pressed the lever. Her arm kicked back when the shot boomed out. The horse collapsed as though its legs had been snapped at the knees, its great nostrils flared against the dirt. Gussie placed her palm against its bloodied head until its forelegs stopped twitching. She ran her hand over her face and placed the revolver in her belt. One by one the disciples approached the horse and ran their hands against it, smearing the blood over their faces and hands. Bulah motioned for Davey to do the same, but instead she looked off over the valley. Keegan roped the slain horse's feet, climbed onto his pony and dragged the carcass into the firepit.

The sect gathered around the fire in silence. When the smell and heat of the charred horse became too great, they fanned it away with their hats and waited a long while until the fire weakened, grabbed fist-fuls of dirt and dropped them on the fire until it was snuffed out. They mounted their horses. Bulah called the clown but he remained fixed in his spot. She called him again. He raised his head, studied her and the others, and waved at them to move on. One of the dogs barked at a movement in the trees. Keegan raised his rifle. Reverend Brown came staggering out of the woods, scraped and bloodied, with a long weeping gash from his right eye down to his jawbone; another gash intersected it horizontally, making the wound appear as a cross carved into his flesh. His cassock was torn and his chest had deep claw marks scraped across it. He held his knife in his right hand and his face was ashen, his eyes wild. His shoulder was packed with dirt and lichen but the gashes across his chest were black and crusted with dried blood. Keegan lowered his gun. Gussie and two of the men cried out. The reverend stopped, lifted the cedar crown as if greeting his apostles, and placed it back on his head. The clown got up, ran to the reverend and embraced him.

Bulah dismounted, unlaced her saddle and handed it to him. Reverend Brown held her gift. One of the men leapt off his horse, removed the saddle, set it on the ground and led the horse to the rever-end. The man picked up his saddle and went to the rear of the column.

Reverend Brown spoke into the horse's ear, placed Bulah's saddle on its back and cinched it. Gussie offered him one of her bags. Bobby removed his shirt and held it out to Reverend Brown. Keegan brought him a blanket. Another man handed over a fistful of jerked squirrel. One man offered his boots. The clown wiped away the dirt and lichen from the reverend's chest and handed him a wide strap of leather. Reverend Brown clamped his teeth on it. The clown opened his canteen and spilled some water on the wound. Reverend Brown winced and let out a low moan and when the gash was cleansed, the clown gave the canteen to the reverend; he took a long gulp of water before handing it back to the clown. Reverend Brown grunted and his eyes flashed white. The clown tore a sleeve off the shirt Bobby had gifted to Reverend Brown and dressed the wound. He tore the other sleeve off, bunched up the fabric, poured water over it and gently wiped the slashes on Reverend Brown's face. He helped the reverend into the sleeveless shirt and when he was done, he bowed.

"It's good to be home," the reverend said, "reunited with my brothers and sisters." He turned to Davey.

She sat upright on her horse and shifted the quiver against her shoulder.

"You saved my life," Reverend Brown said.

The clown flapped out the blanket, slipped it over the reverend's shoulders and helped him pull on his boots. Reverend Brown picked up his knife, climbed onto the horse.

"What happened to the bear?" Davey said.

"I avenged what it did to Bulah." Reverend Brown slipped the knife into a sheaf on his waist.

"Where is it?"

Reverend Brown studied Davey for a long while and smiled. "Up there."

Davey looked up the trail from where he had come.

"Where?"

Reverend Brown swung his horse around and urged it forward. Gussie sneered at Davey and followed the reverend. The rest of the crew fell in. The man holding his saddle ran for a ways and passed Davey before he tossed his saddle to the ground and leaned over his knees, winded. Bulah stopped and offered her hand. He waved her off.

"Come on, no sense in holding everyone back." She pulled him up and he sat behind her. She stopped beside Davey. "If this is the worst thing that will happen in your days, you're going to have a pretty good go of it."

"Was there a part of you that was relieved when he didn't come back?"

Bulah stared off at the horizon.

"I've never heard that man utter a truth," Davey said.

"That's between him and his maker," Bulah said.

"Is it? Haven't his falsehoods caused enough harm? What if there are more horrible things to come?"

Bulah shrugged. "What if there are better things to come?" She kicked her horse in the sides and rode on in a westerly direction.

Davey turned her horse east and raced up the trail. None of the brush was crushed; there were no tracks or blood on the path. She turned around and galloped westward, where soon she caught up with the others.

"Well?" Bulah said.

"There was nothing," Davey said, "no trace of anything. Like it never happened."

———————————

The sect journeyed through country where the wind scrubbed the alpine clean and the cirrus sky was tufted with streaks like mare's tails, the land yellow and tawny, lacerated by brown trails and the green river. They rode along a trail strewn with shrivelled turds from mountain sheep and sought solace in the shade to cool their horses, the clink of the harnesses as the animals jerked their heads against the blackflies. Davey stopped and pressed her palm against the coarse bark of a towering fir on an outcrop of chunky rock. She considered the thinning trees, the oiled dark of the river below, the slope of the mountains. A raven flew between the trees, its wings beating softly. Davey tapped the tree and moved on.

Clouds rolled in and thunder rumbled in the distance. They kept watch for rain, threading through a deep scar in the mountains, pressed close against the prehistoric grey rocks pockmarked with the acne of shell fragments. Then they rode into a clearing over compact, sun-baked land; Davey felt the pound of it shudder all the way up through her shoulders, her neck and teeth. The reverend raised his hand and she stopped along with the others. A deer chewed grass on the far side of the meadow. He reached for his rifle, held the deer in his sights, and when the animal lifted its head, the reverend pressed the trigger. The rifle kicked back and he shouted out, dropped the rifle and held his shoulder. The deer bolted into the brush. Keegan thrashed his reins, alternating against his pony's shoulders and rear, rode hard across the meadow into the woods. A shot rang out; Keegan let out a loud whoop.

The sect camped along the riverbank with a clear run of water and good grass. They butchered the deer, carving off sheets of muscle to roast over webbed pine sticks laid across the fire.

At dusk, Reverend Brown walked along the riverbank. The moon rose swollen over the mountainside like a lucent egg. There was no wind, only the faint rill of water running over the rocks and their horses snorting lightly as they pulled grass and chewed it.

He joined his disciples and picked up a fistful of sand, letting the granules sift through his fist onto his palm, and then did it again until the dust of the sand itself was all that remained. He confiscated another fistful and stuffed it into his pocket and wiped his palms on his cassock.

The wound on the reverend's face glistened in the firelight. It appeared quartered in the shadows when he turned in and out of the light. Bulah gathered the blanket tight over her shoulders.

"A man only has as much as he can fit in his palm," he said. "All our lives we try to keep the sand from leaking out, yet we're stunned to discover that we've run out of sand and time."

Davey lifted her head and squinted at him. "I didn't save you."

"You saving me or someone from above saving me or another man saving me. It's not the point for discussion. It's been done. Our time has been predetermined. Preordained. Prescribed, if you will. It sets up more decisions and actions, cause and effect, dribbling from our clenched fists the duration of our days. The decision you made back there is recorded." He waved his arms in the air around him. "Deposited into the world's memory. Like these grains of sand."

Davey picked up a twig and traced shapes in the dirt.

Reverend Brown smiled. "Every man, woman and beast is connected in an endless bond of being."

"Everyone remembers what they want to remember." Davey drew a small circle and another circle around it.

"And what memory is that then?"

"Truth." She wiped away the cracks and drew a line.

Gussie and the other ragtags laughed.

"Silence," Reverend Brown said.

The group quieted.

"The lass has had little to test her in her youth. We are who we are, good or evil or both at the same time. The pride we shield ourselves with will be revealed over time. Who a man is and who a man believes himself to be. The truth rests in the gap between the two."

He told them he had once climbed a mountaintop to seek god's counsel. The almighty answered his call and instructed him to remove the clothes that shielded him from himself and told him he must stand alone and naked before the lord and that it was up to the lord to grant him amnesty. The reverend said he stood on that mountaintop and shivered until the sun sank below the horizon. His teeth chattered throughout the night and he held his elbows to keep warm but it did not help and by morning his skin was pebbled from the cold, but it warmed when the sun rose. "I stayed on that mountaintop until the truth of who I was and who I wanted to be were one."

He paused, turned his head away from them. A long moment passed before he faced them, his voice low. "You don't know what truth is until you do."

He removed a shin bone from the fire, raised the backside of an axe and cracked the bone into pieces over the rocks that ringed the fire. The marrow hissed and bubbled on the stones. The reverend offered these scorched bones to his followers but no one accepted his gift. He tilted the troughs and slurped out the marrow, tossed them to the dogs skulking nearby. "It gets inside you, courses through your body, leeches into your blood and bones, quiet and profound and mysterious. Its power is unlike any other force you'll encounter in your lives, and no other can take it from you except you, yourself." The reverend watched the dogs tussle with the bones and turned back to the crew around the fire. "Most men live between truth and untruth, a half life, not realizing that they are doing so because they lack the courage to face this reckoning in themselves."

"I don't see why we have to climb a mountain to see god and find the truth." Davey drew a square.

Reverend Brown pulled a kerchief from his pocket and wiped his mouth. He grimaced and rubbed his shoulder. "I never told you I saw the lord. I said I spoke with the lord. Note the difference, lass. You're already changing the referents of my story."

"You tell me to never doubt that which I cannot see. But if I cannot question the unknown, how will it become known to me? How will I know what is true and what is not?"

"It's everywhere," Reverend Brown said.

"You tell us that. You tell everyone, everywhere we go, the same thing. But you offer no proof. You preach that god is everywhere and anywhere. And everyone listens in fear, waiting for him. We're judged by a witness we can never see or hear but one we must believe in. Because you tell us it's so." She cleared her throat. "Why should anyone believe you when you don't tell the truth?"

Reverend Brown stoked the fire and watched the red embers rise into the night sky. He laid the stick on the ground. "Everyone says they want the truth until they hear it. Who do you think has it easier? The one with the truth, the one without it, or the one with half of it? Listen carefully, lass, to what I'm going to tell you so you can decide for yourself. A boot cobbler once kept shop in the eastern Rockies, on the District of Alberta's side of the Pass. He was new to the country via England and he had learned boot making from his father, who had learned it from his father, and he intended to pass it on to his son. He established a humble homestead at the toe of the trail that men used to travel over the Pass."

"You talk and talk and tell stories but you don't answer our questions. You talk to avoid the truth."

"Patience, lass. There's plenty of truth in what I'm about to tell you."

Davey shook her head and studied the ground.

Reverend Brown continued. "The men who travelled along this goat trail did so for it was a shorter route over the Pass from the District of Alberta into British Columbia. To circumvent the Pass added another ten days of travel. Now, the cobbler was desperate to earn, so he dressed in the likeness of a woman and waited near the trailhead, where he asked whoever passed if they would pay him money for carnal favours he would bestow upon their person before granting them the right to continue on. He was not a large or strong man but he understood that the men he bequeathed his favours upon were lonely and that they suffered from the shame of what they had conspired in by engaging with him. As such he held a morally higher ground than they, for he had taken away their honour, their own idea of what it meant to be a man. In this way, over time, he controlled the flow of travellers who travelled over the Pass and amassed a small fortune, more than provided by shoemaking, an honest skill he had learned from his father and his father's father and so on. He kept his earnings concealed in the hollow of a tall fir tree near the entrance to the Pass.

"But deceit has a way of eroding a man's soul while infecting those around him. One day, his son brought him his midday meal on a warm, bright day and witnessed his father dressed as a woman, teetering in the women's shoes that his father had made, and he saw his father's face grimace against the bark of a tree, his dress bunched up around his waist, while another man rutted him from behind. When they were done his father straightened his dress and accepted the coin from the traveller, and after the traveller had had left, he slipped the coin into the hollow of the tree. The son left the meal at the trailhead and ran home, troubled by witnessing a truth that did not add up to how he saw his father, a truth that his father had carefully concealed from him.

"The next day, the boy waited behind the tree. An old man came by, and the boy's father, in his dress, hat, and woman's shoes made by his own hand, accosted the old man and asked him for money. The old man refused and told the cobbler he would give no money to any person for the right to use the trail. He told the cobbler that the land belonged to no one man or woman. That all people were custodians of the land, not proprietors of it, and that any man seeking financial reward for something that was not his own was no different from a common thief. The old man asked the cobbler if he had a son, and the cobbler nodded yes. The old man asked the cobbler to remove his disguise and be seen for who he was. He did as he was told. The old man asked if the cobbler felt any different from before. The cobbler replied that he did and he did not. Here, the old man paused before replying, 'Give yourself an honest chance, rather than promulgating falsehoods through any disguise you might employ.'

"The old traveller said the cobbler's son would either be the man the cobbler was, or his own man. And that if he were to become his own man, the residue of his father would still cling to him, for many men had spent their entire lives trying to shed that cloak, and that concealing his nature would place an unfair burden on the son as he sought to find his own way in the world. He said, 'If a man acts at being someone he is not, then what hope is there for his progeny? How will any of them know what is true in themselves and others if the very well they all drink from is poisoned?'

"The old traveller continued on his way up the Pass without paying the money the cobbler had solicited for. The cobbler smacked his forehead against the trunk of a tree again and again and shouted insults at himself, called himself a "common thief," slapping his face with his palms, and when he was done, his forehead was bruised and bloodied, tears streamed down his face, and he sat against the tree studying his hands, turning them over. His son returned home deeply troubled by all he had observed.

"Soon after, the cobbler fell ill and was relegated to his cot for a period of time. His son went to the trail on his own. The first time a traveller came up the path, the boy greeted him, but the traveller passed by without a word. When the boy saw another traveller approach, he looked in the hollow of the tree, found the women's garments, and slipped them on. He took the jar of rouge and smeared it across his cheeks and stood at the side of the path as he had seen his father do many times before. When the traveller reached the boy, the traveller smiled and offered the boy two coins, double what the boy had seen his father receive, and the boy lifted his dress and bent over. The pain was unlike any the boy had ever experienced, and when the traveller was finished, the boy tottered in his shoes and straightened the fabric of the dress and stood unblinking in front of the man. The traveller handed him another coin and went on his way without a word.

"The boy wept like the child he was until the next traveller approached. He composed himself and smiled at the traveller, and so, the boy began the pattern his father had subscribed to, offering carnal favours to all men who travelled over the Pass. The boy hid his coins in a hole he dug with his hands, and he covered it with a large rock.

"The cobbler recuperated and was determined to take the old traveller's counsel and shed his disguise. He returned to the trail and resumed his boot repair services, but was surprised to find that the travellers asked for his son. One day when the boy brought his father his midday meal, the father inquired what the boy had been doing in his absence. The boy replied that he'd kept shop as he had been commanded. The father asked if the boy had ever been untruthful to him and the boy said no, he had not. He asked the boy again and the boy replied that he had always told his father the truth. At this the father sighed and asked the boy a third time, and when the boy repeated what he had already said, the father slapped his son's face. His son held his jaw and stared at his father, who told him not to cry. The son's eyes were wet and his father slapped him again, this time much harder, and told the boy that if he shed a single tear he would slap him senseless until the tears drained out of him so that he would never cry again. The boy's eyes twitched and his face tightened before he ran off into the woods. The father sat and wept. Eventually he rose and started a fire. He retrieved his dress, shoes, and the jar of rouge and placed them onto the fire. Through the night, he stoked it and added wood until all evidence of his sordid activities had turned to ash.

"The next morning, he summoned his son and declared they would ride over the Pass in search of gold, which he knew from the other travellers was abundant farther west. But the truth he withheld from the boy was that he intended to locate the coal deposits indicated on a map he had stolen from a traveller. Father and son stopped at the trailhead. The cobbler dug out the coins and the map and told the boy he had been saving for this moment when the two of them could go into business with each other, and eventually the son could go into business with his own child when he married. It would be the old man's legacy and the son's inheritance, and then the son's legacy, and so forth. The boy noted the firepit and did not retrieve his own money. He left it behind, deposited into the earth itself.

"Father and son rode for two days. It rained continuously, and the cobbler became sick and weak as they made camp in the evening. On the third day, the son confronted his father about disguising himself as a woman, and in his anger, he crushed his father's head with a chunk of wood, a weapon of the land itself. As his father lay dying, he forgave his son for murdering him. The son replied that he could not be forgiven, that he was prepared to live out his days however he deserved according to his actions. He told his father that he knew the truth of who he was, and with these final words, the cobbler died.

"The son searched his father's body for the map, but it was not on his person. The son howled and cursed his father's name and cast him on the fire. In the morning he headed west, where he eventually discovered the coalfields and earned his way in the world through deceit and crime."

Here, Reverend Brown paused and smiled at Davey. The group sat in silence, staring into the fire. Keegan turned to Davey and then to the reverend and back again but neither person moved nor blinked.

"Can somebody tell me what kind of man thinks dressing up like a woman will fool another man?"

Bulah sat next to Davey and glared at Reverend Brown. The reverend stood and put a finger to his lips and in a low voice said, "Quiet. You can't think straight if your blood runs hot. Hold thy tongue and cool your opinion. The cobbler's son was taken in by a caravan of pilgrims travelling to the coast. These travellers had no reason to take him in other than for their benevolence, and yet they did and treated him as one of their own. He married a woman who bore in her womb a young child who would become his daughter. But the son abandoned his bride and her people before this girl was born, for his bride had shown him the fields of black rock and made him promise not to use this knowledge, a promise that he broke. The pilgrims did not hunt for him. They believed him to be damned, something he had confessed to his wife, and they accepted the fact that he had dishonoured the kindness they had bestowed upon him. Sometime later, when he called for his bride to join him, she and the rest of her people were killed on his orders. His orders. But his daughter, an infant, survived."

He looked around the fire at his audience and resumed. "Can any of you tell me what that son inherited from his father?" Reverend Brown paused and shook his head. "What did his daughter inherit, whether or not she knew her father or mother? She did not learn from or see her parents live out the days of their lives. She did not witness their love or struggle. She was born beneath the weight of a man condemned at birth, one who fulfilled his fate as a thief and a murderer, one whose word was worth less than this dirt you squat on. She was broken from the beginning."

Bulah glared at Reverend Brown. She rose and left the fire.

"The pilgrims' history? They were travelling west across the country to reach the coast and endured many hardships along the way. That is their story, the spine of truth that connects them from generation to generation, passed down through the stories they tell one another at night around a fire. The story of their lives. Their histories. There are peoples of this land who believe that the sun created the earth. We have not one but two creation stories of our own: god created the world in six days and rested on the seventh, and from dust he created Adam, and from Adam he took a rib to create Eve. Other peoples have their own origin stories that shape who they are today. Can they all be true, these conflicting tales? Which one is the true story? Which one is the historical antecedent of the daughter?" He paused and looked at his disciples. "Does it even matter? The pilgrims saved that cobbler's son, and in return for their largesse they were betrayed and slaughtered by that same man, one whose life had been fated long before they saved him. All lands, wherever you go, whether inhabited or not, are possessed by those who have walked upon the ground, regardless of where they come from, regardless of who they are. Hush now. Can you hear the echo of their spirits crooning across the land? Listen carefully. Can you hear the clamour as men like the cobbler and his son mine tourmalinite and chert and hammer out knives and spearheads to protect that which they've taken? What is the sound of fear? An unknown rage, a ruthless rejoicing. I said listen carefully, brothers and sisters. The world does not lie. There's your hard-earned truth."

"You claim the man was damned from birth, yet what does that man say himself? You tell us your version and ask us to believe you. To trust you," Davey said, "to trust you when you have never been honest with us."

Reverend Brown wiped the sand from his hands. "I hold the facts, lass. The facts are accountable."

"Facts or falsehoods? What facts do you hold?" Davey said. "You offered no evidence, nothing but a story, one that blames a man who is not here to refute whether you are telling the truth or not. You are not accountable for anything you've ever said. Now or before. All you tell is stories with no regard for how they might shape someone's thoughts and opinions."

"Look to the bible, a book whose many stories and truths are founded on violence," Reverend Brown said. "Every portentous event that advanced man? Founded on violence, predicated on what individuals hold as their truth. From the beginning. Look at Adam and Eve, Cain and Abel. Their original sins blackened all of mankind. A malfeasance that has corrupted every one of us since." He placed a palm against the ground. "We cannot see them, but the dead are here, beneath our boots that tread over them with each step, grinding them to dust that rises and falls when the wind blows, that clings to our clothes and gets into our eyes, our noses and throats and settles within us, that we carry throughout our lives. Wherever we go, we will all eventually, nay, inevitably, become part of the land that others will trample across."

"What are you suggesting?" Davey said.

"The curse of Adam and Eve and the curse of Cain defiled all of mankind," Reverend Brown said. "Many theologies rest their foundation on this. 'Put up again thy sword into his place: for all they that take the sword shall perish with the sword.' Man produces violence through his own actions, in service of this original curse and all that proceeds from it. Man's children are infected by it and unable to escape it's pernicious influence."

"What does any of this have to do with your tale?" Davey said.

"We are born and inherit the transgressions of the world, of those near and far, known or unknown. Have you ever witnessed a doe raise up on her hindquarters and slam her forelegs down on a young deer, smashing its skull, for the only reason that it fed from the same area as her own offspring?" Reverend Brown said. "Male black bears kill their cubs. There is infanticide by either father or mother. There's patricide. Matricide. Murder. There are more hurts than any man can catalogue. It's the way of the world. It's a nasty, brutish, brief business. So is the duel every man must confront within himself: the riddle of existence and survival. That is a man's life. We bloom and flower and die. We achieve and we fail. These mountains, rivers, valleys and soils you see have been wondered at by all peoples that preceded you and me, from all denominations and cuts of cloth and turns of tongue. This is the story of all mankind—wonderment and rage. Some men see themselves as belonging to the land and want to leave it in better shape before they move on, while many do not. Many see the land and all its artifacts as their personal possession and hoard as much as they can. Wonderment and rage. There will be a whole planet of new people one hundred years from this moment. Think on that. And think on this: the residue, the echo of your life will be part of that original sin, your existence, just like"—he picked up a fistful of dirt and let it dribble from his hand—"just like it is for these souls who have preceded us and now bear witness to our lives."

Bulah returned to the fire. There was a long silence before Davey replied. "Don't we also inherit the goodness of the world? If falsehoods and violence only make more falsehoods and violence, if it only makes more evil, how can it stop? How does a condemnation end?"

"It doesn't," Reverend Brown said. "If god is willing but can't prevent evil, then what kind of almighty and powerful god is he? If he can prevent evil but doesn't want to, then what kind of altruistic god is he? He's either feeble or evil himself. As is man."

"How do we know that a damnation, as you've told us, was placed on that man by his father's father? Did you see or hear it yourself?" Davey shook her head. "How do we know your version is the truth?"

Reverend Brown squinted at her. "God is my witness. Always. As he is yours."

"A god that is either feeble or evil? You told us a story that blames a man and the families he travelled with for inflicting harm on the rest of us. A story that through your telling perpetuates itself with no basis of truth attached to it."

"We believe that which we see, that which we don't," he said. "All men are thirsty for belief and are willing to take up arms for that belief. They are also willing to lay down their arms. But a belief is not a truth. If a belief comes from a curse, can it be considered the truth? Nay, it's a true measure of who a man perceives himself to be."

"What if a man utters an untruth?"

Reverend Brown smiled and stood. "Give me your bow."

"Who's my father?" Davey said.

"Listen carefully, lass. Hand me your bow."

"Who's my father?"

"Lass, I'm not yet done my tale." He held out his hand.

Davey turned to Bulah. Her head was lowered. She appeared to have aged considerably in the slouch of her shoulders. Davey handed the bow to the reverend. He asked for an arrow; she drew one from her quiver and handed it to him.

"It's all a cycle that runs on its own. We have no control in any of it." He pushed the head of the arrow into the fire and turned it over and waited for it to glow and ignite and once it did he removed it and held it out in the darkness where those assembled could see it glowing red. "Our days, our actions, our lives are already preordained and to try to alter the course of that is simply part of a predetermined path that lays before us. It does not matter what fork you choose, what you believe, it will still lead you there. There's no escaping it. Everything one does or does not do is a decision one makes." He smiled, drew the arrow, pointed it overhead into the black sky and released it.

The crew leapt up from where they sat and ran shouting into the darkness, taking cover in the trees.

"Have you learned nothing?" He spread his arms out as his follow-ers scattered about. "To move is already part of your fate. As much as it is to stand still. Quiet, you blubbering fools."

The crew stopped shouting and looked upward and from the dark-ness came silence and then a faint whistling that grew shriller as the fiery glow of the arrow appeared, whizzing as it plummeted toward them and struck the ground behind the reverend.

Keegan shouted out, "It must have been my time." He gasped and crumpled to the ground. He laughed, rolling around in the dirt. The arrow was ten feet to his left, smoking in the soil. Others in the group laughed. The clown mimed shooting an arrow into sky and held out his hand as if he caught it. Another opened his mouth and pretended to have caught it with his teeth. One mimed shooting another man.

Another man mimed shooting the arrow into the sky and looking upward for a very long time and then stopped, shrugged his shoulders and began to walk to the fire before he collapsed as if hit on the crown of the head by an arrow.

Reverend Brown sat and the others approached the fire, laughing and slapping each other on the backs. Davey retrieved the arrow and slipped the head into the shallows of the river. She slid it into her quiver and stood in the shadows. Reverend Brown lifted a palmful of sand and trickled it through his fingers and pressed his hand flat on the ground as if to make the sand solid and hard so it might stay that way for generations.

"You men laugh to shield yourselves from the truth," he said. "Which one of you did not seek to escape that arrow? Not a single man here. You are not indestructible because of your belief in god or anyone else. God has his own rules. There is no man who can claim to know these rules." He nodded to Keegan. "Man's rules are in response to god. More specifically, in response to what they deem are god's rules. You believe yourselves to be free. Every decision you make in life is couched in hierarchy. How can you ever possibly be free?"

"Who's my father?" Davey said.

Reverend Brown looked at Bulah and back at Davey. "I am, lass."

"In all of the stories you tell, you're telling the story of yourself. Do you ever tell the truth?"

———————

In the days that followed, they crossed the high country and rode through forests of hemlock and pine with immense fibril branches fanning overhead. At night they ate fistfuls of berries, roasted rabbits and squirrels, tossing the carcasses to the dogs. A sickle moon rose over the dark mountains and along a nearby ridge, red rows of flowering paintbrush moved in the ever present wind. Stars salted across a black sky.

One day they came to a clearing where a lake encrusted in ice lay like a grimy plate. Steep scree slopes flanked it on three sides. Goats criss-crossed the bluffs and rocks popped loose, tumbling onto the lake. Damp glossed the frozen surface. The lake burbled through small holes and cracks; water flowed here and there. It lay white and opaque in spots, slushy and mottled in others. Dark brown tannins leeched throughout the ice.

"Thick and blue, tried and true," Bulah said. "Thin and crispy, too risky." She climbed down from her horse, took a length of rope from her pannier and secured it around her waist and her horse and then walked a few steps onto the ice, a cracking sound split up and down the lake. She paused after ten feet, leaned down and chipped a hole in the surface with a pickaxe, slipped her hand into it and measured it. Bulah turned around and held up her hand to show the others. "Three inches." She returned to the crew, untied the rope from her waist and the horse, pointed to the slope on the left. "We'll go that way."

Reverend Brown dismounted and led his horse behind him and walked on the ice. The ice cracked and moaned with each step and after a hundred yards, the reverend stopped and knelt down. He swept away the snow and slush and considered the fish labouring below the surface, slow and lethargic like prehistoric versions of themselves. "You can't trust any being that can stay alive while entombed in ice." He leaned his ear against the frozen surface as if he might hear the fish swimming, their dorsal fins scratching the bottom of the ice above them.

He grabbed a palmful of slush and pressed it against the wounds on his chest, stood and directed his speech to the shoreline where the crew waited. "The instinct for these fish to breathe underwater is as strong as it is for man to not breath underwater. The impulse is so strong in man, not to breathe underwater, that he risks running out of oxygen. Brothers and sisters, you shake your heads, but humour me. While running out of air, man chooses not to breathe. He chooses not to breathe. He chooses a slow, horrible death. The world darkens around him as he realizes he is drowning. He has no experience in this regard, for he does not know how to die gracefully. What man does? Instead, he dies in utter awkwardness, flailing against the water and exerting himself to get above it where he can take a breath, fighting within himself, reviewing the most banal parts of his life in those last moments. Maybe he experiences regret, for what man will not encounter regret when he takes stock of his life's work in his final moments? And his final thoughts may be that he has squandered a great fortune in this last, greatest act of foolishness in his life."

The crew shifted behind him.

"Once again, you've reached a fork in your paths today. Either way your choice has already been determined. It is the burden we must all bear in our every hour. Keep that in mind. I'll leave it to you to decide what to do, for that choice is irrelevant. There is no mystery to it. You can choose to follow me or not." He turned and marched across the lake.

Gussie climbed down from her horse and led it behind her as she followed the reverend's footsteps on the ice.

Keegan slid down from his saddle and Bobby joined him. They affixed a rope to one another and began to tread behind Gussie in single file, careful to follow her steps. The ice cracked and moaned all around them. Keegan cussed, Bobby sniffled quietly. Reverend Brown turned and called them fools, pointed out their cowardice, their lack of grace in what might be their last moments. Had they not learned anything from what he had told them? He said that they put each other's lives in their own hands by tying their destination to one another and that in doing so it was just another link in the chain of events that would mark out their final moments, or their days to come if they should be so fortunate to survive the crossing. The two men pivoted and returned to the shore where the others waited.

Davey, Bulah, and the rest of the crew traversed the slope. Rocks and scree tumbled down and rolled across the ice. They met up with Gussie and the reverend at the far end of the lake. Their boots were soaked through and their horses were twitchy. Gussie's face had tightened with the strain of the journey they had completed. Reverend Brown's face shone as if he had become more youthful.

"Did you make the right choice?" he said.

"I made the obvious choice by not playing your game," Davey said.

"You abandoned Gussie and me to preserve yourself."

"I wasn't the only one," she gestured to the rest of the crew. "Why wasn't that my predestination, as you've said?"

"Why indeed."

"You speak in riddles, as if you are above the truth."

Reverend Brown shrugged his shoulders and smiled. "I move in mysterious ways."

"You're not the god of me. You're not my father."

"How would you even know?"

Davey regarded him. "I've always known."

SEVEN

FOR THE NEXT THREE DAYS the sect rose each morning and rode through rain and hail and rain and sleet and rain that slanted sidewise and rain that pummelled down like spikes. They crossed the valley bottom in grey light and stepped their horses over two tracks of glistening steel that appeared like an aberration across the valley. Reverend Brown disembarked from his pony and leaned on the iron rails. He ran his hands along the smooth luminous tracks nailed into chunks of timber sleepers and palmed fistfuls of ballast. Tracks, like sutures, mutilated the belly of the land. He climbed onto his pony, steered it away from the rails. The crew followed.

They chased the valley bottom over rolling grasslands where the river twisted into oxbows and small birds chattered in the tall grasses and an immense raven laboured up to ride a thermal before floating downwind. At dusk the weather broke and the pallid land before them transformed into bright ivory before fading into jaundice. They passed through carpets of wildflowers, acres of golden groundsel and zinnia, deep purple gentian, and wild vines of blue morning glory reaching onward, while the red sunset on the river beside them flowed like an opened vein.

Gussie and Keegan shot deer from their mounts, slashed their throats from jaw to jaw, and left the limp heads to rot on the ground.

They butchered the animals, cutting out flank and top round steaks that they roasted on the fire and divided among the men and women. They seared forelegs and hindlegs, pulled them smoking from the fire and handed them to Reverend Brown who snapped the bones over his knee and slurped the hot marrow.

The next morning, the rain started again. The country tapered between the capes of mountains on either side, shuddering in humps like the backs of immense sea beasts. Rain rinsed all around them. They veered off from the river and went up through the hills and they climbed these shoulders where rain pelted the pines and great cedars, their horses stepping through juniper and bunchgrass. They heard a faint whistle in the distance and lifted their heads, squinting into the rain to ascertain the origins of the foreign clatter that echoed over the sodden land but could see no evidence of the sound.

The rain ceased and in a while the wolves called out from the dark and the dogs trotting along with the men and women moaned in reply. Here and there, the sect caught wisps of whistles and metal clanging, grinding, chugging across the land. They passed the night without fire, each man and woman at the foot of their horse, seated upright against the trunks of pebbled bark on the primeval firs canopied above them.

They all crossed the Stag except Davey and Bulah who followed it on the south side and rejoined the others when the group crossed it again later in the day. The valley bottom opened upon a broad alluvial plain and they rode in silence and encountered no other souls. They climbed a hummock, leaning over the withers of their ponies, urging them up the steep slope.

That night hail pounded down on them. The horses shied and groaned, the men dismounted and stooped beneath firs while the hail recoiled on the ground around them like translucent roe. Then the hail just ceased like it had been cinched tight. The clouds cleared and stars began to appear. The land fanned out from the crew, pebbles of ice glistening in the dark.

They started early and the hail melted as the sun rose. By mid-morning a black locomotive pulling cars laboured across the horizon below them. A trill whistle called out and a plume of steam rose from the train as it puffed along. The group altered their course and headed northwest and soon smoke appeared thinly on the horizon. They descended the rocky switchbacks and crossed a shallow stream where small trout wimpled their pale fins and algae blushed in shaded pools. The crew paused; their horses pushed their noses into the stream and drank. Sheets of mist rose out of the river, crossed over them, and floated through the valley. They nudged the horses through the stream and by late afternoon, they rode into the hamlet of Hosmer.

Reverend Brown climbed down from his horse and walked out into the woods alone and looked out upon the darkness downcountry. The group spoke among themselves in low murmurs and when he returned, he led them into the woods where they waited out the night in the dark as the sounds of Hosmer rolled toward them on the breeze. Firelights against the sky wavered and shimmered. Men yelled. A child cried. Dogs barked. Piano music tinkled from afar. Roasted meat and the swarthy pungence of beer and tobacco smoke.

In the morning, they entered town, clattering over a wooden bridge that creaked and bent beneath their weight, and rode up the street. The hills above town were tunnelled, scaffolded and scarred with drifts and tailings, and along the edge above it all glowing fires rimmed it out, an ancient Dantean pit.

The sect was greeted by the howl of dogs and merchants who swept the front of their establishments. Through the doorways there were bouquets of dried sage, pine and juniper berries; clusters of tin wares hung from low rafter beams like mute chimes. There were shops with pickaxes and wide-bottomed tin pans, shovels and knives, hammers and saws. Stores bursting with bolts of fabric and folded shirts, hats and boots. A dress boutique. Davey stopped in front of a tea salon. Inside, women in hats and long dresses sipped at tea with gloved hands holding small china cups. Bulah rode up beside her, paused, and clucked at Davey to move on. One of the women turned to Davey, but her smile faded before she turned back to the woman sitting opposite her. She said a few words, and both women brought a gloved hand to their mouths and laughed.

The ragtags advanced down the street and passed an unmarked storefront where dark brown bottles of whisky were displayed upright in wooden boxes. They passed the hotel and a tavern. As they rode up to the livery, Reverend Brown nodded toward the end of the street. They cantered up to an empty lot and disembarked and unrolled a large canvas tent, oblong with rounded ends, and lashed guy ropes to stakes in the ground. Keegan, Bobby and three others stood inside the structure and they erected long flagpoles through the caped hoods while the others lashed the ropes. They rolled up the sides and set up a simple rostrum and an upturned whisky crate with a tin pitcher of water placed on top. Behind the proscenium, a large wooden cross was pounded into the dirt, the top of which was crowned with black hawthorn branches twisted into a wreath.

Gussie sent the clown into the street with a trio of musicians. They played and sang tuneless hymns and orated advertisements about the evening's revival but no man or woman showed up and the large tent remained empty, flapping in the breeze. Reverend Brown turned and strode up the street toward the tavern. The others followed. Bulah remained behind with Davey.

"Can you still hear them?" Davey said.

Bulah didn't reply.

"I can't get the sound out of my head."

"I know," Bulah said.

"It was awful, the most awful sound I've ever heard."

"Hush."

"Their pain, rising above the tree they climbed. The tree they climbed to be safe. The tree where they could see their mother get shot. By me," Davey said. "I'm ashamed to have been a witness to it. I don't know how to rid that from me."

"You had nothing to do with it."

"I didn't stop it."

"Hush, child. What would you have done? Climbed the tree?"

Davey reached for the small leather sack that hung off her waist. "I think this is what my mother must have felt," she whispered, "in her final moments."

"Hush."

"All I feel is pain. Like it's squeezing the breath out of me. All of the time."

Bulah was silent. She removed her hat, fidgeted with the brim, and glanced at the sack. "I don't know," she sighed. "All I know is that ruminating seems to make it worse."

"What else are we supposed to do?"

Bulah watched the sect congregate in front of the tavern. "Try to forget."

"What if I can't?" Davey set the sack against her waist.

"Try harder." Bulah put her hat on.

"Well, go on then."

"I won't be long." Bulah left Davey alone in the tent.

Upon entering the tavern, Bulah, the reverend and the rest of the ragtags were welcomed by Wilfred Beaudry, who poured them all shots of whisky. "For men of god!" He reached beneath the counter and lifted a case of whisky bottles and left them on the tabletop for the group to help themselves.

A man arrived wearing an oversized wool suit that seemed to weigh him down, as if lead fillings were jammed in his pockets. He had fantastically misshapen teeth and hair pasted back with pomade, and in a grand gesture, he bowed with one arm forward and offered his girls for discount. One of the ragtags tossed a half-dollar coin at him. The man snatched it in his palm, considered it and placed it in his breast pocket. He turned and one by one his girls sashayed into the shanty as though they were emerging from the decrepit walls themselves. An accordionist crouched in the doorway leaning his chest against his instrument where the bellows groaned a papery sigh. Reverend Brown strode across the floor, lifted him by the arm and led him into the shack.

The whores were dressed in tattered taffeta dresses. Their bosoms were powdered, their faces red with rouge. They flounced between the men and laughed when their dress hems were lifted and the men rubbed their coarse beards against their stockinged legs. Keegan had one of the women, who went by the name of Lenora Bell, lying face down across his lap and he spanked her rump.

The accordionist sat next to the reverend, fitted his grubby fingers against the keyboard and pressed and released the bass buttons, opening and closing the bellows with a slow rhythm. Reverend Brown pulled two large rib bones from his cassock and held both in one hand with a finger between them to space them apart and struck them against his thigh. He nodded to the clown, lifted his crown and pulled two more deer bones from his cassock and, with bones in each hand, clacked them against his knee and his chest, producing double and triple clicks as he and the accordionist played together. The clown stood and began a series of jerky movements to mime waltzing with a dance partner, silently pirouetting through a skiff of sawdust on the floor. Reverend Brown picked up the pace and smacked the bones against his body more briskly and he slammed his boots on the boards like a man possessed by the music, possessed by the act of performing for an audience. The accordionist scowled, pressed the keys and buttons to keep up, and the reverend smacked the bones over the musician's skull and the musician ducked to avoid the strikes and Reverend Brown laughed and struck him on the shoulder, nodding at him to play on.

"Bobby," the reverend shouted, "sing for us!"

Bobby finished his glass of whisky, cleared his throat and began to sing. His voice rose like a broken bird, fluttering in a tone that sounded as if he were a small boy. The reverend smiled and clapped his hands. He dumped the bones onto a table and offered his hand to Lenora Bell, and he spun her around the shabby room and her face flushed red beneath the rouge that she wore. Keegan rose from his chair and stomped his boots on the boards and he jutted out his hand with great ceremony and Lenora Bell took hold of it and she spun by the crook of her elbow interlocked, laughing, her face beaded with sweat, alternating between Reverend Brown and Keegan while the occupants of the tavern shouted, their voices drowning out Bobby's song, and slapped their palms on the tabletops. The clown retreated to a corner and stood, his face absent of expression.

Late in the evening, Davey left the empty tent and went through the camp. Around her, men lurched, fought among themselves, shot their pistols in the air. She stepped aside into a doorway to make room for a procession that crawled down the street. Reverend Brown led, holding high above his head a crucified christ that had been appropriated from the clapboard church, chanting fragments of Latin that were echoed in a strange sing-song by his drunk disciples whose melodic cadence betrayed any indication that they knew what they were uttering. For no one in that hamlet understood the reverend's incantations, whether they were words of import or gibberish. The troupe followed in a skimmington of clattering pots and pans and animal bones that they banged together. Two of the disciples broke rank to address a man who heckled the procession. They prodded him obscenely with their spoons and cuffed his head as if he were a small child being disciplined. Others raised their bottles and drank to him.

Some of the sect had wandered into the cold waters of the Stag and splashed in the shallows. They lurched back into the street and stood dripping in the dim light of lamps, like centaurs in a dark fable. A few of them made it to the livery where they flopped down into hay-lined stables reeking of horse urine. Others drank themselves into a stupor, anointing one another with loquacious sobriquets, shouting senseless epithets at the sickle moon.

Keegan rented a room above the tavern for ten cents. He peeled off Lenora Bell's stockings, bound her to his bed, caressed her bosom and stomach with a chunk of coal. She thrashed wildly, chafing her wrists and ankles, pummelled Keegan's head, kicked him in the ribs. He slapped her face and jammed the coal into her mouth. "I'm paying for you, you'll do what I want. Understood?" He moved the rock like a hinge up and down to make her nod her head. He removed the coal and laughed.

"Get me out of here," Lenora Bell said. "Get me out of this godforsaken place. Take me to the coast and I'll do whatever you say."

Keegan pulled her face toward him. "I'm paying for you. Lick it." When she stuck out her tongue, he moved the coal against it. He unfastened her, took her from behind and when he was finished, he tied the ropes from her wrists to his own so they were bound together. He fell into a drunk slumber while she lay awake listening to voices call out across the steep hillsides where men toiled at the coke ovens.

Davey returned to the tent, where Bulah lay against the cross, snoring deeply. She prodded her; Bulah opened her eyes and pushed her away. "Go on, git out of here."

"You're drunk."

"I ain't got time for your questions. Git."

Davey knelt next to her. Bulah roused herself and pushed her away. She pulled out her pistol, held it to Davey's head and whispered, "Go, git out of here. I'll be along in the morning."

Davey studied her.

Bulah pressed the gun harder against her head. "Now. Git."

Davey rose.

"A little peace and quiet. That's it. Now git out of here." Bulah put her pistol back in her belt and waited until Davey had left before closing her eyes.

Davey walked around the tent twice. Each time she passed the opening she checked on Bulah. She went to her horse and rested her palm against the animal's neck. The horse shifted and blinked at her. Davey stroked its neck and withers and pressed her face into the hair and inhaled. She turned and entered the tent, sat upright against the rostrum, faced Bulah, tilted her hat over her eyes and waited out the night.

In the morning, Bulah tapped Davey's foot to wake her, then they left the tent in silence. A funeral procession snaked up the street, trailing a horse-drawn cart that bore a pine box atop a wagon that creaked with each jostle of its wooden wheels. The procession was led by a barefoot boy holding a wooden cross; a priest followed ringing a bell. A group of mourners clothed in black marched in the rear, their heads bowed. The coffin groaned past. Some villagers knelt and blessed themselves, while others stepped forward and kissed their fingertips and touched the casket. The procession trundled past.

Reverend Brown smoked his pipe in a doorway. He squinted through the smoke and lifted his crown to the priest but the priest did not acknowledge his greeting. The reverend tapped out the pipe and toed the spent tobacco into the ground. He waved at any child that walked by but none returned his gesture.

The boy that had led the funeral procession walked up the street; the cross leaned against his shoulder while he kicked at the puddles. Reverend Brown stepped out from the doorway of a closed shop at the end of the street and smiled at the boy.

The boy held up the cross. "For sale."

Reverend Brown looked up the street.

"Jesus is for sale," the boy said.

"Is he?"

"My father said you was selling him."

"That so?"

"He said no man has the right to sell him. My father said no man can afford him."

"Do you believe everything your father tells you?"

"I got no reason not to."

"How much?"

The boy studied the cross. Two planks affixed by a worn rope with a figure made by straw twisted together in the shape of a man. It wore a small wreath of thorns, its face had lines of red thread running down from the thorns and its limbs were splayed out on the cross. He thrust it forward. "Fifty cents?"

Reverend Brown sought the coins from the pocket of his cassock and pulled out a silver dollar. He placed the coin in the boy's palm. "It's yours. Take it."

The boy turned the coin over and held it up in the light. "I don't have change."

A swarm of swallows cruised overhead. "Did you know that when birds flock like that, they never hit each other?"

The boy shook his head. "That's cause theys birds."

"Thousands of them, tens of thousands of them migrating across the world in flocks that darken the sky and yet they never hit each other or get lost."

The swallows dove and flew upward in a large shadow before dipping out of sight behind the livery. Reverend Brown seized the boy's hand. "It's all a ritual, a predetermined pattern, isn't it?"

The boy didn't reply.

Reverend Brown placed a hand on his shoulder. "Has your father not taught you to be a man?"

"I'm not old enough to be a man."

Reverend Brown scanned the windows of the squat wooden shacks that lined the street. "To become a man is one of life's greatest rituals. We all know there's an ending. The ritual that marks it is a funeral. But when does it begin? Birth is a ritual but it's not the first. There's a mating ritual that precedes it and that ritual is made up of hundreds of decisions, each one their own minor ritual. And what's next, after birth? What are the events along the way that shape a man? How are they marked, recorded, honoured? All of them, all actions and decisions ..." Reverend Brown trailed off. "All of them truths that reveal the man. And so, man is the ritual of himself."

The boy stared at him with a confused look on his face.

"It's yours," the reverend said. "Follow me." He strode up the deserted street holding the cross in front of him. He walked to the end of the street, reached into his cassock, turned and held out another silver dollar coin and smiled. The boy ran toward him.

"What events indeed." The reverend held the boy's hand and led him into the woods.

———————————

In the early afternoon, at the western edge of town on the main street, Davey and Bulah stood to the side of a deeply rutted mud pit where teams of dogs had assembled in a line with the crack of a quirt. They stood with a group of men barking out instructions to the boys whose dogs were situated shoulder to shoulder, yipping and snarling, each team harnessed together and tied to a sled of thick planks behind them, where each boy stood with his legs apart, holding reins. One of the men raised his pistol and fired it in the air; the dogs raced forward, zigzagging up the street. The boys whipped the dogs with their quirts and the animals lumbered forth, scrapping with one another. The mud was thick and the boys whipped their teams with renewed vigour, the dogs lashed out at each other and when the boys trudged through the muck to set the team free, the dogs clawed and bit at the boys. The teams laboured sluggishly up the street howling, and when the first team broke the twine that two men held across the street, the dogs commenced to fighting with each other again until they were unhitched from their sleds. They bounded off down the street, into the woods where they could be heard barking. The boys tended to the welts on their arms.

Davey turned to Bulah. "Can't we just go?"

"Where?"

"Anywhere."

"Then what?"

"Can't we sort it as we go? Ain't we all doing that anyway?"

Bulah regarded Davey.

"We could go now. They wouldn't know until tomorrow morning."

Bulah nodded her head. "Except we'd know. And he'd know."

"We'd be far away."

"No place is far enough for him. We'd live out our days with him chasing us in our thoughts."

"We already do that."

"This would be different. It would be a betrayal. I can think of no worse way to incite that man. Do you have the stomach to deal with that? For the rest of your days?"

The boys struggled to fight back their tears. They walked off in a group except for one who remained sitting in the mud, his head resting on his forearms.

Davey turned to Bulah. "Yes."

———————

Later in the day, a man went up and down the street asking anyone he encountered whether they had seen his son. A shopkeeper told him that he had seen the boy lead the funeral procession earlier that morning. A search party convened and the man, shopkeeper and a few others commenced to look for the boy.

Keegan woke alone. The stockings had been cut and his wrists were still bound together. He held his wrist over the lamp and shouted out as the flames burned through the stockings and singed his skin. He shook the stockings free and stumbled out of the room into the street.

The search party found the boy in the woods, sitting next to a crucifix. His face, arms and legs were clawed and bleeding. When the men approached him, the boy raked his nails against his bare skin as if scrubbing himself clean. A man offered his hand and the boy stared at the man for a long while. Another man stepped forward, removed his hat and knelt down. He held his arms open. The boy scraped his skin and shook his head. The man said, "Shush now, Samuel, it's going to be okay."

Samuel sank into his father's arms and held him tightly. One of the men grabbed the crucifix and followed Samuel and his father back into town. At the base of the tree, the silver of a dollar coin winked in the dirt.

———————

Keegan mounted his horse, rode to the end of the street, turned and entered a side street, stopped in front of the brothel and called out. The door opened and Lenora Bell appeared on the threshold.

"Let's go," he said.

"Why the change of heart?" she stood with her arms crossed.

"Why not?"

"Give me your word."

"I ain't got all day," Keegan said.

"Tell me."

There was shouting up the street. After the search party had found Samuel, it had grown in size and many of the men held knives, pistols and axes. They were marching up the street toward Keegan. "I give you my word."

"Say it."

A man called out to Keegan.

"Fine, I give you my word. I'll take you to the coast."

Lenora Bell smiled and clapped her hands. "I need to gather a couple of essentials." She disappeared into the brothel.

Keegan nodded to the men approaching him and smiled. Lenora Bell re-emerged and stood in the doorway with two suitcases and a stack of hatboxes. Keegan cussed, disembarked from his horse and ran up the steps of the house. She threw her arms around his neck and kissed him. "This is the most romantic thing anyone has done for me." He grunted and snatched up her belongings and she followed him to the horse, where he fastened the cases. He climbed on his pony and offered his hand. She took it, and he hauled her up by the elbow to sit behind him. "Hold on." He turned and tipped his hat to the mob, who were now shouting and jogging toward him. Two of the men broke into a run. A man raised his pistol in the air, fired a shot. Keegan kicked his horse and galloped up the street. Another shot rang out. Keegan thrashed and kicked his horse, and when they reached the outskirts of town, he slowed and turned around. There was no sign of the search party. He smiled at Lenora Bell and they rode on. In twenty minutes, they caught up with the rest of the crew. Two new men had joined the group, Beaudry and James Blundell. Keegan reached back for Lenora Bell's neck, pulled her close, ran his tongue against her ear, and let out a loud whoop. He fell in with the rest of the crew and they all rode on.

EIGHT

THE SECT RODE WESTWARD in silence through the night. Moonlight shone off the river, and at dawn red streaked the eastern sky. They took cover in the woods, watered their horses and rested until they started riding again by mid-morning.

The river was up and boiled against the rocks, churning mud and foam that floated in shallow fords where the ragtags crossed and then crossed it again, chasing it on both sides, the river between them. Davey and Bulah departed the crew at each ford and turned their ponies up scraggy game trails into the woods. They tracked the river from precipitous slopes and then descended to rejoin the trail where the crew's ponies left markings on the shoals. Pale cascades hung down the sheer mountain wall above them, blowing off the high ragged rock like the breath of an immense beast. The ragtags' trail was on the opposite side of the river; at other times the trail was on the same side as Davey and Bulah. The sun rose and any evidence of fording, the slurried river, the damp rocks, evaporated in the heat. Davey and Bulah tracked the crew by displaced rocks whose undersides were caked with dirt and tailings of beetles, and on occasion the faint dent of a seashell fanned out, evidence from a prehistoric time now scattered in the bright sunlight far from its place of origin.

They rode on. There were eagles and other birds in the valley and many deer and there were wildflowers and brakes of blackberry bushes. The river here was sizable and it swept past enormous boulders, and waterfalls fell everywhere out of the high tangled forest. Reverend Brown rode with Gussie at the front. He shot at birds throughout the day and the birds that he retrieved hung upside down from the sash around the waist of his cassock. In the evening he dumped them at the foot of the fire where Bulah plucked the birds and drove a thin branch through the length of their bodies and roasted them over the flames. Keegan and Lenora Bell's grunts and whimpers floated in the air from the woods behind them. Blundell, Beaudry and the clown stared into the fire. Davey sat across from Reverend Brown, an arrow notched in her bow, resting on her lap.

"What now, lass?" Reverend Brown said.

Davey lifted her bow; her mouth was tight. "I know what you did."

Reverend Brown studied Davey. The woods ticked with squirrels chattering and random birdsong.

"Those children. That boy."

"What facts do you hold, girl? Opinions and subjective conclusions hold no value. What you know is what you see and what you do and what you learn by seeing and doing. What did you see, girl? What did you do?"

Davey glanced around but the others did not meet her eyes, except for the clown whose face remained cheerless. Bulah turned the birds over in the fire.

"You not saying so does not make it so," Davey said. "I know what you did. Others know, too."

The reverend pressed his hands together and passed them down over his nose and mouth, tracing the scar that intersected his face. He placed his hands palm down on his knees, straightened his back and faced Davey.

"I am a man of the cloth. A man of god. I have a fiduciary duty to man and god. A delicate stewardship between man and god and the land we inhabit."

"A foodu—" Davey said.

"Fiduciary. A man who is entrusted with power or property for the benefit of another." He nodded at the birds cooking over the low flames and drew a line in the dirt around him. "Men travel across the land by foot or horse. Every hour, every day. From time immemorial. And so it will be until the end of time. These men, every man, believes he is moving of his own accord. That he is free."

Davey sat with her boots crossed before the fire. "I don't see what that has to do with those children."

"Tell me, who is truly free? Children? Wolves? Women? Birds?"

"All animals are free. Same with women."

Reverend Brown smiled. "There's a fundamental flaw in your reasoning, lass."

"What flaw?"

"That freedom exists."

Davey turned to the others but they kept their eyes on the fire. "We are all free to leave or stay. To choose for ourselves."

"And yet here you are. You are not yet old enough to know the basic truth the world affords you. No man is free."

Beaudry snickered. "Are you telling me anything I do or say is not of my own accord? Look, I can lift my hands in the air. Do I not have the power to do so?"

Reverend Brown tilted his head back and gazed at the stars and let out a deep exhale. "You're missing the point. Any action you take has been preordained."

Beaudry looked around at the others. "You all don't believe this, do you?"

No one raised their heads. The clown pinched his thumb and forefinger together and drew a line across his lips. Beaudry shook his head, mumbled something as he turned to the fire.

Reverend Brown resumed. "All men do not accept this truth easily. It's a hard-earned one that men spend their lives puzzling over. You're just encountering the idea for the first time. Your reaction is as predictable as it is preordained."

"The messenger. That beats all ..." Beaudry said.

"That is why we all have our gods and why people will believe anything you have to say that comes from their god." Reverend Brown faced Davey. "And why they will do anything in their god's name. Because"—he paused and slapped his thighs with his palms— "because without that belief man accepts his own fate and any man that chooses his own fate over the path laid out to him by his god severs himself from the tribe. He is alone. Separate from his fellow man, separate from his god. A truly solitary being."

"You've never made any sense. I choose my way in everything I do," Davey said.

"Do you, lass? How do you know you're choosing on your own volition or as part of something larger than you can imagine? The illusion for all men is that they're choosing for themselves when they are not. For if they accept the truth of this, they no longer know how to act, how to live."

"Why does man's freedom insult you?"

"Because it's illusory that there is an order to all beings. It's not what it seems."

Davey turned a stick in her hands. Beaudry shook his head and stared into the fire.

The reverend stood and placed his hands on his chest. "I'm a man of the cloth, standing on the other side of the cage, looking in. Carrying out god's orders, spreading his word. Keeper of all."

Davey pushed another stick into the fire. "And the rest of us?"

Reverend Brown smiled. "In the cage, lass. The cage."

———————————

The next morning, they waded across the Stag while Davey and Bulah climbed and descended through steep forests of pine and firs. The country opened up and they came upon alfalfa grass on the broadening valley bottom and here they spotted cattle in clusters with wide white faces, browsing on the grass. At the edge of the clearing there were log huts and a smattering of small fence corrals. Reverend Brown, Gussie and Keegan crossed the meadow at a gallop, raised their rifles and opened fire on the herd.

"Stop it!" Davey yelled.

Gussie and Keegan laughed. Davey turned to Bulah. "Make them stop."

"How?"

"Do something," Davey said.

More shots rang out. The cows buckled beneath their weight and fell to the ground and others limped away and the trio continued to shoot at them until all of the cattle were lying in the grass in large lumps. Thirty cattle slaughtered, some still twitching and crying hoarsely and those that were not moving the ragtags worked in pairs to butcher and sling slabs of meat over the necks of their ponies and those that were still alive they slit their throats to bleed out into the earth. They left twenty-five behind in bloodied heaps.

Davey wiped at her eyes. "You disappoint me."

"There was nothing to be done," Bulah said. "You know that."

"No, I don't."

The crew climbed on to their horses and rode west into a chiaroscuro landscape and by late afternoon they arrived at the town of Bull Head. Davey lagged behind.

Keegan looked back at Lenora Bell; she stared ahead, her pony weighed down with slabs of a cow's carcass draped over the pommel of her saddle, swinging against her hatboxes.

A wedding procession approached them, the bride's gown dragging in the mud. She clung to the groom's elbow, her face stricken. From the doorways, merchants and grubby children and women dressed in their Sunday finest threw fistfuls of dried flowers and rice at the newlyweds.

The sect rode opposite the wedding party toward the river. At the terminus of the street Reverend Brown led them to a meadow where they stopped and disembarked from their ponies. This end of town was quiet, all the shops closed except for the hotel and saloon where man bent over a broomstick and swept the boards outside, clearing off dried detritus and debris in the dirt street.

They waited in front of a weathered clapboard church with a large tarnished cross on top. Bulah was about to speak but the reverend held up his hand and closed his eyes. The wind came off the river, sending ripples over it and up over the tall grass, dandelions and daisies that spread across the meadow. Behind the church, simple crosses and rocks posed as tombstones in a patch of worn, hard-packed dirt, the powder of flower pollen scattered about here and there.

They entered the church and were greeted by a man who wore a white dalmatic and a white stole draped over his left shoulder, cinched crosswise at his right side.

"Welcome." The man bowed his head. "On behalf of our humble parish, I am at your service."

"Greetings, my fellow brethren of the cloth." Reverend Brown took the man by both wrists. "A true man of god. You don't know what a rare specimen you are."

The man smiled. "The honour is mine, sir. I am but a servant, a novitiate, a temporary employ of the church. You, my good man"—he gestured to Reverend Brown's cassock—"you are what I aspire to be."

"That so?"

"Yes." The man bowed again. He studied the reverend's cedar crown and tattered cassock.

"Delivering the word of god is not spared of the world's vicissitudes." The reverend smiled.

The man nodded and gave another small bow. "Please, call me Deacon."

"Jesus, all this bobbing is making me dizzy," Gussie blurted out.

"Forgive her," the reverend said. "She knows not what she says."

Deacon and Reverend Brown shared a laugh. Reverend Brown introduced himself and held the deacon's wrists and he introduced Bulah and Gussie, who held his wrists in the manner that Reverend Brown had done.

"The house of god is everyman's home." Deacon raised a hand toward the front of the church. An altar constructed from a wooden table sat covered with a wrinkled white tablecloth. A tall candlestick stood on either side holding a partial candle with streaks of tallow running down its sides. On the middle of the tablecloth sat a thick, ornate book. Behind the altar a gaunt, naked figurine of a man was nailed to a cross, a wreath of thorns drawing blood from his forehead, his open palms bleeding from where spikes had nailed him to the wood, his feet bloodied likewise.

"A fine place to do god's work," Reverend Brown said.

Gussie spat. The reverend glared at her.

"My good brother, can you give us a moment?" Reverend Brown said. "We'd like to pray."

Deacon nodded and left, closing the door behind him.

The reverend rested on the pew for a long time before he stretched out and stared at the ceiling. Bulah and Gussie sat on the pew behind him. Gussie leaned her elbows on the back of the pew where Reverend Brown lay.

"You want to hold up for a while?" Bulah said.

"It's as good a place as any."

Gussie spat between her feet. "I don't see why we can't keep on westerly."

"Woman, have you no sense of the sacred?" Reverend Brown said.

Gussie wiped her mouth with her sleeve.

"How long?" Bulah said.

"As long as it takes," the reverend said.

"Takes for what?" Gussie said.

"To reap the rewards of our efforts."

"Our efforts seem to have become disrupting the efforts others have in making peace," Bulah said.

"You sound like the lass."

"She's sensible."

They sat in silence staring at the crucifix.

"We'll do what we've always done and ride on to the next settlement," Reverend Brown said, "and start over again."

He rose and made for the door. Bulah and Gussie followed him out. They were met at the door by Deacon, who held out a clean, folded black cassock. The reverend took the cassock and informed Deacon that they'd be setting up camp in the churchyard, that their first revival and baptisms would be conducted later that evening.

"I'd like to be the first," Deacon said.

"That so?"

"Yes. It will instill faith in our flock here."

The reverend clasped Deacon's shoulder. "As you wish, my brother. As you wish."

Reverend Brown baptized Deacon, Beaudry and Blundell. The three men stood shivering naked on the riverbank, but no villagers came.

By early evening a gathering had commenced behind the church. Chuck steaks and clod roasts dripped fat that sizzled in the flames, and carcasses of ribs and crudely butchered shanks and marbled steaks, some with bones in, some without, and long strips of flank and skirt steaks draped over latticed willow branches. Cast iron pots steamed with stews of lower round cuts cubed and simmering in a broth of bones, onions, carrots and wild mushrooms. The ragtags played their fiddles and snap drums, clacking bones, and one on a flute gambolled in strange, erratic movements, his shadow against the land like a sprite.

Deacon followed Reverend Brown into the church. Here, there were women of ill repute crying out against the men who took them on the pews. Blundell and Beaudry drank whisky from the bottle, the alcohol dribbling off their beards. Beaudry smashed a bottle on the floor. Blundell commanded two hussies to take turns slapping his face. He roared with laughter, poured whisky over his face and shook his beard. The women wiped their palms dry on their dresses.

Davey entered the church. On the altar, Keegan laid out Lenora Bell and fastened her wrists and ankles, dragged a piece of coal along her bosom. He set the coal down and unsheathed his hunting knife. Held the long knife above his head in both hands, laughing. "Who am I? Who am I?"

Lenora Bell screamed and struggled against the restraints. "Stop. Please stop."

"Abraham. Call me Abraham."

Davey removed an arrow from her quiver, notched it and held up her bow.

"You want a go, girl?" Keegan said.

She pointed her arrow at him.

Keegan sliced the restraints and Lenora Bell ran past Davey, out of the church, clutching her robes against her chest.

"Just the reverend's property, then," Keegan said.

"I ain't nobody's property," Davey said.

Keegan laughed and took a long drink of whisky from the chalice. "We all belong to someone else, girl." He emptied the chalice, sheathed his knife, and lay on the altar, stared up at the vaulted ceiling of the church. "Every single one of us." He reached for his gun and held it against his chest with both hands as if in prayer and soon began to snore.

Late into the night, Deacon and the reverend walked through the churchyard.

"This behaviour is blasphemous," Deacon said.

"Sinners sin before they repent," Reverend Brown said.

"There's no respect for authority, for the sacred."

"Indeed."

"Why aren't you doing something about it?"

"What do you suggest, my dear brother?" Reverend Brown said. "These men are acting on their own and as such will be judged."

Deacon studied the reverend for a moment. "And so, shall you, too, be judged."

"Indeed, my dear brother. Indeed."

An hour before sun-up, the church reeked of the rank brine of men and women sleeping, their clothes tangled around their limbs. Keegan lay immobile on the altar. The victuallers and their carts were gone and the blackened rings of the burned-out fires lay in the meadow as if falling stars had smashed into the earth. At a solitary fire Reverend Brown, Deacon, Davey and some disciples sat, smoking and exchanging tales.

Reverend Brown jabbed a stick in the fire and moved the wood so that the flames glowed red. "How do you know of Adam and Eve, my good man?" he said. "Let any man speak who knows them personally."

"Now hold on, are you suggesting a thing is known only if it is seen?" Deacon said.

"We know our histories as have been passed down over the centuries. But who's not to say the storytellers along the way added or subtracted from the version that was recounted to them?" He leaned back and shifted on the ground before facing Deacon with a wide grin. "My holy friend, all truth in the world is embedded in untruth. It's what separates man from beast. Beasts cannot deceive you. You can read it in their bodies and decisions. Always. Man lies all the time, has since Cain and Abel. This, too, you can read in his body. A pulsing carotid artery. The glancing down to the left. A hard, defiant stare. Man teaches himself to forget those moments of his life that do not add up to the man he envisions by hiding them in an untruth, by neglecting to face it, by telling a new story to cover over it, and so that truth, the essential ingredient in every man's life, is erased from the ledger of his days. Excised as if it never occurred. What is remembered and recounted is simply what a man chooses to remember, what others choose to remember according to their own character, always based in self-interest and self-preservation. So, tell me then, how can we ever know who a man really is in this light?"

Deacon waved his hand. "If what you state is true, and that is up for much deliberation, then your line of reasoning rests on a shaky foundation. Are you deceiving us now?"

"What do you think?" Reverend Brown said.

"It's just crazy talk," Davey said.

Reverend Brown started to laugh and swept his arms outward in a grotesque gesture of goodwill. Behind the church the dogs tore down the latticework on the fires and dragged the charred bones across the churchyard. The cook pots were upturned in dark pools of their own broth, damp in the dust that dogs licked.

"My brothers in arms. Joining as two to find strength as one."

Davey shook her head. "You haven't answered his question."

Deacon rose. "It's all right. There is some truth in what he says."

"That don't make it mine," Davey said.

Reverend Brown chuckled. "Girl, you believe what you believe. No man makes you believe anything that you don't already want to believe."

"He's a clever one." Deacon bade them good night and drifted away. The mountains to the east carved themselves out of the dawn. Davey walked to where Bulah lay against a tree at the far edge of the fire, her eyes open, a blanket pulled over her. Davey sat against the tree next to her. Bulah handed Davey her blanket. Davey covered herself with it, and Bulah reached for the coat behind her head and draped it over herself. She laid her head on the ground, shifted and closed her eyes. Davey rested against her as the blue-grey light spread across the horizon.

NINE

THE FOLLOWING DAY they rode out of town to Morrissey to host a revival for the miners. They trekked along the train tracks beside the river and then swung west where the tracks led them to the mine in a deep well of shade, slopes soaring upward on either side. Horses covered in grime dragged carts of black coal out of the mine. They wheezed and the drivers in their ragged and blackened costumes led them by frayed ropes. A group of men stood leaning on shovels and when the horses cleared the mine, the men proceeded to unload the animals and shovel coal into hopper wagons that sat waiting on the tracks.

Reverend Brown inquired after their foreman and the men pointed to a man on the slope above the mine. The reverend squinted against the glare of the sun and recognized the man as Will.

"Well, well, well," Reverend Brown said, "reunited, once again." He turned to Keegan and Gussie. "Go on. Git." Keegan and Gussie pulled at the mouths of their horses and rowelled them toward Will.

Will climbed on his horse, swivelled it in a tight arc and whipped the reins on either side of its shoulders and charged up the slope. He leaned over his horse's neck, shouting in its ear as it laboured, the sweat on his pony's flanks glistening in the light. He reached the summit of the slope and turned.

Reverend Brown tipped his hat to Will and smiled. Will swung his horse around and galloped over the rise into the woods.

Keegan and Gussie lashed their horses and chased after him.

A waterfall thundered out of the forest behind the shacks surrounding the mine, tapering into a thin river that ran through the camp. The miners sat at the foot of their horses nearby, their mouths tight and grim. Reverend Brown motioned for the men to join him at the stream, where he would baptize each one of them, but no man moved. The day's light faded; Davey and Bulah built a fire. The early part of the night was clear and the moon climbed over the mountain. A small black bear wandered down and paused at the far side of the river, tested the air with his nose and turned back.

At daybreak Gussie and Keegan returned with Will. They crossed the stream; the water sloshed against their horses' bellies and the horses picked their way over rocks and glanced upstream where the waterfall pounded down. They had found Will in town, in the churchyard, hiding beneath a pew inside, his horse cropping grass in the graveyard. Now he was stripped naked; a nub of coal hung from his neck. He stumbled beside Keegan's horse with a rope around his neck, shivering, his hands cupping his privates.

The miners rose to their feet but Will did not meet their eyes. Reverend Brown greeted him with a length of rope curled from his left hand.

"My good brother, here we are, reunited once more."

Will kept his head down. His shoulders shook.

"Get him a blanket."

Blundell handed the reverend a blanket and he placed it around Will's shoulders. Bulah approached with a cup of hot coffee. Reverend Brown nodded, and she held the cup out to Will. He drank from it with one hand, the other still against his privates. When he was done he tossed the tin cup aside. "I know what you did."

Reverend Brown smiled. "You know what, brother?"

"You took my child."

"That is a serious accusation you're making."

Bulah seized Davey's arm and pulled her toward the miners. Davey shrugged it off. The clown tiptoed around the group in a slow exaggerated walk.

"It's not our concern," Bulah said.

Davey turned to her. "You sound like him."

"I'm not him."

"Well, you sound a lot like him."

Reverend Brown stepped closer, leaned into Will's ear. "Hanging a man is one of the most ignoble, gruesome things one can witness or experience. Give me one reason not to hang you now."

"You took my child," Will said.

"That's not a reason."

"They won't work for you," Will said. "My men are loyal."

"Any man will change allegiances to ensure his survival."

Will spat.

"Give me a reason." The reverend pushed the rope against Will's shoulder twice.

"I won't talk against you."

"That's not a reason. If I hang you now, you won't talk against me." Reverend Brown studied him. "What do you love most?"

"What?"

"It's a simple question that requires a simple answer."

"You've never been a holy man." Will turned to the ragtags and miners. Bulah and Davey regarded him. The clown moved in and out of the group silently.

The reverend laughed. "And yet, you confessed your crimes to me like a child seeking forgiveness after the fact. What do you love most?"

"You can't just take what's not yours."

Reverend Brown pressed his nose against Will's ear. "You slaughtered your own family. You took what they cautioned you not to take and have been profiting from it ever since. Yesterday, you fled from your men and left them on their own." He grabbed Will's hands and turned them over. "You're fulfilling your grandfather's prophecy. And yet, when faced with one of life's most fundamental questions, you cannot provide an answer." Reverend Brown put his arm around Will's shoulder and pulled him close; the rope grazed Will's cheek. "You are a soulless, cowardly man, beyond reproach. But I will help save you. I give you my word. In return, you'll give me your men."

Will tried to pry free of the reverend's grip.

"This is not a negotiation, my brother. Do we have an agreement?"

"Where is my child?"

"What makes you think that infant survived?"

Will considered the reverend's words. "Are you telling me the truth?"

"It's a simple yes or no answer," Reverend Brown said. "Do we have an agreement?"

Will nodded.

"Is that a yes?"

Will turned to the reverend. "Yes."

"Excellent." Reverend Brown gripped Will's neck and led him to the river. "It's time you are cleansed of your sins. You and your men." Reverend Brown nodded at Bulah and Gussie. The women passed Davey, ushering Will's men single file to a rocky, flat length of land next to the river. Reverend Brown led Will to the river's edge and entered the shallows with him. The reverend tightened his grip on Will's neck, forced him to his knees and dunked his head into the water. He held Will for a long count before dredging him out. Will gasped and spit out water. The reverend pushed him below the river's surface again and held him for a long count before lifting his head. Will coughed up water and inhaled and the reverend pressed him down again and Will thrashed beneath him before Reverend Brown lifted him up, made the sign of the cross and shoved him into the water. "You are cleansed of your sins," the reverend said. "Finally."

Will lay on his side, coughing and spitting up water, wheezing hoarsely.

After the baptisms, they rode back into Bull Head, Reverend Brown and Gussie at the lead, Will tethered to the reverend's horse, then Keegan and Bobby. Davey and Bulah brought up the rear of the group. They rode past the small train depot to the church where Deacon came out to greet them.

"Please," Will whimpered. "You must help me."

Deacon glanced at Reverend Brown and scurried away. The reverend, Gussie and Bulah left Will in Keegan's care while they conferred inside the church. Davey sat atop her horse outside.

Keegan whistled and Lenora Bell came out of a tent with two other women who carried clothes and a wash basin. He darkened when Lenora Bell glanced at Will's privates. The women bathed Will with a sponge and scrubbed his body and when they were finished, Lenora Bell lifted Will's feet, washed each foot and rinsed them with water. She tossed the sponge in the wash basin and helped the women dress Will. She turned to leave. Keegan pressed the barrel of his rifle against her neck. "Let me see some."

"You gave me your word."

Keegan snorted. "The coast is a long ways off."

"You gave me your word."

Keegan smiled and nodded. She pulled the blouse off her shoulders and stood naked from the waist up in front of him. Davey looked away. "You leave her be," one of the women who had been sponging Will said.

Keegan pressed his rifle against Lenora Bell's chest. "Or you'll do what?"

"Just leave her be."

Keegan pulled back his gun. The barrel had left two circles imprinted on her chest.

"A man's only as good as his word. Remember that." Lenora Bell pulled up her blouse.

"I seen you looking," Keegan told Will.

Will shook his head.

"I seen you looking, all right."

"I wasn't looking."

"Why wasn't you looking?"

"I wasn't looking."

"She not pretty enough for you?"

"No."

"No? No, she's not?"

"No. I wasn't looking."

"I'm asking something else. Answer me, man."

"Yes."

"Yes what?"

"Yes, she's pretty."

Keegan rested his forefinger on the trigger and pushed the barrel against Will's head. Davey lifted her bow, notched an arrow, took aim on Keegan. He laughed and turned back to Will.

"What kind of man are you?"

Gussie called for Will. Keegan used his rifle to push Will in her direction and released his finger from the trigger. Gussie pulled out a knife and gestured for him to raise his arms in front of him. She cut the rope that bound his wrists and shoved him through the church door. Keegan turned to Davey. "Lower your bow, girl, I ain't no animal."

Davey kept her arrow sighted on Keegan.

"Jesus," Keegan said, "what in hell is wrong with all you women?"

Bulah came out of the church and stood at the church door. Davey slipped the arrow into the quiver and joined her. The reverend spoke to Will and told him how they had saved his life years ago and that in return Will would work for him, ensure the mine continued as it had, and that Will would manage the workers, that all proceeds would go to the reverend. "Consider it a donation. Penance. God does love the generous man."

"What if I don't?" Will said.

Reverend Brown lowered his voice. "Brother, this is not a negotiation."

"Where's my boy?"

"There was no boy."

"I saw it. I heard it cry."

"There was no boy."

Bulah went out into the churchyard and waved at Davey to join her but Davey shook her head.

"Is my boy alive?" Will said.

"Patience, man," Reverend Brown hissed in a whisper. "You ensure your men work for me and we'll raise this issue later."

Bulah waved again. "Let's get a move on." Davey stood for a moment longer at the door. She crossed the churchyard and joined Bulah.

"Is what that man's saying true?"

Bulah let out a long breath. "If it were, would it matter?"

"Yes."

"He slaughtered his own people. His wife and her family. He would have killed the child." A light breeze riffled over the river; a fish rose and dimpled the water.

"The child should know," Davey said.

"It's up to the men."

"That's the problem. The men are making all the decisions for the rest of us."

The next day, the reverend baptized Will's miners in the river behind the church, his black cassock swirling in the shallows. He plugged their noses, dunked them into the water and blessed them, and each newly baptized citizen dropped what money he had into Gussie's hat and stood naked on the riverbank. The reverend gestured for Davey to come to the river but she sat on her horse.

In the evening, Davey and Bulah passed Will in the street at dark, stumbling with a bottle in his fist, shouting at anyone who crossed his path.

"He's got no fight," Bulah said. "Any man that can't stand up for himself ain't a man at all."

"We broke him."

Bulah spat. "He was broken long before us."

Will swung his bottle at the air in front of him, spilling liquor over his shirt. He brought it to his mouth and drank. "Barbarian," he said. "Your holy man is a barb—" He stumbled toward Davey and Bulah. Davey raised her bow. "Heathens." He slapped his chest. "Right here. Go on." He fell into the dirt and lay murmuring. "Took everything. My child, my mine. I ain't got nothing left."

"Leave him be," Bulah said. "Ain't no fight except the one he's got with himself."

Davey lowered her bow.

In the days that followed, Keegan and Gussie sat on their horses outside of the mine as the miners trudged through the darkness. Men with clunky headlamps smashed away at the earth, breaking it up in front of their blackened faces, inching forward, digging out a new land beneath them. At dawn a whistle cried out and the men staggered into the sunlight blinking like parolees crawling out of dungeons, their eyes empty and hollow as if they had witnessed unspeakable horrors.

Keegan appropriated Will's home, built at the edge of town. Now, Will slept in a small pyramid tent a hundred yards downstream from the entrance to the mine shaft where a rotating shift of ragtags kept watch on him. He fought anyone who brought up the subject of wages, which had not been paid since the reverend seized the operation. He brawled with bottles and knives, grunting like a beast, smashing in the faces and skulls of men who didn't understand why he was fighting them, standing over each one as they bled out into the mud. He pushed the men aside with his foot, as if to dare them to get up and challenge him once more, and moved on toward the saloon each evening after his shift, his boots sucking up mud beneath them, limping as if the ground had a deeper hold on him.

One afternoon Davey and Bobby left the crew at the mine and went into town. They walked past the livery, the office of the *Free Press* and the saloon. Mothers shopped with their children. Vendors with whisky carts called out. Horse-drawn carriages rattled down the mud street. Davey tipped her hat to a woman in a long grey dress carrying a small stack of books tied together in binder twine heading to the schoolhouse. The woman returned her greeting with a smile and carried on. When Davey and Bobby reached the hotel, Davey stopped. Inside the tea shop, women in hats and dresses of all colours sipped from small china teacups and nibbled on tiny sandwiches from white-gloved hands. A young couple sat across from one another smiling, holding hands on the tabletop, the man's hat hung off the back of his chair.

"They look so handsome," Davey said. "Like dirt might not ever stick on them."

Bobby nudged Davey. She stood for a moment longer before they continued on and arrived at the train station as a locomotive pulled in, hissing and steaming. Deacon strode in carrying a basket. A few passengers alighted and among these was a young couple who had arrived after sailing from England and then suffering through the long, punishing train journey from Halifax. Deacon greeted the couple, offered them a bible and a basket of bread.

Bobby stopped a man in uniform wearing a blue cap. "What time does it leave?"

"Same time every day. Ten. In the morning." The man helped a woman negotiate the steps off the train.

"A man could go a long ways away on this," Bobby said.

Davey nodded.

"See what else there is to see."

"What if it looked the same?"

"Well, a man could always come back. On the train."

They both laughed.

"Where to?" Bobby said.

"The mine."

Bobby shook his head. "I'll follow along in a bit." He turned and walked farther up the platform and spoke to another man in a blue cap.

Davey went back into town and retrieved her horse.

At the mine, men hauled carts of coal out on wagons dragged by horses covered in black dust. The men squinted into the light, their faces blackened with streaks of sweat running down from their temples. Davey stopped a man and inquired about Will. The man pointed at the ground.

"When's he coming out?"

"In the morning. When the shift changes over."

Davey tipped her hat and rode back into town.

———

A rangy dog followed Deacon as he led the young English couple to their company house, sandwiched between slavtown and dagotown. He informed them of the daily service and baptism, that the church would welcome them to the community formally at Sunday's service.

Deacon acquainted them with Reverend Brown and his crew and he told them the reverend was a man to be feared, not to get on the wrong side of him, but that he was also a man of principle and men of principle attracted followings because they instilled hope in those who joined the group. Deacon recounted stories of the baptisms and music and theatrical productions and told them how he had seen many of their own convert their views after witnessing the reverend's sermons. When they reached the door of their home, the woman turned to Deacon and said, "Do you fear him?"

Deacon removed his hat and bowed slightly. "I am perhaps not the best person to ask. I fear everything."

"I am sorry to hear that," the man said.

Deacon nodded.

"If you would?" The woman lowered her head.

Deacon held his palm in front of the door. "Bless this home and this couple. May they know no fear. Keep them safe. Amen." He made the sign of the cross.

"Simple. To the point," the man said.

Deacon nodded and smiled.

"Thank you," the woman said.

Deacon pushed a disc with a strand of twine looped through it into the man's hand. He looked at the disc and showed it to his wife. Number 212.

"Put it on before you go to work," Deacon said. "I'll say good night then." He walked up the street.

"Your dog," the man said.

Deacon turned. The mutt sat a few feet away from the couple. "He's not mine." He waved and continued on.

The woman glanced at her husband. He shrugged and they went inside.

After unpacking their trunks and eating a light meal of bread and cheese, the woman kissed her husband goodbye. He laughed as he walked up the road, the aluminum of his lunch box bright against the darkening land. When he reached the mine's entrance twenty minutes later, Keegan stopped him.

The man dug into his pocket and pulled out his disc.

"Around your neck. In your pocket. Wherever. It don't matter to me."

The man shrugged, slipped it back into his pocket and entered the mine.

Lightning scored the dark sky with furious tendrils that flashed open the valley, the vast expanse of trees covering the mountainsides, the wooden buildings throughout the town, the silver cross on top of the church, before the sky went black again. The woman stood in front of her home looking out over the town. She fanned herself with the *Free Press* and glanced down at the dog. Its ears were alert; its gaze intent toward the horizon.

The dog bolted off the porch before the sound hit. An explosion ripped open the damp air and drove coal dust back through the fanhouse, wrenched loose the roof of the building that Will and his men had built and flung it away; it sailed across the sky, a dark patch, and crumpled when it smashed into the treetops. A grey-and-black geyser spouted from the ground. Fir posts and timbers tore away, blasted from the mouth of an old tunnel into the bathhouse. A dark column foamed upward and then dropped, desecrating the mountainside with shattered coal and splintered debris, the clothing shorn from the bodies of souls working underground, their buttons ripped off and strewn nearby.

One long cry of the whistle sounded. The woman leaned forward, waited for two more bursts, but the whistle continued to bleat one long note.

Stillness hung in the air for a brief interval before crashing and jarring the world around the woman into the chaos of men shouting, dogs barking and women screaming for their children. The woman lifted the hem of her dress and sprinted down the street as horses and wagons clattered past; she pushed past people and followed the crowds heading west. When she reached the mine, she bent over her knees and gasped to breathe, the panic solid and hot in her throat.

The girth of the crowd jammed the mine's entrance; everyone clamoured for information about the men inside. The woman clasped the backs and shoulders of strangers and threaded herself through them until she reached the front. Here, the entrance was cordoned off and a few men guarded against anyone from entering the mine. The deceased were laid out in the dirt, covered with bolts of fabric, dull black boots poking out. At the mouth of the mine, a car filled with bodies emerged, the arms and legs drooped over the edge. The crowd pressed the woman into one of the men blocking the mine. Someone barked out orders to calm down. The man gently pushed her back. She turned to the mass of people behind her. The white glow of Deacon's dalmatic came toward her through the filth and dust. His eyes jittered back and forth.

Throngs of women behind her wept, their faces frozen in grotesque grimaces.

"Where's my husband?"

Deacon seized her hands but she yanked them away.

"Where is my husband? I need to see him." She repeated the words to a man holding a clipboard with a list of names on it. He handed her a brass disc with 212 engraved on it. She shouted, "No. There's been a mistake, a horrible mistake."

The man with the clipboard closed her fingers around the disc in her palm and turned away. The wails of the women punctured the air; their children clung to them, crying hysterically, terrified by the sounds their mothers made.

Davey, Bobby and Bulah rode up. Davey cantered around the crowd searching for Will.

A gunshot went off. Keegan and Gussie rode back and forth along the crowd with their pistols raised. The crowd quieted. Reverend Brown jumped onto the back of a cart and turned to the crowd, his voice crackling with the intoxication of tragedy.

"Friends." Reverend Brown pointed at the entrance to the mine. "He is here, right now, here in our midst. He has chased the devil from our home and he has spoken to me."

Reverend Brown shifted his gaze toward the sky and cocked his head.

The woman yelled out, "Our men are gone! Where was god when we needed him?"

The crowd fell silent. Reverend Brown smiled, nodded and turned to the woman. He spread out his arms and turned his palms upward.

"He said: Say unto them, this is the time for you to act. This is the time for you to stand tall and love thy neighbour. There is no time for selfishness, no time for righteousness or falsehoods. I said: Lord what should we do? He said: You shall do, and do at once. Give as I have given unto you. I said: Why have these women's homes been stricken? He said: Tragedy tests your faith. Through suffering there is salvation. I said: What of their children? They will be hungry. Tragedy will haunt their every thought."

Reverend Brown looked at the mourners.

"Our men gave their lives," the woman said. "We have nothing left to give."

"Hush, woman," Reverend Brown said. "I am not yet done."

She clenched her husband's disc in her hand and shuddered.

Reverend Brown punched his palm and resumed his sermon.

"I said: Our home is stricken. And he said: You are in the valley of shadows right now but you must climb back into the light. This is not the time to look sorrowful and say, 'May god have pity on me.' He said: I will take no pity on those who offer nothing in return but pity. I reward men of faith in times of despair, men who act on that faith and cultivate hope. And I asked: How can they demonstrate their faith? He said: I will reward every man who donates one dollar or more for the aid of thy brother. There is no man among you who cannot give one dollar. Many can give more."

"Our men are gone," the woman said. "Your words are not going to bring them back."

A man shoved the woman aside. He raised his arms and shouted, "Hallelujah! God is my father!" He emptied his pockets into a hat the clown carried through the crowd. The crown of the fabric bent beneath the weight of coins.

"He is here among us. Give so that you may receive comfort in our darkest hour!" Reverend Brown said.

The woman turned away from the reverend. "I want to see my husband," she told the man who had handed her the disc. He nodded. She followed him past Davey, Bobby and Bulah, wove her way through the crowd to the left of the mine's entrance where several dozen bodies lay covered. Each of the boots had numbers scrawled on them in chalk. They walked along the corpses until they reached 212. The man looked at the disc once again and at the boot. He nodded and handed the woman the disc, knelt down and pulled back the blanket.

Her husband's face was coated in black and he looked as if he were sleeping with a grimace scored across his mouth. She leaned down and placed a hand on his forehead and was surprised that his skin felt cold. She left her hand on his face for a moment, studied the length of his body and stood, aided by the man.

"He was one of the lucky ones," the man said.

"Lucky?" the woman said.

"His body wasn't broken." He coughed. "'Twas the lightning. Struck the rails." He pointed to the lines of the tramways running from the entrance deep into the mines. "Sparked the methane." He wiped his face. "They're calling it an act of god."

Lenora Bell and a few other women from the brothel carried platters of sandwiches and urns of coffee and offered them to the rescuers staggering out of the mine behind the last car. Their faces were smeared with soot; Davy lamps clanged against their chests. One prostitute handed the woman an urn and motioned for her to help. She shook her head. Davey rode up.

"We could use another woman's pair of hands," Lenora Bell said.

"Leave her be," Davey said.

Davey offered her hand to the widow but she shook her head and stumbled out of the crowd and headed to town.

It took two days for the rescuers to drag 128 men out of the mine. In pairs they hauled them out, one man at the foot, the other at the shoulders, carrying the limp bodies out of the earth and laying them out at the bathhouse, near the entrance to the mine. A contingent of women scrubbed the blackened corpses. They washed the arms and legs that were with or sometimes without bodies, stripped off their wedding bands and offered these along with their discs as evidence to the widows waiting to claim them, some of whom sat outside the doors of the bathhouse wailing.

The bodies were loaded onto a train that ran on a spur line into town, and received by families at the depot, their cries an awful chorus as they claimed their dead. Families carried their sons or fathers or father and son, and lurched up the street in silent processions, the deceased held above their shoulders as they marched home. The deceased without family, or otherwise unknown, were carted by horses to the church and laid out on the pews at the front, where families still searching for their men filed past, their faces pale as they lifted the blankets that covered the bodies.

The next day, at Reverend Brown's request, Deacon presided over thirty-five funerals. Included were fourteen unmarked, simple coffins in one long cortège of unclaimed men and boys, those with no family or kin. The procession trudged down the street in a train of wagons with rickety wheels. Deacon led the pallbearers, holding a cross in front of him, his boots sucking up the mud and puddles that stained the street. Reverend Brown and his disciples sat atop their horses. Davey stood beside her pony with Bobby and bowed her head. At the rear, mourners fell in behind the wagons, their hands clasped in prayer and behind them the clown strode forward with his arms extended outward. Behind the clown, a small troupe of musicians, all of whom held their archaic instruments in silence save the accordionist, who pumped out a single, baleful note—the only sound heard over the creaking wagon wheels and Deacon's boots in the mud.

When the procession arrived at the graveyard, Deacon stood on the riverbank and faced the widows and fatherless children of the town. He held up a bible. "There are no words to adequately express what has happened to our little community," he whispered. "I will say this: We have been injured, terribly so. We have all suffered unspeakable loss." His eyes welled up. "The year has been filled with many dark vagaries from which we have all suffered, but which will be but a small interruption in our lives. For god the almighty would want us all to carry on in the face of such unspeakable tragedy and turn it into something like grace to live out our days. That is our challenge. This is what will test us today and shape us for tomorrow. Amen."

They buried the anonymous men in the hard muscle of the land, the shouldered clay of the riverbank, low on the alluvial plain, carved by runoff from violent spring storms and the ruthless snowmelt; a long row of dirt mounds, each with a simple cross nailed, hacked out of wood by river pigs who used crosscut saws to mark the final resting place of the deceased.

The Englishwoman trudged home with a hundred widows and countless children in the twilight along the long rows of miners' cottages, each with their front door darkened by folds of heavy crepe. Davey and Bobby waited outside of the hotel. Their horses twitched their tails against the flies. Bulah and Gussie came down the street and stopped. They disembarked from their mounts, tethered their ponies.

"We're off at first light," Bulah said.

Davey and Bobby nodded. Bulah and Gussie went into the hotel.

"My father," Davey said. "He was in that mine."

Bobby looked at her.

"That man who ran the mines," she said.

Bobby shook his head. "How do you know?"

Davey eyed the street. The Englishwoman came toward them with a dog at her heels. "Just do." Davey removed her hat.

The woman stopped in front of one of the horses, place a hand on its long muzzle. She turned to Davey, her eyes red and damp. "I am going home. Will you be so kind as to accompany me for a little ways?"

When the trio arrived at the front door of the widow's cottage she stood for a long while with her hand on the door. The dog whined behind her. "There's nothing here for me," she said. "Was never meant to be." She started off down the street.

Bobby looked at Davey. "She's suffered enough for both of us," Davey said.

They caught up with the widow and took their time strolling through town. Davey breathed heavily, as if winded.

"Are you all right?" the widow said.

Davey nodded.

It was early evening; the sun had sunk behind the peaks west of town and the light in the sky had faded. The first of the stars appeared. Swallows peppered the air above them. A piano started up in the saloon. Two men stood outside the entrance shouting obscenities at each other. A carriage rattled past.

The three of them entered the train station. The widow sat down and fanned herself. She reached into her pocket, held up a banknote and handed it to Davey. "I'd appreciate it if you could stay with me until the next train arrives."

Davey turned the note over in her hands and returned it to her.

"It don't come 'til morning," Bobby said.

The widow handed the banknote to Bobby. He slipped it into his pocket.

Davey removed her quiver and set it down opposite the widow. She arched her spine and pushed her shoulders forward and rubbed her lower back before sitting next to the quiver, her bow across her lap. She stretched out her legs, crossed her boots at the ankles and leaned her head against the bench. Tipped her hat down over her eyes. Her breath was shallow but it levelled out and she fell into a light sleep. Bobby rolled a smoke and wet it in his mouth. He offered it to the widow but she shook her head. He shrugged and struck a match on the bench, lit the cigarette, drew on the tobacco and exhaled blue smoke toward the ceiling. A breeze had come up and pushed the sulphur from the match and the tobacco smoke toward her. She fanned it away with her hand. Bobby laughed. Davey lifted her head and opened her eyes.

"Get comfortable," Davey said. "Rest."

"How long have you been like that?" the widow said.

"Like what?"

"Tired." The widow offered a thin smile.

The sky was dark and soon the moon appeared, a large fish eye that rose in the doorway of the train station, staring at the trio, lingering for a few minutes before slowly swimming from view, floating high over the land below.

BOOK
THREE

1902

TEN

AT THE PEAK OF THE PASS, Jack Smith turned in his saddle and glanced back at the skinny goat trail he had bushwhacked through from Crowsnest. The land lay bunched in trees; the river snaked its way through the tight valley, a ribbon of tarnished silver. He swivelled around and surveyed the land to the west. A broad valley, splashed with patches of dry fields shadowed in the hulking muscle of mountains stretching westward. Pale blue light, a fallow land that clawed open valley and river, a world come into view, waiting like a dream. Toward a smudge on the horizon, the thin white gauze of a locomotive, its dark brume rising up, drifting to the mountainside and clinging to the firs and lodgepoles that flushed the land beneath him in a wash of smoke and deep green. A raven floated, then dipped sharply and soared away. He leaned over the withers of his horse. "C'mon. Let's get a move on."

The path cut down the heat-stricken granite face of the Pass in treacherous switchbacks that narrowed into a winding game trail. Bursts of alpine flowers and gnarled brush crowded the way. Smith cautiously descended, zigzagging the mountainside, the click of his pony's hooves on rocks, its snorts punching out short gasps. It took most of the morning to reach the bottom. He stopped at the river, dismounted and watered his pony. Smith bent down and splashed the water on his face, scrubbed his neck and drank handfuls of water he scooped up. The water was clear and cool. He reached into it, laid his palm on the pebbles, some smeared with a verdigris of algae. The rocks had settled here long before him; they would continue to rest long after he was gone. He lifted his hand and wiped his face.

At sundown, Smith made a fire on the riverbank and when it could burn on its own, he set off and found his mare cropping grass. He removed the saddle, an old slick fork with pecan stirrups and wrecked, sour, rawhide housing. The mare's head twitched sideways and then was still. Smith left her to graze.

He unspooled his bedroll and cut a chunk off the venison leg he'd stashed inside it. Jammed it on a stick and propped it out over the fire. The grease from the meat sputtered and smoked on the coals. He broke open his Lee-Metford carbine, a single shot breechloader. Slipped four cartridges into his jacket pocket and set the gun down. A coyote yapped. Smith removed the venison from the fire and ate it from the stick and slurped river water to put a bottom on his stomach. He laid down and chewed on a twig of sage. The mare shuffled, pulled at the grass. Smith looked at the stars for a long while before closing his eyes and drifting to sleep.

————————

At sun-up, he crawled out of his bedroll and stripped off his shirt and trousers. He laid them out with his red jacket on the rocks along the shore, the brass buttons on his jacket glinting in the sunlight, and walked through the cool morning air to the river. A thin sliver of moon hung in the west over the bluff, a crisp, bright star above the tip of it. Smith stepped into the water. He waded out past the smaller pebbles until he was up to his thighs, dropped down into the water and shot up gasping as the cold knocked his wits loose. He paddled around some and scrubbed his body with fistfuls of sand, dunked under again before he waded out of the river, sat on a rock and dried in the morning chill. He put his clothes on, pulled on his boots. Tore a piece of meat off the deer leg and chewed it. Fish rose and poked rings on the surface of the river. A hawk circled above.

He watered his horse, flung his gear on it and lit up on top. Kicked his heels against her belly and headed up the valley.

Smith travelled steadily through the morning. The valley narrowed and he rode up on a burbling stretch of water. After that, he veered away from the river and in an hour the valley bottom forked and he took the right fork, westerly. The air was hot and sticky, the sky the colour of whisky. He removed his coat. His shirt was soaked with sweat. Loosened the collar on his shirt and unbuttoned it to his navel. The sky got darker as he rode and the wind lay low. Great rags of clouds tumbled down from the northeast and piled up overhead. By noon they had assembled into dark thunderheads. A breeze had picked up and the air cooled.

He led the mare up a deep, rocky ravine between scrubby, fir-splotched mountainsides. The sky blackened. Clouds turned over themselves, whipped into a sinister froth. Gusts of wind shook the brush and treetops. Smith came out of the draw into the open.

Sheet lightning soundlessly spread through cloud cotton. The clouds simmered, churning greenish-black under. It was dark except for the thin, whisky skyline ahead of him.

Fat drops of rain plumped the ground. The rain turned to hail and pelted Smith's thighs and shoulders, stung the back of his hands. He lowered his chin to his chest and rode quickly, hail slapping the back of his neck. He shouted. Hail smashed and recoiled off the ground, roared like buckshot, the air hissing and bawling. Smith led his mare to a large fir; they stood beneath it until the storm had quit. The hail had shorn leaves and branches from the aspens and firs. Everywhere the tang of damp dirt and shredded flora. There were whole hailstones as far as he could see; the land pelted in white ice like millions of glistening quail eggs waiting to be hatched.

Smith jabbed the mare's belly and they lumbered on, crunching over the hailstones until they topped the ridge. Snow-capped peaks rolled like ocean swells beneath bright sunlight. And the trash of the storm: melting ice, sheared-off brush, broken trees, scraps of splintered trunks.

———————————

The ragged land lifted and fell and cut through forest shredded and torn, blazing a trail for Smith to follow. The mare perked her ears and strained to see ahead in the cool shadows. They cantered steadily, threading their way through the woods with occasional bursts of openings where they stole views of the valley ahead.

Toward evening a breeze came up, cool and sweet. Grey flecks of ash floated down and landed on Smith's arm. He made camp at an opening just up from the river where the ground was flat and his horse could crop grass. The air was fresh and smelled of cedar and river. Stars circled overhead.

He woke the next morning covered in a thin film of ash, and the air tasted of charred creosote. He brushed himself off, saddled his horse and chased the river. To either side, snapped pine trunks stuck up like spears. Rough fescue, hawthorn, bunchgrass and small hemlocks lay ripped and mutilated on the ground. The valley widened and trees receded up the mountainsides. Smith followed this expanse with the sun blistering his hat. Smoke rose in the distance. The unmistakable clang of the blacksmith's forge, voices, dogs yapping. Ash floated down from a flawless sky.

———————————

Smith brushed the soot from his boots and polished the buttons on his coat, straightened his hat, rode to the edge of town. He followed the smoke and stopped at Morrissey. Two or three wooden buildings were blown apart, their sticks scattered everywhere. A mess of timber and signboards, broken glass, tin roofing. A grey film of ash on everything. Men loaded debris onto a wagon. Wagons stuffed with detritus or waiting to be filled up. Saddle horses everywhere—Coggshalls with brass-covered trees and stirrups, silver concho accents and Montana flat plates, and high-backed Albertan trail saddles with scrolled work on toasted leather. There were canvas wall tents erected behind the mine and bundles of clothes covered in ash spread out to dry on guy ropes. Men and boys worked to clear the debris off the ground, and others carried armfuls of torn timber, piles of broken glass, and smashed lanterns from the mine. They worked in silence except for an occasional "Gimme a hand here," "That's it, easy does it," "Lift on three. One, two ..." A crew of men lugged wreckage from the wooden hull of another building. Smith lit down from the mare and tied her to a leafless tree. He slipped the spurs off his boots, hung them on the saddle horn, walked over and pitched in.

The men's faces were grimy with sweat and dirt and they squinted in the sunlight at Smith's brass buttons and scarlet jacket but didn't speak to him.

Smith helped where it was needed. He hefted broken beams and timbers and helped knock apart a wooden partition and dragged out railcars loaded with debris and coal. A woman came around with a pot of black coffee and handed him a cup. He sat with the men on a stack of broken timber and drank.

"You come over from the coast?" the woman said.

Smith shook his head. "The prairies."

"I can't believe my eyes." Her voice wavered. "Oh lord, I tell you it feels like the end of the world." She started to walk away, turned back, offered her hand to Smith. "Lenora Bell. Friends call me Lennie."

Smith sipped his coffee. The men rolled cigarettes. One was offered to Smith. He shook his head.

"You come from the Pass?" the one who offered him the cigarette said. He was tall with a black moustache.

"More or less."

"You seen that storm?"

"It was hard to miss."

Another man leaned forward with thin, clean fingers. A small notebook protruded from his breast pocket. He was the only one whose hands and face weren't sun-browned. His eyes were dark and sunken. A pencil nub tucked behind his ear. "One hundred and twenty-eight men. Good men, many of them young."

"My sincere condolences," Smith said.

The man shook his head. "Members of the same family were killed. Men and boys. Fathers and sons working side by side down there." He jabbed his thumb over his shoulder to where the bulk of the wreckage lay. "Wounded people everywhere. Men injured hauling out the bodies, men gone missing like they stepped off the face of the earth. It blew up on us out of nowhere." He stared off. "And then that storm roared in like a revenge. It's got folks sleeping in the church. In tents. Under wagons. Ain't no point in writing about it. People are in the midst of living it. Will be for a long time."

"I'm truly sorry to hear that," Smith said. "Seems each place I'm going, I'm seeing god's work in the world."

"His work?" the man with the black moustache said.

"Wrathful work. His footsteps crush everything in their path. Some believe it amuses him to see what he has kicked up."

"What do you think?"

"It's just a storm," Smith said.

"Well, at least he spared the church," the newsman said.

"He always does."

"Ain't no luck in this place," the man with the black moustache said. "Some say Will brought it on—all that bloodshed he caused—and that we're all going to die in blood to pay for his sins."

Smith tipped back his hat, wiped his face and looked around. Women poured coffee and carried platters of sandwiches. Men smoked, ate and drank. Some rested their heads on their arms and knees.

"You may be right. I can't speak for a man I have not met," Smith said. "But being chained to another man's fate, well, that's another matter. It's just an idea that takes hold. It gives us something or someone to pin the blame on rather than accepting the consequences of our actions. The question is, where is it in the goodness of our days? 'Cause there's plenty of that, too. What's it called then?"

"Lady luck." The newsman chuckled. "Wait 'til you meet the one who calls himself Reverend Brown."

"He calls himself Reverend Brown?"

"Yessir."

"What do others call him?"

"Reverend Brown."

The men laughed.

"They call me Jack Smith."

The newsman reached for his pencil and scribbled in his notebook.

They laughed again. The man with the black moustache cleared his throat. "You're saying that the misfortune we carry because of Will ain't real?"

"I'm saying it's real if folks believe it's real. What we believe in seems to make the belief real. Or, we can choose to have faith that there's something else to all of this. Either way we have a choice. There's some solace in the fact that it's up to us. What we believe, how we act." Smith brushed soot from his sleeve. "What does this man, Will, say about it?"

"He died in the mine he built."

"Well," Smith said, "I can go to hell then."

The men laughed.

"You here for the relief efforts?"

"You might say that," Smith said.

The man with the black moustache looked toward the shattered mine. He wiped his face slowly with the palm of his hand and dried it on his chest. "Ain't no luck here, none at all."

They finished their smokes, got up and smacked the dust off their thighs. Smith pressed each of the nubs into the dirt with the toe of his boot until they were good and extinguished.

Toward the end of the day, the men quit their work. Some went to their tents. Others wandered into town to find the saloon. Still others mounted their horses and rode off. A few men kept on working, stacking broken timbers and planks. Daylight frittered down to a slash of orange. Dim scatterings of birds flew across the sky.

The man with the dark moustache told Smith his name was Dutch Peters. Smith, the newsman and Dutch Peters talked for a while. Bellevue, Cypress Hills, the Pass. No rain for weeks. Wolves killing livestock. The reverend's baptisms. River low and clear and fish caught in shaded oxbows here and there. The strange music and theatrics of the reverend's followers. A workhorse at the mine screaming after the explosion hit, hurtling and bucking all over the town. Shards of coal and wood scarring its side.

The newsman bid them both farewell.

"Where do you aim to spend the night?" Peters said.

"The hotel."

"It's plumb full up."

"In the woods then. Don't make much difference to me."

"You can put up at my place. Hay for your horse. I'll cook up some grub."

"No need."

"I got to cook it for myself. It's no chore to cook for another."

"Well, I won't argue with that."

Smith untied his horse and followed Peters. Cooking fires burned here and there. Canvas tents glowed like chines of white from candles and lamps within. The night sky pinpricked with stars. They stopped in front of a large tent.

Peters nodded to a clearing where a baleful sheep stared at them, its back leg cocked, and went into the tent and lit a lamp. Smith unlaced his saddle and dropped his gear to the ground. Staked his horse out. Peters came out of the tent and shook some hay out in front of the mare. He reached to pat the sheep but it skittered away. Peters walked over to the cookfire. "Take a load off." He went back into the tent and came out a few moments later with some jerked elk and two bowls of canned pears. They ate together, shovelling the pears into their mouths and then licking their fingers. Peters tipped back his bowl and slurped the juice; Smith did the same.

After their meal, Smith fetched his gear and followed Peters into the tent. A cot lay along a side, with a rumpled blanket on it. There were canned goods, a stone bottle, plates and a pan stacked on top of two overturned boxes.

Peters sat on his cot and pointed to the ground next to him. "Space enough for you to set up there."

Smith unspooled his bedroll and lay back.

Peters reached across him for the stone bottle. He removed the cork, tipped back the bottle and took three long swallows. He held it to Smith. The bottle was heavy and Smith noted the glisten of Peters' saliva on the rim.

"I'm all right." He handed it back to Peters.

"Helps me sleep."

"I don't need help in that regard. I seem to sleep fine enough."

Peters tipped it back, took three more long swallows. "That'll have me counting sheep in two shakes." He chuckled and took three more long drinks and rested the bottle on his knee. His eyes were red, watery. "Tell me your story then."

"No story to tell. I've been summoned to investigate a preacher and his sect bilking folks out of their money." Smith had his hands behind his head and stared at the flickering light playing on the canvas. "Sound like your Reverend Brown?"

Peters grunted. He took three more swallows from the bottle. "If I could just get up the cash I'd set up farther west, on Joseph's Prairie," he said. "Gold. I'd chase gold."

"Is there still gold out there?"

"Heaps of it."

"Why aren't you there now?"

Peters was silent. He took three more gulps and began to snore sitting upright. He woke himself and muttered, "It's a terrible thing to be a failure."

Peters stumbled as he stepped over Smith and left the tent. Smith's horse snuffled and Peters slipped off his suspenders and a moment later the sheep bleated. Smith stood and peered out from the tent. Peters had his trousers down at his ankles and was staggering around the clearing, cursing at the sheep that evaded him. He stopped with his hands on his knees, breathing heavily. He turned away from the sheep and lurched toward the tent. Smith lay down. Peters reached for his trousers and fell to the ground. He raised himself, pulled up his trousers and snapped the suspenders over his shoulders and entered the tent, wheezing lightly.

Smith got up and helped him to his cot.

"I appreciate that." Peters held Smith on the shoulder.

Smith blew out the lantern and lay down on the floor. Outside, the murmur of men, crack of a log in a fire, snarling dogs.

———

In the morning Peters fried two eggs in a skillet and laid them over chunks of potatoes that he yanked out of the low fire. The men ate in silence and afterward they went into town, Smith on his horse and Peters walking alongside.

There were several horses tied in front of the saloon, a man sweeping in the doorway. Clang from the blacksmith's. Dogs lazing to the side of the street. The newsman came riding up. "Off to help out at the mine?"

Smith nodded.

Peters scratched his jaw. "I've plenty cut out for me here."

The newsman shook his head. "Better to work one off than sleep it off."

Peters walked back in the direction they'd come, and Smith rode with the newsman to the mine.

"One thing he'll never be accused of," the newsman said.

"What's that?"

"Work."

Smith helped clear debris out of the crushed passages within the mine. He kept to himself, sweat dripping from his eyebrows and chin. In the afternoon a wagon rattled past with two bodies wrapped in blankets, their feet sticking off the end. A small, numbered disc was tied to the big toe on each.

At dusk, Smith left the mine and rode back into town. Peters sat on the front steps of the saloon.

"You look like you could use one," Peters said.

"No need."

A young girl with a bow and a quiver slung over her shoulder stood outside the saloon. Men laughed and joked among themselves. She walked along the boardwalk. An older woman burst from the saloon and chased after her.

"He's got no claim on me." The girl glared past the woman at Smith. There was something dark and fierce in her eyes. She continued along and picked up her pace and the woman followed. They veered off to the left at the end of the street, toward the church, and disappeared from view.

Smith turned to Peters and raised an eyebrow.

"Believe me, you do not want to mess with them," Peters said.

———————————

Smith tried the hotel and rented a room. He gathered his gear at Peters' tent. Peters wasn't around, but the fire burned low and the stone bottle stood uncorked on the ground. Smith went to the hotel and lay on his cot, stared at the ceiling for a while. There was a knock on his door. The front desk clerk identified himself and said that Smith had a friend in the lobby, waiting on him. "I ain't got no friends."

"He goes by the name Peters."

"Tell him I ain't here."

"He said you'd say as much. He said to tell you he'd seen you enter the hotel."

"Tell him I'm sleeping."

"He said you'd say that, too, and told me to tell you that you can sleep when you're dead. And that you ain't dead. Not by a long shot."

Smith rose and rinsed off his face in the wash basin and went out. "What do you say?" Smith glared at the clerk. The man wore a patch over his right eye and stood on one leg, leaning on a crutch. The trouser for his missing left leg was pinned up at his waist.

"I say what I'm told to say."

"The next time he comes around, tell him I'm not in. Can you say that?"

The clerk lowered his head and stood silently.

"Jesus." Smith dug into his pocket and handed the man a coin.

The clerk raised his head and nodded. "Yes, sir, I can tell him that."

Smith descended the stairs. In the lobby Peters held up a ceramic bottle and grinned. They walked across town to Peters' camp and sat in front of a low fire and each time Peters drank from the bottle he offered it to Smith, who waved him off.

"Who was that we saw today?"

"I saw a lot of people today," Peters said.

"The girl and that woman. Who were they?"

"You like 'em young and full of firewater?" Peters scratched his thigh and let his hand rest against his crotch.

"Trying to get a straight answer from you is like teaching a stone to talk."

"I told you, you do not want to mess with them."

"Where are they from?"

"Beats me. They came in town one day with the reverend and a crew of misfits and the meanest men you ever met. Rumour is they robbed the mine."

"The mine?"

"Yessir. Before the tragedy."

"Women robbed the mine?"

Peters chuckled and squeezed his crotch. "Can't get past that lively little bundle, can you?"

"What's her name?"

"Dunno. The reverend's been giving baptisms at the river, taking folks' money and then gambling it in the saloon."

"I ain't seen them about," Smith said.

"Well, you will or you won't." Peters took three long gulps from the bottle.

"Why's that?"

"On account of mischief."

"What's she got to do with those men?"

"I told you." Peters smiled at Smith. "Mischief." He lifted his buttock, passed gas and sighed.

Smith shook his head. "Can't you just act like a man for a moment?"

"I am."

"Try acting like a different kind of man then."

Peters drank from his bottle.

"What's this crew, this reverend look like?" Smith said.

"Short, skinny as a goat. Hair all frizzy and wild. Clean-shaven. He wears a crown made of twigs, like he's the second coming of christ. His followers are a bunch of misfits that resemble something you've never seen before. Like they've rode to hell and back and are headed plumb straight in that direction again." Peters lowered his voice and looked up the street in either direction. "That man"—he paused—"got folks around here thinking he hung the moon and stars with his bare hands. He's got the meanest scar on his face you ever seen." Peters made a sign of the cross over his own features. "They're saying it came from killing a bear."

"Jesus. You've got something dying in you." Smith waved to clear the air in front of him. He covered his nose and mouth with his palm. "Where do I find him?"

"That's a different man, trapped inside me, dying to come out." Peters laughed. He tipped back the bottle and when he was done he belched. When he was finished, he lowered his voice. "Where else? Try the church."

Smith awoke in the hotel. Dim orange light slanted in from the shutters. A church bell clanked. Butchers sharpened their cleavers, steel sliding on steel. Boot heels stamped on the boardwalk below. A man shouted. Whip of leather against horse flesh. Horse hooves, rattle of wooded rims in the street. Smith's shirt, coat and jacket were laid over a chair in the corner of the room. He swung his feet down onto the floor and looked out onto the street. A lone woman stepped aside so two drunk men holding each other up could pass. Men clambered and stormed along the worn boardwalk. Women pounded and slapped laundry against timber beams. Laughter of children sprinting in the street. A dog barking and then another. The moan of a whore and grunt of man in the room adjacent.

Smith rinsed his face in the basin, put on his shirt and jacket and pulled on his grey pants and tucked them into his long brown boots. Combed his hair and waxed the ends of his moustache and fetched up his holster and fastened it; his Deane and Adams revolver hung on the left-hand side. He grabbed his hat and stepped out into the long hallway. Walked down the stairs to the lobby and went over to the front desk.

"What's the time?" he said.

"Eight thirty, sir." The clerk cleared his throat. "That man came around looking for you. Late." The clerk stopped writing in his ledger.

"And?"

"And I told him you weren't here."

Smith glared at him.

"I'm just telling you."

Smith shook his head and walked out.

In Deb's café on the north side of the street, Smith ate a breakfast of steak, fried potatoes, onions and coffee. He went back out into the street. The sun was already well up.

Two butchers, their aprons bronzed with blood, talked and gestured with their knives and set to carving a carcass laid out on a worn cutting table. A cart piled with fresh blocks of uncut ice clunked across the street toward the railway station.

Smith wandered up the boardwalk, worn in ruts, spattered with tobacco spit. A short line snaked out of the butcher shop. Ducks and rabbits hung from twine lashed over ceiling beams. Tongues and saddles and quarters of beef. Sausage rings in loops like lariats. Next door, a sign that simply said, RICHARDS. The shop had barrels of dried fruit, beans, grains, spices and onions. Dried garlic hung from their fronds. Swallows swarmed in and out of the shops. A woman wandered out of the butcher shop, clutching a small package wrapped in brown paper.

In a tea shop across the street, three women sat at a table, laughing. Smith walked to the next street and turned.

There were no people here and the street was shaded. He walked past a blue door, a yellow door and past a house with an immense thick fir door with a wooden balcony overhead. At the end of the street, a white clapboard frame house with pink lace curtains. Small, white picket fence. Vegetable patches between the front steps and the fence, the black dirt freshly turned. Stakes of flowering snap peas green in the light. Two women fanned themselves on the porch, smiling through rouge-painted faces. He tipped his hat to them and turned the corner into bright sunlight on the main street. When he reached the river, he climbed the steps into the church and opened the door. The altar was askew, as if someone had tried to move it out of the way, and there was a length of rope on top of it. A pair of pants and three shirts lay draped over a pew. A hat lay on the ground, its crown crushed flat. There were empty liquor bottles upright and on their sides in between the pews and the air reeked of body odour and booze. He called out but there was no answer. He returned to town.

There were more people out now, walking up and down the street, going about their business. Smith noted a woman and her child enter a shop with miniature doll heads and playthings. Two women entered a candy shop. He passed a general store where pans and pickaxes were displayed in the front window. Stopped at a doctor's office and read the flyer tacked up on the door: *Mother Seigel's syrup to cure windy spasms.* There was another notice that claimed a cure for loss of vitality for men. Smith grinned and passed a tonsorial parlour. He looked through the window; the barber chair was unoccupied. He pushed the door open.

"Come on in," the barber said. "Frank's catching me up on things. Daily state of the union." He nodded at an old, bald man leaning on his cane, sitting on a stool. Tall-necked bottles, mirrors, marble sink, smell of lavender and antiseptic. The barber had a white sheet draped over his forearm. He gestured to the chair. "It'd be an honour to do you the honour."

Smith removed his jacket and hung it with his hat on a piece of hardware against the wall. He sat in the chair and the barber flapped out the sheet, up and over Smith, fastened it behind Smith's neck with a safety pin. He picked up a pair of scissors, stood behind Smith, placed a hand on his shoulder and looked at him in the mirror.

Smith ran his hand along the whiskers on his cheeks.

The barber set down his scissors, reached behind the chair and cranked it lower. He tipped Smith back. "Shave it is, then," he said.

The barber poured water that steamed into a cup and used a brush to mix it. His back was turned to Smith and he worked up a lather like he was beating the band and when he was done, he laid a hot towel over Smith's neck and unrolled it up his chin over his nose to the bottom of his eyes, pressed it against Smith's skin.

"They got most of it cleared away. They're talking 'bout starting it up again in a few days," Frank said in a raspy voice, like he was gurgling rocks. "Men still ain't been paid"—he cleared his throat—"since the new management took over."

The barber lifted his eyebrows. "Is that a fact?" He removed the towel and spread warm lather across Smith's face with his palms.

Frank nodded.

The barber held up his lathered palms. "Here to keep the peace?"

"I am and I'm not," Smith said.

The barber wiped his hands on a towel on the counter and stropped his razor. He turned to Smith.

"You might say it's a case of being in the right place at the wrong time. On account of what you folks have all endured," Smith said.

"The sound of that whistle shrieking, I tell you, it gets up in your head where it can't get out." Frank pointed his cane toward the street. "Women, children, dogs and horses, all of them stampeding up and down the streets, screaming and crying like it was a day of reckoning." He coughed. "Which, I suppose, it was."

"Now then," the barber said, "that's all in the past now, isn't it? The sun's shining and it's a glorious day to be alive." He laid a warm towel over Smith's eyes and stropped his razor again.

"They're saying that reverend wrestled a bear to his death," Frank said. "That he hunted it down for days and killed it with his hands."

"That a fact?" The barber leaned over Smith. "I heard he had a knife."

The old man said, "Dick Cartwright was just in the other day, telling me he swore he saw the reverend stare down a goat and willed it to just drop and die, right there in front of everyone."

"I didn't know we had any goats around," the barber said.

"There ain't anymore."

"There's a lot of stories about that man," the barber clucked lightly. "One thing I know for a fact, it's turning out to be a nice day in our fine little town. We got boarded sidewalks. Plenty of wood, coal and water. More animals than you can fit on the ark." He tipped Smith's chin toward him; he rested his palm against Smith's face and shaved in short strokes, pausing after each pass to wipe the blade on the heel of his palm. Tobacco and antiseptic on his breath. "We got the Crow's Nest line coming in over the Pass. They're pushing track as far west as the coast. We're on the map now. Business is set to boom. Any person can stop in."

"Anyone," Frank said, "but not everyone."

"Now then, any person can leave, too. There's a lot of world to see now, isn't there?" The barber set the razor down, picked up the scissors and trimmed Smith's moustache. He trimmed his nose hairs and his ear hairs, wiped his face, up under his nose, near his earlobes and the rest of his neck. He stood back and studied Smith's face and tossed the towel on the counter.

Frank waved his cane at the window. "The Reverend Brown and his crew are holding a revival tonight," he said. "First one. Since."

"Is that a fact?" The barber rubbed cream into Smith's face that smelled like lilac and gently slapped Smith's cheeks.

"He put on some show week before last. Folks still running off the lip about that."

The barber stood back and tilted up the chair. "How's that suit you?"

Smith studied himself in the mirror and nodded.

The barber smiled, turned the chair to face him and removed the sheet. He shook it out to the side.

Smith stood. He placed three coins in the barber's palm.

"That's mighty generous of you. I thank you."

Smith buttoned up his jacket and put on his hat. "Where's this reverend hosting the revival tonight?"

"The church," Frank said.

Smith tipped his hat to the men, opened the door and looked up and down the street. He turned to his left and closed the door with a soft click as the old man rasped, "He's a strange one."

"He's a generous man," the barber replied.

Smith walked back to the café where he had a plate of eggs, sausages and fried potatoes for lunch. He sipped his coffee, grimaced, and tossed a pinch of salt in the cup, stirring it and gulping it down.

Evening. Children played next to buildings. Shopkeepers lit their lamps. In the saloon, men smoked their pipes. Boots scuffed on the floor. The piano sat unoccupied. Smith knocked back a shot of whisky. He left and ate at the café again—pan-roasted trout dusted in flour, salt and pepper, fried potatoes and stewed tomatoes. When he came back out there was a crowd of people talking about the revival. He asked a man where it was held and the men pointed in the direction of the river, where the silver cross stood atop the building.

In the hotel lobby, the lamps were lit and the glass globes placed overtop and the wicks turned down. Dim lemon light. The clerk sat behind his desk reading a paper, lifted his head when Smith entered and nodded. Smith started up the stairs. A woman flushed in the face hurried on her way down. She had a large welt beneath her right eye; her nose was red and stuffed with cotton.

Smith took off his hat.

"You don't remember me," she said.

"Lenora Bell. You make the best coffee I've had the pleasure of drinking in this town."

"Lennie."

"Lennie." Smith nodded and smiled. "Are you all right?"

She nodded and lifted a hand to her face, turned her head away from him. "I am now." She descended the stairs, walked through the lobby and out. The clerk raised his head from his newspaper and scowled. Smith climbed the staircase and went through the hallway to his room. He drew a match against the wall and lit a lamp. Murmur of voices in the street. Dogs barking. He closed the shutters, wriggled off his boots, climbed onto the cot and stared at the light flickering shadows on the ceiling.

An hour passed before he rose, pulled on his boots, blew out the lamp and descended the stairs. He strode past the clerk, who picked at his teeth with a sliver of wood.

"Off for an evening of"—the clerk shifted the toothpick and pointed it at the door—"entertainment?"

Smith glared at the man.

"Or maybe you're off to be saved?"

"Any man who puts his saving in another man's hands is not a man."

"Isn't that your job?" The clerk tossed the toothpick to the ground, hopped to the door, turned and faced Smith.

"How about I give you a dollar not to speak to me anymore?" Smith said.

The clerk nodded and held out his palm. "That friend of yours, Peters, comes around, I suppose you're not in?"

Smith walked out into the street and headed to the river. The evening air thick with raw yellow cedar and saw boards. The church stood footed on a flat meadow along the river, tombstones like decaying teeth sprawling out from the cemetery, the grass in front worn and scabbed with patches of dirt. There were a few people standing in the churchyard. Smith tipped his hat to them and entered the church. Two parishioners knelt with their heads bowed over their clasped hands. The altar had been straightened out and there was no sign of the disarray he had seen earlier. The parishioners made the sign of the cross, stood and left. Smith followed them out and asked them about the reverend but they shook their heads and wandered away toward town. Smith asked others waiting in the churchyard but they shrugged their shoulders. He walked back into town.

A mother and her boy struggled to push their cart through the mud, filled with limp leafy greens, potatoes encrusted in dirt, the wilted tops of carrots. They moved together like they were leaning into the wind and when the woman placed her hand on the boy's head and stroked his hair, Smith turned away and headed toward the white clapboard house with the pink curtains.

There were several women on the front porch fanning themselves. They called out from the dark, their pale faces mocking him, coarse pink mouths open in laughter. He noticed one woman sitting against the stairs, head down, knees splayed open, her dress a ruffle of white. She lifted her bruised face and smiled. "You miss my coffee?"

Fires glinted in the dark as he led Lenora Bell through the streets. Carriages clattered past, men shouted and snapped leather switches against the horses' lanky frames. The clamber of the train whistled low across town. She walked a few steps behind him without being told to do so. Smith noted the livery and the *Free Press*. The breeze had a raw edge to it; leaves scattered by and skeltered on. She followed him into the hotel. The clerk nodded to Smith but his face darkened when he saw Lenora Bell. They climbed the stairs and pushed the door open to Smith's small room.

"Why Lennie?" Smith handed her a banknote. "Sounds like a name fit for a man." He lit the lamp and closed the door.

Lenora Bell stood at the foot of the bed and unclasped the top three buttons of her frock, folded the banknote three times and slipped it into her bodice, raised a finger to her lips to silence him. "You're not paying me to talk about my name, are you?" She lifted her skirt and lay back on the bed. He glanced at the tuft of dark pubic hair that poked out of a tear in her bloomers and peeled back his suspenders.

"Honey, can you blow out that lantern? I'm not looking my best."

Smith did as he was told, unbuttoned his fly and crawled on top of her, pushed himself between the folds of her cloth and waited for her to respond. He thrust into her and rained sweat on her face; she turned away. He pulled off his shirt and wiped her face.

She wrapped her thighs around him and drew him in tight, her breath in his ear. He pinned both of her arms above her head and held them with one hand. He balled up the shirt, tossed it behind him and placed the other hand on her throat. A gold crucifix lay against her warm skin, the bones and ligaments in her neck spongy like those of a small bird. He lifted the cross, unclasped the chain off her neck and dropped it on the floor, rested his palm against the side of her neck. She stared back at him. The blankets slid back and fell off as she stood. She walked to the door and straightened her dress and then her hair. Knelt down and ran her palms over the floor until she found her cross and necklace. She stood, affixed it around her neck.

"What is it with you men? Need to hurt something to possess it and then feeling bad and all so we have to console you only to be hurt by you again."

He came up against the door frame. She caught hold of his hand and laughed. "This is going to cost you more."

He nodded and nipped her shoulder.

She led him through the dark. "Can you be a gentleman? At least until the introductions are over?" They bumped up against a small chair. He sat her down. The grate of wood as she leaned back against it. He lifted her legs up.

Their hipbones knocked. He clenched the chair back with his hand. His other hand gripped a stockinged leg that flopped against his shoulder. He reached for her chin but she jerked her head aside and kept her face turned away, avoiding his eyes. Rotated the crucifix to the back of her neck, held her up and eased out of her. She gasped. He eased back into her. "There," she breathed. "Keep still. There." Fingers scraped at his back, heels banged against his shoulder blades. His body shuddered and beneath him Lenora Bell trembled as if to ward off a chill.

Smith led her to the bed. The moon was up. Her knee brushed against him and her eyes were wide open now and he rolled back on top of her. Neck straining in the white light, violent eyes, mouth open, biting his neck. Her buttocks bounced against the mattress. He grunted and she gripped his hips tighter, grinding him into her. She held him there and was still for a moment before her body convulsed beneath him and then slackened. Her mouth tasted of tobacco.

"Lennie was his idea."

Smith rested his forehead on the pillow beside her.

"I'm alone," she said. "Since I can ever remember. Born alone. All the time alone. I'll probably die alone. He came into Hosmer with all those misfits. It wouldn't surprise me if he was riding a dead man's horse. I don't think that man ever worked an honest day in his life. He come out one day when they were shooting up the place and picked me up onto that horse and I was thinking we were going to the coast like he promised and here I am, a few miles down the road. Lonelier than ever."

"How's that?"

"There isn't anything lonelier than being with someone who doesn't want to be with you."

The bed creaked. She pushed up against him, her chin up, her head straining back, and let out a long, tight-throated yell.

Smith placed his palm over her mouth. A faint footstep hopped up the staircase and grew louder as it approached the room. Three palm slaps on the door. "Everything all right in there?" the desk clerk said. He banged on the door again.

"Tend to your own business," Smith said.

"This is my business."

"Well, I'll contribute one dollar to your business if you go on and git."

"Any business that operates on credit ain't in business."

"Is tomorrow near enough?"

The clerk sighed as if he were considering the offer. "You have yourselves a good night then." He hopped along the floorboards in the hallway and paused.

Smith removed his hand, kept a finger against Lenora Bell's lips.

The clerk hopped down the staircase, reached the bottom and hopped to the front desk. The chair creaked as he sat.

"Wanted to see the ocean," she said. "Gave me his word."

Through the window, the red moon rose trembling out of the earth like translucent roe.

———————

The next morning Smith slapped a coin down in front of the desk clerk. The clerk held it up, studied it in the sunlight. He removed his eye patch and studied the coin again before tucking it into his pocket. He slipped the eye patch over his other eye and went back to his ledger.

"You got a leg hidden in there as well?" Smith pointed at the man's pinned-up trouser.

The clerk kept his eyes on his ledger. "Only a man with two legs would say such a thing."

Smith headed out east and walked through town. The sun was bright; the aspen trees fanned out like umbrellas on each side of the street, dropping puddles of shade. He returned to the church but there was still no sign of the reverend. Near the train station he noted a blacksmith shop. A train sat on the tracks beside the platform, hissing, steam rising from its wheels.

The train tolled its bell. Smith ambled over the tracks. Trill of a whistle. Steam billowed from beneath the wheels. An iron door slammed shut, a gust of dark smoke boiled out of the stack. The train began to roll. Two boxcars, one mail car and two passenger cars grunted past.

A man's face in profile at the window.

The girl's face. Same eyes, same fierce look shielded beneath her hat, a quiver on her back. She sat with a woman wearing black and, opposite, a mean-looking man.

The woman's gaze moved across Smith. A black glove lifted a white kerchief to her nose and mouth. The girl and the man stared straight ahead, their mouths tight, their eyes narrow.

"Out to Hosmer and then Michel," a man in a dark cap and uniform told Smith. "Then up over the Pass into Alberta, all the way to Lethbridge."

Smith and Lenora Bell lay on the ground at the edge of a treeline. Their bellies were slick; Smith's hand traced Lenora Bell's hip. She rolled onto her back.

"That big blue sky just scatters my little mind," she said. "How does god do that? It's like one big, perfect bowl turned upside down and we all are trying to find our way back into it. Some folks think heaven's up beyond that blue. I don't know. The harder I look, the farther away it seems." She shivered. "But what if those up there in heaven are looking at us right now like we're looking at them and they're saying the same thing? Oh, I tell you, it hurts some to think on that." She shivered again. "Do you think I'm pretty?"

He touched her face, caressed her cheek and her chin. She had long, soft lashes. Blue irises, brown streaks flaring out from the centre. The lines on her face softened. He traced the bruise beneath her eye and kissed the tip of her nose. His hand browsed on her belly.

"I do."

The river murmured. Squirrels chittered in the trees and tossed pine cones that plunked on the ground.

"I'm tired of this life."

"This here life, now?"

"No, this is nice. Real nice." Tears spilled from her eyes. They streaked down her temple and pooled in her ear. Her shoulders shook. "I don't have no children. Any woman without children ain't a woman. She's just lonely."

"What's a man without children then?"

"Lucky."

Smith held her close. A squirrel darted up a trunk and disappeared behind a branch. Smith closed his eyes.

An ant ran across the back of Smith's hand and woke him. The air was warm and smelled of pine and the green treetops flushed against the sky. Smith pressed his head against the needles and closed his eyes.

"Honey, I can't stand that man," Lenora Bell said. "He ain't ever said a kind word. Day and night he took me. Whenever and however he wanted. Usually from behind. Like I'm some animal that he don't want to face."

Smith opened his eyes. A breeze moved through the pine trees.

She propped herself up onto her elbow. "Listening to him chew like he's some hog in the pen. Watching him fondle that pistol of his, loading it with bullets and spinning that chamber and snapping it into place. It gets the hair up on my neck, I tell you." She cleared her throat. "No telling what's on that man's mind 'cept hurt. He's aiming to hurt the world. Ever itsy bit in it. Not a strip of kindness in him." She squirmed against the ground. "I'm going to die in this place. All alone. I know it."

The sun blazed, a smeared yellow yolk against a blue bowl sky.

The next day, after a brief late-morning rain, Smith walked to the church. The front doors were open and inside a man in a white robe lit candles and smoothed out a cloth that covered the altar. The man smiled at Smith. "I know you." He came toward Smith. "You're the newly arrived law. Been helping out over at the mine."

"You must be the one they call Reverend Brown. The one everyone is talking about."

The man laughed. "I'm newly arrived myself. Up from Pincher Creek." He offered his hand. "Father Dan."

"Jack Smith."

They shook hands.

"The reverend and his followers left a few days back. Our deacon, too, if you can believe it."

"Where?" Smith said.

"Up valley. West."

"They coming back soon?"

The man looked beyond Jack Smith toward town. "Folks around here certainly had their share of it. God's testing us all in these dark times."

Smith nodded. "Thank you for your time."

"No need to rush off," Father Dan said.

"I got things that need tending to."

"Okay, then," Father Dan said. "May god be with you always, no matter where your journey takes you."

ELEVEN

DAVEY AND BOBBY SAT with the widow as the train inched out of town. Davey reassured the widow they'd get off at the next stop and leave her to journey on her own. The widow dabbed at her face with her handkerchief and looked out the window. On the platform a man in a red coat with a pistol on his belt studied them. Davey stared straight ahead. Once the train was on its way and town receded, Bobby got up, walked to the front of the car, pulled out his revolver and declared he was robbing the train. He unloaded two bullets into the ceiling of the coach.

"What are you doing?" Davey said.

He waved his gun and threw his hat to her. "Collect their money."

Davey tossed his hat back to him. "This has nothing to do with me."

Several of the passengers screamed and sobbed. Bobby moved quickly through the car and held out his hat, instructing people to drop their valuables into it. One man held up a whisky bottle; Bobby grabbed it, and he continued to gather cash and jewellery from the other passengers into his hat until the crown sagged. He relieved the conductor of his 23-jewel Elgin pocket watch and ordered him to keep the train moving. He stopped at Davey and the widow.

"What are you doing?" Davey said.

"Making my own way," Bobby said.

Davey shook her head. "This ain't the way to make."

Bobby grinned and dumped a fistful of cash on her lap.

"We can get far away from this," he said. "From him."

"What about Bulah?"

"Forget Bulah. You either come with me or you stay on this train as an accomplice. They'll hang you."

Davey considered his words. Most of the passengers sat with their heads bowed. Two women wept. She turned to the widow but the widow refused to acknowledge her. Davey dropped the banknotes on her lap. "You're going to need this."

"You can't keep acting like you got no one else to care for," the widow said.

"I've been caring for myself all my life."

Bobby snatched the banknotes from the widow's lap and stuffed them into his pockets. He emptied his hat and jammed the jewellery and money into his pockets and put the hat back on. He marched to the rear of the train. Davey stood and removed her hat. "I am truly sorry for your loss and suffering," she said.

The widow gazed out the window.

Davey put her hat on and followed Bobby down the aisle to the rear of the train.

Near Michel, they hopped off the train and rolled down the embankment and sprinted for the woods where they waited out the day sitting against a tree trunk. Bobby offered to split his haul with Davey, but she shook her head. He drank the bottle of whisky and offered it to Davey; she turned away and pulled the brim of her hat over her eyes.

In the morning they rose at first light. "Well, what do you want to do?" Bobby said.

Davey looked down the valley. "I'm going home."

"You ain't got a home."

"I'm going back to Bulah."

"I ain't going near that man again," Bobby said. "You could come with me."

Davey shook her head.

"She's not your blood," Bobby said.

Davey stared at him. "Neither are you."

"We've got all this." Bobby gestured to the money and jewellery weighing his pockets down. "I can be your Bulah."

"No, you can't. You've already proven that."

"That man is the devil, through and through."

Davey considered his words and was silent for a long time. "I've made up my mind. I'm going home."

"You've always been stubborn, like you always know what's right."

"Knowing what's right is not difficult."

"Well, this is it then. Safe travels." Bobby walked eastward and then doglegged it into the woods.

Davey advanced westward. She kept a relentless pace all day, keeping to the woods. At night she walked in the open and by sun-up she staggered into Bull Head. She went to the church. Father Dan told her that the reverend, Bulah, Deacon and the rest of the crew had moved west, that the Mounted Police had been by, a man named Jack Smith. He fed her and let her rest on a pew. Later that night, she sat up in the dark, empty church and set out west by foot.

———

The sun broke in the east and Davey woke under a dwarfed pine on rocky ground covered with patches of lichen. Pikas called out. A raven floated in the sky in front of her. Downslope a deer browsed in a draw before darting into the brush. She jammed her hands under her armpits and hugged herself. Sat up and pressed her chin tight against her chest and rocked herself until the sun got into her bones.

She followed game trails through the firs and hiked along a range that rose out of the land like a serrated knife. In the valley to the west lay shady draws pocked with snow, and on exposed terrain, there were green patches of pine and fir trees. The sun dropped over the range and a wind blew in. Stars stuffed the sky and seemed to draw near in the dark.

She slept chin to knees on the ground, shivering, her bow clutched to her chest. In the morning she woke and retched until her throat was raw and dry. Her hands numb with the cold. She lay staring up at the pale sky; clouds moved across in the shape of animals whose names she mumbled to herself. She cupped her hands against her mouth and blew on them and soon they began to tingle and she was able to flex her fingers.

Davey stuck to the alpine and moved west all day. In the fading evening light, the land lay low and dim, distinguished by ragged peaks that held the sun's afterglow. Clouds gathered overhead and the breeze whipped up off the valley. The sky lowered and she moved on through a veil of fog. The tops of twisted evergreens hissed in the wind; she started down the face of the mountainside.

Thunder rolled across the land to the north. A cold wind kicked up the smell of wet grass and stone. She shivered, zigzagging down the slope, skating over the scree, stumbling on tufts of grass and mounds of dirt left behind by pikas until she reached the valley bottom. It was warmer here but the air had a dark, ferrous look. Like it was going to rain. Like it was pushing hard to rain. The air packed and still, pressed against her like a sack bursting at the stitching, and all it needed was the sharp point of a blade to split it. Lightning struck the land in front of her. Gusts of wind churned up dirt and sheet lightning flashed overhead. A cluster of paintbrush bloomed in the dark. The air shattered all around her as a deluge of fat rain drops smashed the ground. Then hail, stinging her shoulders, head and hands. She crouched over the flowers and shouted, hail punched the land and ricocheted like marbles. Then it quit. The clouds moved on and a few stars appeared. The flowers were intact but clusters of ice lay on the damp soil around her.

A thin fang of a moon lifted. She studied the terrain before her, blowing into her clawed fingers and trudging on. Soon she came across tracks that blurred into each other, criss-crossing and in tandem, cloven hooves alternating with half-circle holes stamped into the dirt. An elk appeared at the edge of a knoll. It turned its immense head and was still for a moment before bolting. Three wolves sprinted after the animal. The elk ran across the bottom of the knoll. Two of the wolves kept to the flats while the other veered off up the hummock and then they were gone. Davey hurried along and a half-hour later she came upon the elk, its head trapped in the boughs of a gnarled cedar tree. Its neck was scraped and bleeding and a chunk of flesh was missing from its hindquarters. The bones of its leg were visible in what remained of the muscles and ligaments. It wriggled lamely and bleated against the tree branches when she approached. The wolves patrolled silently fifty yards away. Davey put a hand to the elk's neck and stroked it for a long while. Mosquitoes and horseflies hovered in clouds, congregating on the tender skin around the edges of the animal's eyes, pulpy crusts of blood and pests. Many alighted on Davey's arms and neck and the back of her hands. She yelped. Smacked the flies off. The bites began to swell immediately. She pushed her blunt fingernails down into the bites to reduce the swelling. The elk's black eye stared at her. In the dark expanse of land in front of her, a faint fire burned and twisted in the breeze. The wolves paced in the dark. Davey stepped away from the elk, raised her bow, notched an arrow and released it. The arrow thumped into the animal's chest and it collapsed in the bough, its eye still open but unblinking. The wolves skittered off and then trotted toward the elk when Davey moved on toward the fire.

She came across an old man standing next to a hole in the ground. He stood leaning on a spade, sweating and grimy in the firelight. His long, white beard was stained yellow around his mouth and bits of twigs and grass were trapped in it. A mound of dirt lay next to the hole. He motioned Davey over with a wave of his withered hand.

"Can you help a fellow pilgrim?" he said.

"Are you hurt?"

The old man smiled. He handed her the shovel and wiped his face. He eased down into the hole. "If you could be so kind as to grant a man his final wish, I'd be grateful."

A bat flew over them and then another. "Where you from?"

"Nowhere special." The man began to weep. "I ain't been nowhere special, ain't done nothing special."

Davey dropped the shovel. "Well, you have a chance to do something special now."

"What could I possibly do?"

"Stand on your feet." She offered her hand to the man.

"Where you from?" He ignored her hand.

Davey shrugged.

"Everyone knows where they came from."

"No idea where I came from, who my people are, where I'm headed. I've been on my own from the beginning."

"If that's not the bleakest thing I've heard." The old man cleared his throat and spat. "Maybe you should be in this hole instead of me."

"Are you going to get up?" Davey offered her hand again.

"There's something broken in me," the man's voice caught in his throat. "Always has been."

"Can't you fix it?"

He shook his head.

"I'm sorry to hear that." Davey walked on. She encountered two immense ungulate heads, the blood on them still damp. They were propped up against each other like a vulgar cairn, their antlers interlocked. A low brush fire burned weakly, the ground from the stunted skeleton of a fir scorched a thin path that was still warm and smoking. The shrub cracked and sap sizzled from its spindly branches. The breeze picked up and the fire flared, lifting sparks into the air, and then flamed out.

Two slaughtered elk. Their legs shorn and scattered near where the fire had burned; the bones seared black and cleaned of the marrow. The once great mass of their bodies, limp and eviscerated and burned unceremoniously. Stench of singed animal hair and flesh. A figure moved across the prairie behind Davey. The snap of a twig startled her, then a snort, followed by shallow bursts of breath and then silence. Davey stood still. In the pale light from the quarter moon, the land was one long shadow of trees. She picked up a faint trail of tracks, trailing them for a while before they looped around and she returned to the epicentre of the fire. Walked north some two hundred yards from the tracks and squatted, listening until her eyes became accustomed to the dark.

She woke curled and shivering. Jammed her hands under her armpits and rocked herself silently. The moon had moved across the sky. After a while she rose and stumbled along in the dark, following deer tracks until she came upon them drinking at a pool of water. They darted into the brush. She lay in the wet trampled dirt and drank the brackish water full of diaphanous larvae and black wigglers, rested, and drank again until she retched herself hoarse. She held her side for a long while and drank again. When she was sated she laved mud over her face and arms and hands taking care to leave no bare skin exposed. She walked on; after an hour she came upon a whitetail deer.

It stood in a small draw and then it moved off in the dark and stopped, its tail a snowy flag in the night. Davey drew her bow. The deer trotted past and came back. It moved soundlessly in the brush and when it came back Davey noted urine, sour against the dirt. She crawled along the ground, drew her bow, took in a deep breath, released the arrow on the exhale. The deer collapsed.

She ran over to it. The deer struggled to rise on its forelegs but fell back to the ground and lay twitching. Davey removed an arrow from her quiver and used both hands to push the arrowhead into the deer's neck. The deer struggled, trembling against her. She caressed the deer's neck, the vertebrae articulating under the hide and wept as she jabbed the arrow in deeper. Blood spurted forth and she pressed her face against the animal and blubbered into its ear as it thrashed back and forth. When the deer stopped wheezing and flailing, Davey lay weeping into its damp face.

She searched the ground and found two thin, sharp rocks. She split the hide around the back of the neck and made one long, jagged cut down to the chest. Then she sawed through the hide carefully; the thin watery layer between hide and red meat was visible in the moonlight and she nimbly cut through it. Separating the flashing of white membrane at the top of the neck, she pulled it away from the meat and cut the meat off in coarse sheets. She ate her fill and cut more raw chunks and stuffed them into her pockets. Stretched out next to the butchered deer and woke at dawn, sliced six more pieces off the carcass. Bluing light flared the land open. She packed the remaining pieces of meat before pushing on.

The mosquitoes and horseflies were everywhere, buzzing in her ears, around her eyes and nostrils, but the mud had worked and none were alighting on her. She stumbled along waving at them and by midday she was violently ill. She retched until she dry-heaved and clutched her side, groaning on the ground, picked up a pebble and placed it in her mouth and sucked on it, rolling it around with her tongue, surveying the countryside for clusters of willows that might indicate where the river ran before she stood and stumbled along. Throughout the day she encountered faint elk and horse tracks, but her progress was slow. She keeled over, clenching her stomach and turning in the dirt until the cramps subsided and then lay still. Sometime later, she woke beneath a raging sun, vomited and fell back asleep. In that fever dream, she heard the sound of a horse nickering, the murmur of voices. She woke and lifted her head. Towering over her, the reverend, Bulah and the rest of the sect sat on their horses studying her. She closed her eyes and all was black.

———————

Davey lay before them like a small child, her face covered with the dark red blood of the deer and the mud of the land; strands of her hair were matted on her thin shoulders. Reverend Brown smiled. Bobby stood next to him with his head lowered. Behind them were Bulah and Gussie, Deacon, Keegan and the others. The horse nickered again. Davey leaned on an elbow and pushed herself up to her feet. She grimaced and held her side. The clown sat with his head between his hands. Bobby lifted his head. His eyes were feverish and he gazed at Davey as if she were a stranger, for she was more wretched looking than he. Bulah stared as if not trusting that it was Davey in front of her. Her eyes were damp, and she wiped her face against her shoulder before dismounting. Handed Davey a blanket. Deacon wrapped the blanket around her and held her hands for a long time, rubbing them until they warmed. He turned away when her bottom lip trembled. Davey reached into her pockets and offered up her meat. Gussie and Keegan took it and at the reverend's instructions tossed it to the ground where two dogs masticated it, snarling at each other.

Davey held the blanket tight around her neck and received an update from Bulah. Bobby had gone east and lost his money playing flinch at a tavern in Fort Macleod. He traded in his jewellery, except for the Elgin watch, for a feeble horse. Then he headed south, riding for several days before turning north on account of having no luck in finding anything to eat. He pushed on through the mountains in Montana all night and the day following. His horse collapsed and he continued by foot and came upon the reverend and his followers two days later. They drove themselves west and deliberately doubled back and forth over their trail in order to lose their pursuers.

"Who?" Davey said.

No one spoke.

"The redcoat?"

When they rode out a few minutes later Davey was on her horse. She rode tethered to Bulah's horse, slumped, holding her side as pain radiated through her body with each step of the pony. They rode through the valley, sharp mountainsides soared up into blue sky on either side. The pain receded and she closed her eyes. She woke to the squawks of ravens and plunged into a deep slumber and woke again to her horse drinking from a stream, and when she woke a third time it was night and the wind blew off the mountains, the sky was pitch and salted with stars that fell silently all around her; the wind carried the sound of coyotes yapping from the neighbouring valley long into the night.

Mid-morning of the next day they rode alongside the river where the valley widened at the toe of hulking peaks that rose on either side of them. They travelled mostly in the shade, despite the sun's height, and in the late afternoon smoke from cedar fires drifted in with the breeze. Just before dark they rode into Elko.

This village, like many of the others they encountered throughout the valley, was one of tents, smoking fires and crude outbuildings made from the timber of the woods behind it. Keegan and Gussie rode off. In a few minutes they returned and escorted the group down the empty street until they came to an old porte cochére leading into a fenced-off patch of dirt with tufts of wiry, cropped grass poking out. A squat chicken shed whose walls slanted toward the ground sat precariously near the house. Small skeletal cows and a pony stared balefully at the crew. Chickens clawed at the dirt and scrabbled here and there. There was a cookfire at the side of the lot with a few pots and a kettle on it. A tall, thin man came out of the house. He bowed to the reverend and waved them into the yard.

They dismounted from their horses and were led into the chicken shed by an old woman, a boy and a girl. Dried flowers hung from twine on the wood beams and the ragtags had to lower their heads to avoid them. They sat in the straw. The old woman and the girl brought them bowls of hot broth made from blanched cow bones and a blue speckled plate heaped with thick slices of bread. They were served this with coffee and a small side of salted offal, floating in puddles of congealed fat. The old woman and girl bowed their heads, made the sign of the cross, and bowed again before the old woman left.

When they had finished their meal, the girl and the boy pointed to where they should sleep on the ground. Reverend Brown placed a hand on the boy's shoulder and smiled at him. The rest of the crew got up and returned a few minutes later carrying their saddles and blankets.

Davey lay in a corner, away from the others. Bulah drew near. Davey nodded and Bulah lay down next to her. The girl and her brother left the shed and closed the door behind them. Darkness settled on the crew. Someone coughed twice. One wrestled with their blanket.

"Next time you intend to strike out on your own, you come to me first," Bulah whispered.

"It just happened," Davey said.

"Nothing just happens. Give me your word."

Davey stared up until her eyes grew accustomed to the dark and the rafters appeared in the gloom like the backbone of an immense beast. "You have my word."

TWELVE

IN THE MORNING, after the chickens woke them with their squawking, the crew milled about the courtyard. The same man from the night before came out of the house and introduced himself as Boggs. Chickens scuttled in and out of the shed into the courtyard and scratched at the ground. A dog lay curled, snoozing in a doorway. To the left, a waist-high chopping block sat on the dirt, the base dark with blood. The dog stood and stretched. It sniffed around the yard, lifted a leg, urinated on the block and trotted out of the courtyard.

"I need a drink," Gussie said.

Boggs removed his hat and ran his hand over his bald head. "Bit early, no?" He placed his hat back on and squinted up at the sun.

Gussie glared at him, spat on the ground.

Boggs pointed to the right. "Can't miss it."

Gussie walked through the courtyard, beneath the porte cochére and into the street. The others followed.

Davey waited outside with Deacon while the rest of the group entered the decrepit establishment. It was a simple shack with a dirt floor that looked as if the boards had been slapped up in haste and could be dismantled just as quickly. The ragtags sat on a bench against the wall. Three men sat at a wooden table drinking. The barman was shirtless, his chest and arms and back covered in a mat of black hair;

his belly hung over his belt like an animal pelt cinched around his waist. He perspired heavily, lowering himself onto the bench with his legs splayed open and his hands on his knees.

"You're the holy man everyone's talking about."

"I am," Reverend Brown said.

The barman wiped his face with his palm, dried it against his chest and shook his head. "We could use a miracle or two. 'Tis no good fortune here." He leaned on his knees to prop himself up and walked away from the crew, the hair on his back glistening in the gloom.

After they drank, Bulah, Gussie and the clown left the reverend with Keegan, Bobby, Beaudry and Blundell and went to fetch Davey and Deacon to see if they could drum up enthusiasm for a revival. A man had removed his boots and socks and sat in the dirt against a building with his knife, shaving the calluses off the ball of his foot, tossing chunks of hard skin at a dog skulking nearby. Another man stared off into the mountains as if he were waiting for someone or some sign to come along. A third man stood smoking.

"What all you pretty ladies got going on?"

Gussie turned. The man who'd spoken was propped against a post with one knee drawn up to support his elbow.

"Hosting a revival," she said. "This evening."

The man spat. "Ain't nothing free no more. Not even god's love."

Gussie slipped her right hand to her waist and rested it on the butt of her revolver. "You're liable to catch a chill out here."

"Maybe you'll convert the bear," called another. "But he don't need no saving."

"Why's that?"

"Because," he laughed, "he's already been saved."

———————

In front of a macaroni shop, within a clapboard shed of three walls and a gabled roof, an immense grizzly bear paced. It wore a thick chain looped around its neck, and the length of it was nailed to a stake in the ground. A mitre with a cross embroidered on it sat unsteadily atop its head and the bear was covered in tattered robes like a crazed Nebuchadnezzar. In the back corner of the shed, a clump of sage smoked on the ground. The bear rose on its hindquarters and snorted at the visitors. Its hat smashed into the peak of the roof. The shed shuddered but the hat stayed on the animal's head, affixed by twine that looked as if it had been stitched directly into the fur. The fur around its neck was rubbed raw to the skin beneath the chain collar.

Bulah, Gussie and Davey stood in front of the shed. The enclosure reeked of excrement and damp fur. Davey squatted to study the bear. There was a dark patch on its shoulder and a broken nub, like a small stick, was embedded in the fur.

"Ain't he something?" A man stood to the side wiping his hands with a cloth.

"Are you the owner of this beast?" Bulah said.

The man placed a hand over his heart and smiled. "Yes, I am."

"Where'd you get it from?"

"The bush. He come down from the bush, snarling and mean like."

"You leave it out here all the time?"

"Yes, I do. Keeps guard of the place," the man said.

Bulah looked up the street. Reverend Brown was making his way toward them.

Gussie laughed. "You Indian?"

"Miss?"

"Indian."

"No."

"Why so dark then?"

The man studied Gussie.

"Where you from?" Gussie said.

"The old country."

"Every country is old. Which one?"

"Italy."

Gussie exhaled slowly through her nose. "So, then you're a man who eats macaroni?"

"When I'm hungry. Yes."

"You're a man who eats his share?" She laughed as she looked him up and down. "Is that about right?"

The man's face reddened.

"So, you're a man from the old country, here in our new country, eating macaroni until you're plumb filled up. Is that about the extent of it?"

The man looked at the reverend and back at Gussie.

"Macaroni needs watching over?" Gussie said.

"Everything needs watching over. It's a fact."

"A fact, you say?" Reverend Brown said.

"Yes."

"So, you ain't from here," Gussie said. "And that bear ain't from here. But here you both are, taking from the rest of us and guarding against anyone who might take from you. Is that the extent of it?"

The man looked into the cage. "Big as life. Never hurt him a bit."

"Why?"

"Why what?"

"Why the hat?"

"Makes him look sacred."

"A sacred bear guarding macaroni?"

"Yes, ma'am." The bear paced back and forth; the man shushed him and the bear circled the cage one more time before slumping down on the ground. The man smiled. "I've been his guardian since he came down into town. He would have been shot dead if it wasn't for me. Everyone around here wanted him dead." He lowered his voice. "There's something hallowed about that bear. I know it. Everyone here knows it. Makes them jittery."

"Dressing a thing in robes and a hat don't make a thing holy,"
Gussie said. "Just makes you all more dim-witted than you already are."

"He escaped death."

"How?" Reverend Brown said.

"How what?"

"How did he escape death?" Reverend Brown said.

The man shook his head. "Does it matter? He just did."

"Are you telling me you saved that bear?" Reverend Brown said.

"He came in half-dead. He got some stick stuck here." The man
pointed to the bear's shoulder. "I tried to get it out but it's in there
something deep."

"And you, sir, have you been saved yourself?" Reverend Brown said.

"How so?"

"Have you been baptized?"

The man nodded.

"How long have you had him in your possession?" Reverend
Brown said.

"Few weeks. Give or take."

Gussie looked at Bulah.

"Why does macaroni need safeguarding?" Gussie said.

The man studied the reverend. "That bear came down from the
woods with something in its shoulder. An arrow, maybe. And I saved
him. He's my guardian and I'm his. Saying otherwise doesn't make it
less true." The man faced Gussie. "It needs safeguarding on account
of thieves. They're everywhere. Now, if you please." He picked up a
pile of blankets that were stitched together, tossed them over the top
of the enclosure and drew them down so they reached the ground,
enveloping the bear in complete darkness.

———————

That night, after a revival that attracted three attendees, a fire was lit
at the end of the street and the bar filled up with men drinking and

179

smoking. Despite Deacon's protest, Keegan pulled Davey into the shanty and offered her a cup of whisky; she declined. He pressed himself against her and Davey warned him away and threatened to shoot him. Keegan laughed. He opened a half-filled sack and upturned it on the table. The shanty was quiet as the men in the place studied the money.

Davey quit the bar. Deacon followed her into the street.

"Are you—" Deacon started.

"I'm fine."

They walked together in silence.

In the shanty, the reverend inquired where Keegan had accrued the money.

"The whores," Keegan said. "I didn't have a chance to share it. On account of leaving the last place so fast."

"Is this a good time to share it?"

Keegan nodded. He divided the money in half, scooped up one pile and handed it to the reverend.

"We didn't discuss the terms," Reverend Brown said. "Eighty-twenty. Does that sound about right?"

Keegan placed his hands over the remaining pile of money and halved it again. He gathered one portion and brought it to the reverend.

"That looks like seventy-five-twenty-five. We had an agreement. Eighty-twenty."

Keegan returned for a third time to the table, halved the money again and brought it to Reverend Brown. "A little extra. To make amends."

Reverend Brown nodded.

Keegan turned to the men in the dim room. "Make me an offer." He pointed to the few remaining banknotes on his table. "Anyone. Make me an offer I can't refuse."

Bobby held up the Elgin watch. Keegan grabbed it, turned it over in his hand and smiled. Bobby gathered up the money and slid it into a small sack and tied it shut. "Everyone's got a price." Keegan laughed and the other men joined in. "Money is easier to procure than common sense." He held the watch in the air and put an arm around Bobby's shoulder. "I ain't got no money but I got all the time in the world." Keegan roared with laughter. Bobby wriggled himself from Keegan's embrace, but Keegan grabbed him by the wrist, pulled out his revolver and jammed it against the underside of Bobby's jaw.

"We made a deal," Bobby said.

Keegan pushed the barrel of the gun harder into Bobby's face. "And what, exactly, did I offer you in return?" Keegan said.

"What I took."

"That so?"

Bobby nodded. The dull sound of an axe hacking at a tree reverberated in the woods behind the shanty.

"What makes you think I offered all of it in exchange?" Keegan said.

"You gave your word."

"Did anyone hear me give my word?"

No one answered. He pushed the revolver harder into Bobby's jaw. Bobby's eyes welled up.

"It's no wonder you came scampering back after that train stunt you and the child pulled off," Keegan said.

Outside, a man shouted at his horse. He beat it viciously with a switch and the two of them rolled past the doorway of the shanty.

"Let go of my money," Keegan said.

Bobby released the sack; Keegan pushed him away with his pistol. He jabbed Bobby in the shoulder with the barrel of his gun and laughed. "I was only messing with you," he said. "Buy me a drink and we'll forget about it."

Bobby shook his head and left the shanty. Keegan and the others laughed as they knocked back glasses of whisky.

Along the street, a man led a horse that towed an immense freshly fallen fir, the boughs dragging in the dirt. When they reached the fire, they stopped and the man cut the tree loose and hauled it onto the flames. He led his horse back into the woods and started hacking at another tree.

By morning, husks of great firs lay on their sides, blackened and partially burned.

The sect collected their horses from Boggs, rode through town and stopped at the macaroni shop. Reverend Brown climbed down from his pony and approached the enclosure. He yanked down the curtain of blankets. The bear paced the cage. It scraped at the ground and growled. Reverend Brown stood for a long time in front of the animal.

"Well, look here," the reverend said. "Reunited. My very own Lazarus."

Reverend Brown opened the door to the enclosure and faced the bear. He yanked the chain from its tether and spoke to the animal in a hushed voice. The bear followed him out of the enclosure. Reverend Brown climbed onto his horse with one hand holding the chain, clucked softly and his horse began to trot with the bear keeping pace beside them. The rest of the crew followed at a distance and headed west.

———————

They rode from Elko across the base of the Rocky Mountain Trench above the river in a tight valley through a dogtown strewn with broken buildings in a state of disuse, as if the inhabitants had got up and quit that place all of a sudden. To the south, Sheep Mountain and Wigwam Flats, where the confluence of the Stag and Wigwam inscribed the land.

The bear ambled along with them. In early evening they rode through fir forests up into the hills to the west. The sky was overcast and the fluted columns they passed in the dark were like the ruins of vast temples, silent save for the haunting cries of owls. The terrain was thick with sage and huckleberry; tufts of prickly brush clung to the horses' hocks. A wind rose through the hills and all night it warbled across the land. They reached an abandoned miner camp near the river and settled in for the night.

Davey stared into the fire. Wind fanned the coals and the flames flickered back and forth. The crew kept their distance from the reverend and the bear. The bear's eyes were rheumy and the scabby fur beneath them was wet with clumps of mucus. Davey lay in her blanket next to Bulah, her bow clamped across her chest.

The embers popped and the sparks showered the ground at their feet. Reverend Brown got up and went into the woods and after a while someone asked Deacon how the moon and stars came to be and Deacon eyed the world above them all and said it was a mystery that only the almighty knew. And someone asked if it would always be a mystery and Deacon replied, Yes, for god worked in profound ways and man would always be humbled before the marvel of him.

Reverend Brown returned to the fire holding a rope coiled in his right hand. "The problem with mystery is that man can't leave mystery alone. He has to solve it, make it known. And once he does that, the mystery loses its power." The reverend turned the rope over in his hands. "Mystery is what men believe in when they lose faith in themselves." All listened as he spoke, but none lifted their eyes from the fire.

Davey shook her head. "If what you say is true, then explain yourself."

Keegan laughed.

"You didn't kill that bear," she said. "We all know it."

Reverend Brown smiled. "Is that a fact, girl?" He unravelled the rope and took the length of it, held it across his palms like a great serpent, dropped one end on the ground and stepped on it with his boot. He kept his boot on the rope and in a grand, elaborate gesture, threw the rest of it upward, where it disappeared from the firelight and stood quivering upright on its own accord. He yanked on it; the rope held taut.

"Hold the rope, lass."

She did as she was instructed.

Reverend Brown placed both hands on the rope and began to shimmy up. The rope swayed and Davey struggled to hold it steady and a few moments later the reverend vanished and the rope stood motionless.

Davey looked upward and soon she was joined by the others, murmuring among one another, but they could not see the end of the rope or Reverend Brown in the black sky overhead.

The rope slackened. It fell from the sky and collapsed on her head.

"Good lass." Reverend Brown stood to the side of the fire and smiled when the crew turned around to see him.

Keegan slapped his knee. "What the—" The others were silent for a long moment and then they started calling out at once.

"I'll be damned."

"It's a trick—the rope was looped over that tree."

"It's a miracle. I seen it with my own two eyes."

Deacon raised himself from where he sat and studied the air above him before turning to Reverend Brown, who had begun to speak.

"There was a time when nothing existed," the reverend said. "Not a single thing or being. We are told this in the bible and in all origin stories from all peoples. But consider this: there is nothing which did not have a beginning."

Many of the disciples scrunched their foreheads in thought.

He continued. "A thing or being cannot cause itself. It must be caused by another. In order for a thing to exist, it must be caused. And since it can't cause itself, it follows that another must cause it. Each event is caused by another, ad infinitum. And it's this sequence, stretched out like a rope in the night sky, whose end you cannot see or fathom—that needs no support, as if suspended by nothing. If a thing cannot be proved or verified then the question of that thing is based on nonsense or mystery as you like to call it. Everything around you has come into being as the result of the activity of other things. Your mothers and fathers have procreated to produce you. This is how you are here today, whether you know who they are, whether they are alive or not. Their mothers and fathers produced them, and those mothers and fathers produced those, and so on. But this sequence cannot go back to infinity. There must be a first member in this cause-and-effect path, one not caused by any other. It's uncaused. It's the first cause. It's here, at the first cause, that you either believe in the mystery of god or you believe there is anything at all. Tell me, then, if you can't prove it, should you believe it?"

"Why can't they trace back to god?" Davey said.

"How can man verify it? You're forgetting the cause and effect I spoke of earlier. It holds that if you can't verify it, it does not exist."

"So, god does not exist?" Davey picked up the rope. It was warm and heavy in her palms. "Why are you preaching about god everywhere we go if you don't believe in him?"

Reverend Brown snickered. "Why indeed. The message, lass. Remember the message, not the puzzle of it. The mystery is merely the carrier pigeon hurtling toward you with the message."

"I exist because god exists," Davey said.

Reverend Brown studied her. "You're staking your claim as a being in the world on a being you have never met, blind faith in that he exists and that you are the result. It that about the sum of it?"

Davey nodded. "We all need something good, something beautiful, something true to believe in. Isn't that what you've been preaching all along?"

"You'd stake your life on it?"

She nodded. "Belief doesn't need proof."

"When you seek to put the world in order, you do so in terms that fits your view of the world. You can't decide the speed at which the world will let you do so. Some events come so quickly you don't have an opportunity to evaluate them. Your default is your own world view, your experience." Reverend Brown smiled broadly. "You're just a young girl. What experience of the world do you have to inform you in life's gravest moments if you stake your life on the mystery of it? Is that the belief you speak of?"

"Yes," Davey said.

Reverend Brown laughed. "What do you fear?"

"Nothing."

"Everyone experiences fear. What do you fear?"

Davey considered the question. "Pain."

"Real or imagined?"

She weighed the two options. "Real."

Reverend Brown smiled and nodded. "Real because that pain is a memory of a long-forgotten pain you once had. So, not real but imagined."

"That's not true."

"No? What about death?"

"I don't know anything about it except it's final. So, real, not imagined."

Reverend Brown turned to Bulah. "What do you think? Real or imagined?"

Bulah glared at him and spat in the dirt.

———————

At first light, Davey studied the ground from where she had held the rope, looked up and then down at the ground and found nothing. By mid-morning, she was riding with Bulah at the rear of the crew.

They crossed a vast dry patch of valley bottom with rows of dirt clumps ranged beyond it, the work of prairie dogs. They led the horses upon the alluvial plain, crossed a land of caked slurry and powdered pebbles, and climbed a low range of grassy hills to a barren promontory where the reverend surveyed the peaks around them. He held up his palms and measured eight fingers from the horizon to the sun and pointed westerly to set their course. The river snaked and stretched away before vanishing into the hard folds of the mountains. They eventually reached a lake. Davey sat on her horse at the shoreline next to Deacon. Each man and woman shed their clothes and jumped into the lake, scrubbed their filthy skin with fistfuls of coarse sand and pumiced pebbles until their bodies glowed red. They scoured their garments with larger rocks and rinsed them in the lake, twisted them of excess water and slapped them against boulders. They laid their clothes out on the shoreline gravel and stretched themselves out beside them, dozing in the warm light.

Davey and Deacon slid off their ponies. Deacon took out his bible and handed it to her. She turned the worn leather over in her hands and traced the stencilling on the cover with her finger and handed it back to him. He read her a story about Jonah and his reluctance to go to Nineveh, the storm, Jonah's helplessness when thrown overboard, his anger with god. "A man cannot run away from the lord, from anyone else, especially themselves," Deacon said. "When Jonah was tossed into the sea, it became calm and the storm stopped. When Jonah spent three days in the belly of the fish that swallowed him, his prayers were answered." He stared at the lake and said, "People who worship worthless idols forfeit the grace that could be theirs."

"That must have been a big fish."

Deacon laughed. He placed his bible against his chest and leaned back against the rocks. "Indeed, it was."

"Ever feel like the world was made without you in mind?" Davey said.

"You just haven't found your place yet."

"What if it doesn't exist?"

"Then god didn't consider you."

"Do you believe that?" Davey said.

Deacon shook his head and laughed. "If I'm being honest, then I'd say we're all thinking the same thing for much of our lives."

"That don't seem right."

Deacon nodded. "We're all born into this world and inherit all the grudges and rivalries and hatreds and sins of those that preceded us. But we also inherit the beauty and joy and goodness of our forebears. We're not here for long, but our decisions matter because they form the inheritance of those that will walk on this earth when we are gone."

"And if I make bad decisions? What then?"

"You always have a chance to make a good one again," he said. "It's no small thing."

"What?"

"Your life. All that you do. All that you don't do. It's no small thing."

Keegan and Gussie wandered off and a while later a single shot reverberated across the lake. They returned carrying a limp deer laid out upside down, its feet bound, swinging between them on a pole.

"They ain't happy unless they're killing something," Davey said.

The night was cold and to the north the mountains lay corrugated. They sat around the fire, each in their own cone of darkness. Reverend Brown led the bear and staked it to the ground near the fire with a braided horsehair rope. The reverend cracked the shin bone of the deer with the back of an axe. After he slurped at the marrow he tossed the bone to the bear.

"The most eloquent olfaction sense in the world of terrestrial beings," the reverend said. "When that beast sniffs at the air, it humidifies the air, and that warm air then enters its brain through a cribriform plate. And so it is with people. It's the way we smell and distinguish odours. But it's miniscule in comparison to that beast. He will travel tens of miles tracking the scent of another. When you see him stand

and he is larger than any beast you've ever seen, he's not looking at you, he's smelling you."

Keegan chuckled.

Reverend Brown said that an elm tree produces over 330,000 seeds a year but very few of those seeds grow into trees. He espoused spiders and spoke of how they deposit up to three thousand eggs into the egg sac but very few of those actually hatch and survive.

"So, too, for humans," he said. "Thousands of Boyles, Clarks and Newtons have been lost to the world, they've lived and died in ignorance and meanness. No one dies for naught, for the world makes a note of all that contribute to its history. Its people keep it alive through the stories they tell. But that doesn't mean suffering is fair or can't be protested. Suffering takes seed and grows. We nurture our suffering. There is evidence all around us in this regard. Look no further than to yourself. Do not blame another man or god for the cross you bear. Suffering comes from a single source the world over."

"Where's that?" Deacon said.

"God's providing plenty of misery for me," Keegan said.

Reverend Brown outstretched his hands to all those seated around the fire. "From oneself. Of course."

Davey sighed.

Reverend Brown studied her for a moment, rose and moved away into the darkness beyond the fire.

"There's no mystery in that," Deacon said. "The man finally speaks the truth."

Three days later they reached the Flatbow. The day was warm and the crew sweated at the edge of the river. The clay-coloured water came down from the north, flat and steady. Two blue herons rose from the shore and swung away. The horses trotted down the bank into the eddying shoals and drank, their muzzles dripping into the passing current.

Upriver at some distance, the crew circumnavigated the Ktunaxa's camp. The Ktunaxa moved about their cookfires and stared at the sect riding up out of the willows. The men wore their hair long and braided; the women were clothed in deer hide speckled with beadwork, some with infants clinging to their backs.

Bulah rode past with Davey alongside. Farther upstream a derelict camp of migrant miners swam their ponies across the river. An old man, shirtless with a long white beard, sat with his boots at his side and his feet in the water. His skin hung off him like stretched leather.

"Where you headed?" Bulah said.

"Home."

She looked across the river to where the old man gestured. "What's delaying you?"

"Sometimes I like looking at it. Like I can't believe my luck."

Bulah considered the miners on the shore. "Maybe it ain't luck."

"Maybe," he said. "Maybe it's just too much for one's eyes."

Bulah nodded.

The old man turned his face toward her. His eyes were cloudy and faded blue. "Can you spare a dollar?"

Bulah waved her hand in front of him but he didn't respond. She pressed two one-dollar coins into his palm.

The man rubbed his thumb over the edge of each coin and over the face before turning them over and rubbing the other side. He smiled, all pale gums, no teeth. "Much appreciated."

"You take care." Bulah and Davey climbed the bank. Davey turned around. The man sat as they had left him, smiling, his thumb tracing both sides of the coins.

THIRTEEN

THE FARRIER FINISHED applying pine tar to the hooves of Smith's horse. Smith spooled his bedroll and tied it on behind the cantle. The Lee-Metford would ride up under his knee. He lit up and headed across town, turned up Victoria Street and arrived at the house with a white picket fence. Women lounged on the front deck, smiling at him. He rested his hands on the pommel; a few minutes later, Lenora Bell came out the front door wearing a wide-brimmed hat fastened by thick ribbons beneath her chin and a long cream-coloured evening gown of ivory silk taffeta and chiffon with lace insertions, chiffon flowers and silver sequins. She held a hatbox and a suitcase and smiled at Smith, stepped down the stairs and picked her way along the board-walk toward him. She turned to the women on the porch. "You all be safe, you hear? I'll write." She laughed, turned to Smith and held out her luggage. He strapped the suitcase behind the cantle and handed her the hatbox.

"We're travelling light," he said.

"Oh honey, I need my hats."

"It's not up for negotiation."

She set the box down on the ground. One of the women picked it up and brought it back to the house.

"I'll send for it when we get to the coast." Lenora Bell offered her hand and Smith took it, pulled her up on the horse to sit behind him. The two made an odd pair. He in his red serge, brown hat and brass buttons; she in her ivory dress and wide-brimmed hat, as if they were heading to a night out at the theatre. Lenora Bell placed her hands around Smith's waist and kissed his ear. "Thank you."

Smith grinned. He snapped the reins and they were off.

They headed west up the valley. Smith followed a series of deer trails that chased the river and then broke free when the river jogged south. The land rose and fell and in the open spots the sun pressed down onto Smith's head; sweat streamed over his face. Lenora Bell pleaded for him to stop. He led his horse to a patch of trees where they rested in the cool shade. Smith turned to look back in the direction they had come from.

A figure topped a rise then fell out of sight then topped another rise. Horse and rider got bigger as they came closer. It was Dutch Peters trotting up on a chestnut horse. He nodded to Smith and raised an eyebrow at Lenora Bell.

"What are you doing out here?" Smith said.

"Riding."

"Just riding?"

"Where you headed?" Peters said.

"West."

"Joseph's Prairie?"

"We're just heading west."

Peters took off his hat and wiped his face with a kerchief. "Lord, it's hot."

A fly sat on the back of Smith's hand. He brushed it off. The horses twitched their tails.

"What the devil do you want to go out west for?"

"Work."

Dutch Peters looked at Lenora Bell and back at Smith for a minute. "Well, best get to it." He jabbed his heel at his horse's belly.

"What's that mean?" Smith said.

"Good luck. You might need it out there." Peters smiled. He turned his horse and rode until he was no longer visible against the eastern horizon.

"Who was that?" Lenora Bell said.

"Nobody anyone cares about."

"Ain't that the saddest thing you've said."

"The truth often is."

Smith snapped the reins and they rode west.

FOURTEEN

ON THE TRESTLE BRIDGE that spanned the river, Bulah and Davey sat on their horses and studied the loggermen working below. Men barked orders and wrapped long ropes around the ends of the logs. They lashed their horses and the horses brayed and snapped their teeth. Their eyes were large and black and the horses frothed long white streams of drool from their mouths as they dragged logs up the riverbank. The man supervising the operation turned, removed his hat and shaded his eyes with his hand. "A pleasure, ladies." He bowed with great ceremony. "It's an absolute pleasure to make your acquaintance."

Bulah and Davey crossed the length of the bridge. Their ponies clopped on the wood deck and the men working below paused and called out to the women. The supervisor shouted, "Get back to work."

Bulah and Davey joined the rest of the ragtags on a bench of sand partially shaded by river willows where they set up their camp.

In the evening, the loggers had gathered into a semicircle where the grizzly bear was tethered to the ground. Keegan held a fistful of banknotes and invited the loggermen to wager bets on the bear to perform a miracle. An empty brown bottle lay on the ground at his feet. Three men poked the bear with thick pine branches until the bear grunted and thrashed about. One man laid dead prairie dogs just outside of the bear's reach. Two men threw dirt at its face. The bear howled, clutched at its eyes and snapped its head around. The rope it had been tethered to was tied around a wood stake. It threatened to snap and the ground shook with the bear's wild gesticulations. One of the men lit a matchstick.

A rifle blast thundered in the air. Reverend Brown pointed his gun at any man who was near the bear. "He that is without sin among you, let him cast the first stone."

The man dropped the match and toed it into the ground. "Give our money back," he said.

Keegan handed him a banknote. The other loggermen held out their palms and Keegan returned their money to them.

The man who lit the match said, "I don't know what kind of circus you're running here, but it ain't one sanctioned by god." He returned to their camp with the others.

Keegan turned to Reverend Brown. "I don't see what interest that bears holds for you."

"I don't remember giving you permission to profit from that animal." Reverend Brown pointed his gun at Keegan. "Speak plainly, friend."

Keegan held up a hand. "Why is that bear joining us?"

Reverend Brown lowered his gun. "My dear brother, you are not speaking plainly. 'Ask, and it shall be given you; seek, and ye shall find; knock, and it shall be opened unto you: For every one that asketh receivith; and he that seeketh findeth; and to him that knocketh it shall be opened.'"

"Did you kill the bear?" Davey stood in the firelight facing Reverend Brown.

"The lass speaks plainly," the reverend said.

"Did you?" Davey said.

Reverend Brown turned to Keegan and grinned. "Yes." Reverend Brown blinked a few times and looked up to his left as if studying the sky.

"That's my arrow in its shoulder."

He strode past Keegan and Davey. When he reached the bear, he grabbed the tether and yanked it out of the ground in one great heave. He brought the bear to the fire. "Where's this arrow you speak of?"

"Just because you took it out doesn't mean it wasn't there."

He turned back to Davey and shook his head. "Prove otherwise."

———————

Reverend Brown dragged the bear along, humming a hymn. Gussie, Bulah and Davey followed.

Reverend Brown led the bear through the loose sand to the river and let down the tether. He stood before the beast and held out his arms.

"Come here."

The bear growled and peered past him at the water.

Reverend Brown raised his hands and murmured a prayer. "Come, my Lazarus."

The bear stopped growling and ambled toward Reverend Brown. A murmur went up from the loggers, several of whom stood in the shallows to the side.

Reverend Brown picked up the tether and led the bear into the water. The bear paused when the river lapped over its paws, stood and sniffed the air and lowered itself. Reverend Brown waded out until the water was mid-shin height; his cassock purled about him. The bear paused. Water ran along its underside up to its chest. The current was slow and Reverend Brown stepped into the shoals and gently tugged on the rope. The bear took another step toward him. Reverend Brown leaned down and scooped handfuls of water and laved it over the bear's shoulders and chanted some words in Latin and made the sign of the cross over the bear's head. The bear shook its coat and sprayed the reverend, and the reverend laughed, and this seemed to placate the bear. Reverend Brown poured water over the bear's wide head. He then drizzled water over his own head and stood facing the bear, both of their heads drenched. "We are bound in our history, complicit in our knowledge of one another."

The current pulled at them. Reverend Brown shifted his feet and stumbled; he let go of the lead and fell into the water, the current sweeping him downstream. The loggers shouted and pointed at the reverend flailing, trying to keep his head above water, thrashing his arms over his head, slapping the river. The bear bounded after him and in one long arching swipe of his paw, caught Reverend Brown's cassock and flung him to the shore. Reverend Brown lay winded on the rocks. The bear stood in the river, the rope around its neck swayed in the current.

Reverend Brown gasped to regain his breath.

Keegan blurted out, "It's a goddamn miracle." He turned toward the loggerman camp and shouted, "A miracle!"

Reverend Brown slowly lifted himself up, gathered the rope and led the bear to their camp. Every man and woman they passed bowed their heads as they passed by. The bear stopped, shook his body vigorously; droplets of water fanned out. Reverend Brown laughed and motioned for it to follow. The bear did as it was commanded. Reverend Brown tied the end of the rope to a tree. He tossed three pieces of smoked trout to the bear and it lifted each fish in its paws and swallowed it, one after the other. When the bear had finished feeding, the reverend spread out a blanket on the ground and motioned for the bear to lie down; the bear did as it was instructed.

Keegan repeated "it's a miracle," but no one paid heed to him for they watched the bear and the reverend.

Later that evening, Davey awoke. Gussie handed the reverend a bough of bright-green cedar sprays fashioned into a crown. He accepted her gift, placed it on his head. Gussie bowed and left him alone. Davey fell asleep, and when she woke much later, she glanced toward Reverend Brown keeping watch over the bear, muttering, "My Lazarus."

FIFTEEN

JACK SMITH AND LENORA BELL rode for most of the day under a blanched sun that smashed down on them. Sweat streamed from Smith's face; he turned his chin and lifted his shoulder to wipe it away. Lenora Bell sat behind him listless, her cheek against his back. She hadn't said anything since they encountered Dutch Peters, which seemed like many days ago instead of a few hours. They rode down from the high country into the valley and followed a deer trail to a cluster of willows ahead. Smith's mare picked up the pace and soon they were in a draw of willows beside the river. Smith helped Lenora Bell down and they drank from the river upstream from his pony. When they were sated, Smith removed Lenora Bell's shoes and peeled off her stockings. He lifted her up, walked into the shallows and lowered her until her bare feet were submerged in the river.

"Oh, you are a gift from heaven," she said.

He smiled and moved her feet back and forth to cool them in the river. She held him tight and sighed.

"I might be the happiest gal in the world. Even though a moment ago I was the most miserable. You did that to me, Jack Smith. You make me happy when I'm not."

Smith swished her back and forth in the river. Lenora Bell kicked her feet against the water and splashed him. He held her in the stream for a moment longer and then returned to the shore where he laid her down against a blanket he had unrolled from his saddle. He placed a hand on her ankle and slid it up her leg.

"Honey, can't we just lay here and watch the sky?" she said.

Smith slid his hands down to her feet. He rubbed each foot and then lay next to her. She rested her head on his chest. High above, a crow soared, its black wings pegged against the pale blue, circling in a thermal. The river flowed silently, rich and loamy with the musk of rocks and sand. They dozed and when Smith awoke, Lenora Bell's eyes were fixed on his. The sun hung low in the west.

"We need to make tracks," he said.

"Can't we just stay put for the night? I'm just so tired."

"We'll ride for another hour or two."

Lenora Bell frowned. He helped her up. She pulled on her stockings and laced her boots. When she was done, she put on her hat and fixed her hair. "How do I look?"

"Really?"

"Yes."

They continued their ride and soon came across boot prints and the paw prints of dogs and the hooves of deer and the shoes of horses but they saw no man. They trotted past a camp where the cookfire was spread out in the dirt and still warm against the palm. Farther on they encountered the carcass of a large mammal, a deer or elk perhaps. They rode on and made camp in the dark and when Smith asked Lenora Bell if she wanted a fire, she shook her head. She walked a few steps and ducked behind a tree, leaned over her knees and vomited.

SIXTEEN

AT THE LOGGERMAN CAMP, in a large wall tent with animal pelts stacked from floor to ceiling and great racks of elk, moose and deer antlers that lay in heaps next to them, the reverend, Gussie, Bulah, Davey and Deacon stood with the camp foreman, Benjamin Bowles, drinking whisky from fine English china cups decorated with floral patterns. Davey declined Benjamin Bowles' offer of a drink and held the empty cup in her hand, rotating it in the saucer by its delicate handle. Bowles informed the group they were no longer welcome to host meetings on the riverbank.

"There's nudity," he said. "Nudity and fear. None of what you preach to these travellers comes from the bible. I do take issue with that."

"We all interpret the words of others to fit our own words and ideas," Reverend Brown said.

"Well, that's debatable. I take that to mean that you misrepresent the words of others. Which, as you well know, goes against the teachings of the great book."

The others were silent. Davey set her cup in the saucer and placed it down on the table. Reverend Brown studied Benjamin Bowles and smiled.

"Each of these men and women lead lives filled with apprehension and despair," Reverend Brown said. "When they reach this camp, it's one more concern, one more uncertainty to their sense of safety. Are they welcome or do they need to move on? While they deliberate their decision, they form allegiances with others and find belonging in those newly developed tribes. How they make that decision is based on their faith, and their faith is based on their own words and ideas." Reverend Brown held out his cup and saucer.

Benjamin Bowles poured more whisky into his cup.

Reverend Brown sipped his whisky. "I provide the faith that gives them hope to cross the river, to pursue their lives with a meaning beyond that which is locked inside of themselves. And while you might not agree with my methods, you cannot fault the results. There are more pilgrims arriving every day."

Bowles nodded his head. "That has nothing to do with you."

"It has everything to do with me." Reverend Brown set his cup and saucer down, placed a hand on Bowles' shoulder. "I propose that you charge a fare for the privilege of continuing on, and that you offer me a percentage of those fares in compensation for the increase in traffic."

Bowles laughed.

"It's a fair offer."

Bowles stopped laughing. "If I understand this to be a negotiation—"

"We're not negotiating, we're setting terms."

Benjamin Bowles studied the reverend. Davey shifted her quiver. A fly buzzed and alighted on the rim of Bulah's cup.

"If I understand this to be a negotiation, then you will offer me a percentage of your collection from the travellers after each of your sermons? When you're passing a hat around?"

Reverend Brown smiled and shrugged his shoulders. "Sure."

"Then what's the difference—if I give you a percentage of the fares you suggest I charge and you give me a percentage of your collection?"

"It's the principle of the matter."

Bulah waved at the fly. It circled in the room and shot out the door. There was an argument outside, down by the bridge.

"We won't charge any fare for a man's right to continue on their travels."

"Their right?" Reverend Brown said. "Who grants them these rights you speak of?"

Bowles smiled. "I'm afraid there's nothing left to be said of the matter."

The argument outside grew louder. "If you'll excuse me." He nodded at the group and walked toward the door.

Reverend Brown seized Bowles by the arm. "Consider my offer. It's more than generous."

Benjamin Bowles pulled his arm away from the reverend. "We will not charge any traveller for their right to stay or carry on. Each man, woman and child is free to travel wherever they like. You don't own the land. No man does. Therefore, no man can deny them their basic freedom to travel as they please, especially not a servant of god."

"My fine woodsman, let me ask you this: Do you consider the men and women in your camp to be sentient beings?" Reverend Brown said.

Bowles pulled at his beard and turned to the men squabbling below, cussing at one another.

"And what if they faced imminent danger? What would you do then to maintain your *fidus et audax* duty as you've just stated?" Reverend Brown said.

Bowles shook his head. "You're a slippery one, aren't you?"

Reverend Brown raised his hands on either side of him as he had done dozens of times while holding baptisms and looked skyward before fixing his eyes on the woodsman. "He works in mysterious ways."

"The only mystery here," Benjamin Bowles said, "is why a man of, shall we say, the cloth, is making these demands, and"—he cleared his throat—"veiled threats. Now, if you'll excuse me, I'm needed down at the river." Bowles strode to the door and turned around. "Yes, they are sentient beings. But you, a servant of god, already know that." He marched toward the river.

The reverend, Bulah, Gussie and Davey left the tent. Benjamin Bowles stood between two men on the riverbank, his head down, as if concentrating deeply on what each man was saying.

The crew rode away in silence. "What now?" Gussie said.

Reverend Brown halted his horse and looked back. Bowles smiled as both men shook hands. The three of them shared a laugh and Bowles walked upriver to a group of pilgrims that had just arrived. "He's a stiff-necked man. You can't say I didn't try to talk sense into him." He clucked into his horse's ear and they rode into their camp.

SEVENTEEN

SMITH AND LENORA BELL bivouacked beside the river for another day, until she felt better. In the morning they travelled on. It was hot. Clouds had gathered and moved swiftly toward them, jaundiced and boiling. Smith noted the rain against the sky to the north. As they rode the rain raced toward them and dropped like a slop bucket, everywhere the sound of rain pounding the landscape and nowhere to take shelter. They cantered on, hunched over the horse, Lenora Bell's face pressed against Smith's back. She clamped her teeth down on his shirt to prevent them from chattering in the cold. They spent a miserable night sitting beneath Smith's horse; Smith held his shirt over Lenora Bell and held her close while his pony shifted from hind leg to hind leg.

The sky cleared in the morning. Smith started a fire, fixed a pot of coffee and poured a cup for Lenora Bell. His mare cropped grass a few feet away. Smith finished his coffee, stood and tossed the grounds out. Lenora Bell sat on a blanket, her hands wrapped around the cup, sipping from it.

"Oh honey, I'm as wet as a dog caught in a storm," she said. "Ain't no part of me that's dry. Can't we just lay up here? Dry out our clothes?"

Smith looked west where the sky was blue. He picked up a swatch of grass and tossed it in the air and watched the faint breeze carry it briefly before dropping. He wiped his hands together. "You're lucky your eyes are so pretty."

They spent the morning on their backs, their clothes spread out and pegged down by rocks. Smith had his hands behind his head and chewed on a piece of grass. Lenora Bell laid her head on his chest.

"I could live like this for the rest of my days," she said.

"Staring at the sky?"

"I mean it. I could live like this, with you."

Smith kissed her forehead.

Lenora Bell traced his ribs lightly with her fingertips. "I think the coast will agree with me. And you, of course."

Smith was silent.

"What do you think?"

"Maybe. I go where they tell me to go."

"Can't you put in a request?"

"It doesn't work like that."

"I don't see why not."

"I go where I'm told. Plain and simple."

Lenora Bell sat up. Her pale skin had started to redden under the sun. "Do you mean to say that once we get to the coast you will leave me there?"

Smith shook his head. "Who said we'd make it to the coast?"

"You did."

"It was you who said that."

"You didn't say otherwise."

"What would the point in that be?"

She startled him with a hard slap on his face. She got up and sat down near a sage bush.

"I can't see what good that did," he said.

Lenora Bell picked at the leaves and rubbed them in her fingers.

They spent the rest of the day apart. Smith polished his boots and the buttons on his jacket. Each time he stole a glance at Lenora Bell, she was staring at ravens in the sky.

Toward the end of the day, Smith checked on their clothes and, satisfied that they were dry, he dressed himself and brought Lenora Bell's clothes to her. "Here."

She didn't respond. He picked up his rifle and walked until he found deer tracks and then dry turds and waited in that place, watching a stand of trees for movement. When a whitetail bounded from the brush, Smith levelled his rifle and killed it with a single shot. He butchered the deer and brought the meat back to camp. He started the fire and set to cooking the meat and when he was done he plated some for Lenora Bell and brought it to her. She sat with her clothes beside her, staring at the sage bush. Her shoulders and back were red.

"We can resume this tomorrow," he said. "You need to eat. Take it."

He handed her the plate. She looked at the meat and the blood that had congealed around it. She set the plate down and doubled over, dry heaving. "I'm not hungry."

"Suit yourself." He looked at the western horizon. "Night's coming on. At least get dressed and come to the fire."

She waited for a while and then dressed herself as the sun slipped behind the horizon in the west.

EIGHTEEN

THREE DAYS LATER Keegan and Beaudry crossed the bridge in the middle of the day, rode up the wooded shoreline and slipped into the loggerman camp. The men were working in the woods somewhere to the north and the women tended cookfires near their tents. On the riverbank, a few children played in the water, chasing each other along the shoreline, laughing. When the children saw Keegan and Beaudry, they stopped, held up hands to block the glare of sunlight. Each man removed a length of rope from their saddle and swung it in the air. They drove the children into a herd and lassoed them together. Keegan reached down and seized one of the girls by the wrist and pulled her up on his horse and rode off, shouting as he crossed the river. Beaudry whipped his horse and yanked the crying children behind him.

They hauled the children into the river and dragged them across, some barely able to keep their heads above the water. They finally landed on the shore, where the children lay writhing on the sand, coughing up water and gagging.

Reverend Brown strode along the shoreline. He offered a hand to a boy who refused it and then turned to Keegan and lifted the girl from his horse by her armpits and set her feet on the ground. She stood tottering as he placed his hand under her chin to lift her face to meet his. "Can you hold a tune?" He smiled, lifted her up onto his back and carted her to his lean-to on a rise above camp. Keegan and Beaudry followed with the rest of the children.

That evening, Benjamin Bowles and several loggers crossed the bridge. The men were tall and had thick arms and long beards and each one held an axe. Reverend Brown came down the hillside to greet them on the shoreline. Bowles demanded that the children be returned, and that Keegan and Beaudry be handed over to them.

"I'm afraid I can't turn my disciples over to you." Reverend Brown lowered his voice. "But what I can do is send them away. Cut them from our tribe, banish them, leave them adrift."

"They will no longer be your men, then."

"Yes," Revered Brown said.

"They will have to fend for themselves."

"That's correct."

Bowles turned to his men. They sat on their horses, their axes across their laps. One of the men spit to the side; a trail of spittle caught in his beard. "The children?"

"I'll bring them over in the morning."

"That's not sufficient."

"Give me a few hours then." Reverend Brown addressed Bowles in a whisper. "To talk to my men."

A dog in camp barked.

"You'll go to great lengths to preserve the façade of being someone you're not," Bowles said.

Reverend Brown shrugged his shoulders. "I'm a man like any other."

"A few hours then." Bowles nodded to his men and then turned his horse. They followed behind and crossed the river back to their camp.

Reverend Brown spoke to Gussie. "Send the boys west. To the coast."

"You're cutting them loose?"

"I'm saving their lives. Draw up a list of food and goods. Have them go to the coast, pick up the supplies and bring them back."

Gussie nodded. "And the children?"

Reverend Brown studied her and smiled. "That's my concern."

———————

Keegan and Beaudry left at sunrise. They rode down the days and through the nights slumped in their saddles while their horses followed game trails that meandered close to the river. They travelled for twenty-five days, before descending the mountainous slopes near the town of Hope. Here, they followed the wide valley bottom for two more days and entered New Westminster in a splatter of sunlight. Mounted Police passed them in the mud of the street and in the distance the Fraser River slapped against a rocky shoreline. They passed a hotel built in stone with a uniformed doorman stationed outside. Beaudry tipped his hat to the man.

They rode past a barbershop, tea room, general store, pawnbroker, café and beer parlour. Beaudry pointed at the general store. Keegan laughed and told him they'd get to that later. Keegan climbed down from his horse and walked into the beer parlour. Beaudry waited in the street before he slid off his horse, tied it to a post next to Keegan's and went inside.

The barman greeted them by towelling three glasses and placing them upright on the worn wooden counter. He pried open a bottle and poured two fingers' worth into each of the glasses. He raised his own glass, nodded to Keegan and Beaudry, and they all drank and set their glasses down. The clerk refilled them and they drank those in silence and set their glasses down again.

Keegan removed his hat. He took two banknotes from inside the headband and set them down on the bar.

"That'll keep you and me satisfied for a long while," the barman said.

"You concern yourself with keeping our glasses filled," Keegan said. "I'll worry about the time."

The barman topped up their glasses and the men drank and set their glasses down and the barman filled them again and left the bottle on the countertop. He walked to the end of the bar and spoke to a man drinking alone.

Keegan and Beaudry took turns tipping the bottle into each other's glasses and after a while both men tottered against the bar. Beaudry removed his hat and set it down next to Keegan's. He ran his hands through his hair. They stared at themselves in the mirror behind the bar. Beaudry studied Keegan; Keegan turned away and drank again.

Beaudry laughed. He grabbed Keegan by the back of the neck and kissed him on the mouth.

Keegan pushed him back and punched him in the jaw.

"You've been like a brother to me, is all I was trying to tell you," Beaudry said. "A brother."

"The hell I am." Keegan wiped his mouth, drank a shot and gargled it and spat it out. He rested his hand on his revolver. "You pull a stunt like that again and it'll be your last, you hear?"

Beaudry nodded. He turned away and wiped at his eyes with his hand.

"Jesus," Keegan muttered.

"I'm striking out in the morning," Beaudry said. "For Nome."

"The hell you are."

"They say there's a lot of gold up there."

Keegan drank and Beaudry filled his glass and Keegan drank again.

"That's the problem with you. You'll believe anything you tell yourself."

Beaudry turned away and wiped his face. He took a deep breath and refilled Keegan's glass and Keegan drank and Beaudry filled his glass again. Beaudry held up the empty bottle to the barman and the barman grabbed another bottle and set it down between Keegan and Beaudry.

"Compliments of the proprietor," the barman said, nodding toward the man at the end of the bar.

"In that case, we'll have another pour and take two bottles, on account of the compliment," Keegan said.

The barman poured two more glasses. He reached below the counter and brought up another bottle and set it down.

Keegan smiled. He drank, set down the glass and refilled it. There was a commotion in the corner. Two men had raised their voices and now stood, their noses nearly touching, jabbing their fingers at each other. Keegan watched them for a while and laughed. He turned to fill his glass. Beaudry was no longer beside him. He looked around; the room swirled in his vision but there was no sign of Beaudry. Keegan turned back to the bar and refilled his glass, drank it and filled it again. He waved the barman over and asked him where the entertainment was and the barman told him there was no one playing the piano until later and Keegan swore at him and told him he didn't care about the piano, where were the whores, and the man poured him a glass and told him that he'd have no trouble finding the entertainment he sought if he went out into the street, turned left at the general store and walked for a few hundred yards. Keegan raised his glass, slung it back and the man refilled it before walking back to the end of the bar. Keegan drank another glass down, reached for the bottle and lurched out of the parlour.

Keegan woke with three naked women twisted around him, the air ripe with the sour musk of their bodies. He had a fierce headache and was having trouble focusing. He kicked the women awake and searched the premises but there was no sign of the hat or his clothes. He grabbed each woman by her hair and slapped her in turn and threw her to the mattress, where they all lay crying. Keegan pushed open the door and stepped out into the mist, the cold damp biting his raw flesh. He made his way to the beer parlour where his horse stood alone, tied where he had left it the night before. He reached into his saddlebags, withdrew the Elgin watch, and sat on the walkway and waited.

When the pawnbroker opened the door, Keegan pushed past him and strode inside. A boy on crutches stood next to the pawnbroker; both of the boy's legs were wrapped in leather braces.

Keegan held out the watch and unfurled the gold chain. "I need to sell this." He unsnapped the front cover.

The watch was encased in ten-karat gold, with a double-sunk Montgomery dial. Twenty-one jewels. A railroad watch. White-faced with the maker's name inlaid in gold: *Elgin Nat'l Watch Co.* No hairlines on the crystal face. The bezels snapped off and on correctly. The lever set moved in and out easily. Quick train. Size sixteen. Front and back lids screw closed tightly. On the back, the engraving *Levi Winston James.*

The pawnbroker handed the watch to his son. The boy turned it over like his father had done and ran his fingertips over the etched script of *Levi Winston James.* He nodded and handed it back to his father.

"Name your price," Keegan said.

"It's a nice watch, but I can't buy it."

Keegan looked at him and then at the boy. "You can't, or the boy can't?"

"Does it matter?"

The man handed the watch back to Keegan. "I've seen a lot of watches in my life but I ain't ever seen a naked man holding one."

"Well, now you have. You can add it to your recollections."

"That I can."

"So, we have an agreement then." Keegan grabbed the pawnbroker's wrist and pulled him toward him.

The pawnbroker shook free of Keegan's grip. "That's not how I see it."

"You shook hands on it."

"I did no such thing." The pawnbroker spoke in his son's ear, turned and left the shop. His son shifted on his crutches.

"I got all day," Keegan yelled after the man. He turned to the boy. "You speak any or are your lips crippled too?"

The boy stared at him without a trace of emotion in his eyes.

Keegan spit on the floor. "This is a helluva family business you all got going on here."

When the Mounted Police arrived with the pawnbroker, Keegan had the watch on the counter in front of him and he stood with his arms crossed. The boy shifted a few paces and stood next to his father. His father leaned down and the boy said something and the father nodded, placed a hand on the boy's head and nodded again.

"What now?" Keegan said.

"Where's your clothes?" the redcoat said.

Keegan shrugged.

"I could arrest you for public indecency." The redcoat considered Keegan and looked at the pawnbroker, who stood at the doorway of the shop. He turned back to Keegan. "What's the problem?"

"I'm trying to help this man make an easy sale," Keegan said.

"Ask him where he got that watch. It's not his, you can wager on it," the pawnbroker said.

"Hold on," the redcoat said, "we're not making any charges. He turned to Keegan. "Is that your watch?"

Keegan picked up the watch by the chain. "It's what you might call a family heirloom."

The boy said something to his father.

"Ask him what his name is," the pawnbroker said. "That watch has a name on the back."

The redcoat nodded to Keegan.

"I don't need to prove nothing to nobody. It's my watch and I want a fair price for it."

The boy whispered into his father's ear.

"Make him read the name," the pawnbroker said.

Keegan glared at the boy. The boy's face remained passive.

"Careful, man, about the charges you are making."

"No one's making any charges," the redcoat said. "This can all be settled if you just read the name on the back of the watch for us."

Keegan turned over the watch and peered at the script. He held it out to the redcoat. "Look at it for yourself. It says my name. Right there."

The boy noted that the watch was upside down and told this to his father. His father raised his eyebrows and the boy nodded. His father whispered this to the redcoat.

The redcoat listened carefully before he handed the watch back to Keegan.

"You know what you get when a pawnbroker and his crippled son run a business together?" Keegan addressed the pawnbroker.

The pawnbroker didn't reply.

"Damaged goods." Keegan grinned and left the shop.

"Do you want me to bring him back?" the redcoat said.

"When trouble comes and then leaves, you don't invite it back," the pawnbroker said. "My son and I thank you for your time."

The redcoat left and the pawnbroker closed the door, slid the dead-bolt across it. He smiled at his son and they exited the shop through the back, locked the door behind them.

"Would you like me to carry you home?"

The boy shook his head.

"Pay no heed to anything that man or any other man says, you hear?"

The boy nodded.

"You have more integrity in a single finger than that man or any other man has in his entire being. Remember that. It's what makes you strong." The man placed his palm on his son's shoulder as they slowly made their way home.

———————

Keegan crossed the street, went down to the beach and sat on a log polished by the river. A tugboat chugged by and grey swells rolled in. He walked to the water's edge and looked up and down the beach but there were no other people. He urinated into the river, turned and went back to town.

In the early evening, Keegan returned to the pawnbroker's shop via the alleyway. He kicked down the back door and stumbled around the place until his eyes adjusted to the dark. A bridal dress hung on a rack over a mannequin. Keegan pulled the dress off and placed it over his head. It tore here and there before he managed to fit it over himself. He ransacked the place and found a cigar box under the counter, concealed beneath a stack of ledgers. The box was filled with banknotes and coins. He closed it and grabbed a pistol that lay in its case and searched the place for a pair of boots, finding two that were slightly larger than his feet. He quit the shop in his dress and newly acquired boots, pistol in one hand, cigar box in the other.

Keegan stopped in at the saloon to buy a bottle and returned to the river. He guzzled deeply from the bottle, reeled from the effort of looking at the stars above him. The river rolled against the shoreline. There were flashes of white on the water and he unloaded his pistol at them, the bullets whizzing into the darkness. After he had spent the ammunition, he clicked the pistol and tossed the gun into the water. He walked back into town.

———————

Keegan woke in the brothel roped to the stove. His head pounded fierce and his mouth was parched. The watch lay on his lap. The room spun before him. He wiped his face on his shoulder and waited for the nausea to subside. Daylight cut through the shabby curtain and the brothel appeared empty. He held the watch, opening and closing the cover, but he could not tell the time for no one had taught him.

A young woman named Sylvie entered the room with a pitcher of water. Her eyes were bruised and swollen and there was a bandage across her nose. One nostril had a piece of cloth stuffed up it. Behind Sylvie was an older woman with a tight mouth and jaw that twitched beneath her skin. Next to the older woman stood a tall man with an immense bald head that appeared to sink into his neck. His belly drooped over his belt and he breathed in short gasps. A bolt cropper hung from his right hand. Sylvie knelt down and ladled Keegan some water. The top of Sylvie's head had dried blood on it and what looked to be strands of hair yanked out on the crown. Keegan showed her his watch. She turned to the woman standing behind her. The woman nodded. Sylvie pulled off each of Keegan's boots, rolled off his filthy socks and washed each of his feet with a cloth. She dried them with a towel, pulled his socks back on and held out each boot for him to pull on. When she was done, she left without a word.

"Do you even understand what is going on?" the woman said.

He handed her the watch. "Keep it."

The woman held the watch but didn't take her eyes of Keegan. "The Mounted Police will be here shortly. I believe you've already met him."

"Be sensible, woman, nobody will know." He looked over her shoulder at the large man.

"I'll know. Sylvie will know. The rest of my girls will know." She took a step toward Keegan. "And you'll know."

"They're just whores."

The woman placed the watch in Keegan's hands and put her lips to his ear and spoke in a low whisper. "Tell me, what punishment do you think you deserve?"

"For what?"

"What punishment do you deserve for what you've done to that girl?"

"I haven't done anything anyone else hasn't already done."

"What punishment?"

The large man took a step toward him.

"My watch. It's all I have."

"That's just a thing. Any man can possess an item. It's a thing you've not even earned honestly."

The large man cleared his throat.

"What are you prepared to give up to atone for your crime?" the woman said. "*Lex talionis?*"

"What?"

"An eye for an eye."

"Wait a minute," Keegan said. "Just wait a goddamn minute. That ain't fair."

The man behind her shifted and moved the bolt cropper to his left hand.

"Are you enough of a man to turn the other cheek?" The woman held up her hand and turned it over in the light. "Incredible, aren't they? Their power to create. To assist another." She placed her palm against Keegan's face and held it there. "They can be eloquent. We can read much about a person by examining their hands, can't we? We greet one another with them. We bid farewell. It's a well-constructed tool. One that can create and caress; one that can destroy." She slid her palm along Keegan's jawline and held his chin up. "A man is his hands."

Keegan offered her his watch again. His fingers trembled and he lowered his head. "It's all I got. Have mercy on me. Please."

"Put that thing away." She turned to the large man. "Pinky." He stepped forward. His breath was laborious and he wheezed in short gasps. The man leaned over Keegan, grabbed his left hand and placed it palm down against the side of the stove. Keegan tried to pull it away but the man's grip was strong. The man lifted his leg and jammed his boot on top of Keegan's hand. His breath whistled in and out of his nostrils, the sweat slick on his forehead. He raised the bolt cropper, opened the jaws, lowered the tool over Keegan's thumb and sheared off the digit. Keegan screamed. The blood was tremendous as it poured from the amputation. Keegan stared at the space where his thumb used to be and then down at the ground, where it now lay. He blubbered, "Please stop, take my watch." The man raised the bolt cropper again and in quick succession snipped Keegan's index finger followed by the middle and ring fingers. The man released his foot from Keegan's hand. Keegan held his hand close to his chest, flexing the lone small finger against it.

The man snatched Keegan's right hand and proceeded to shear off all its fingers as well, save for the smallest. Keegan and the large man's belly were covered in an astonishing amount of blood. The man grabbed the back of Keegan's head and yanked him up, forcing him to face the woman.

"Eight fingers for freedom," she said. "That is your debt. For now. Surely, inevitably, you will die a most horrible death out there." She nodded again to the large man. He raised his bolt cropper one more time and cut the ropes that tied Keegan to the stove. Keegan raised his hands and flexed the small finger on each hand and groaned.

"Pinky. You'll forever remember the name, I'm certain of that," the woman said, "and I'm certain you'll forever remember the harm you've done to Sylvie." She left with the man.

Keegan lay slumped against the stove; his fingers and thumbs lay clustered in a puddle of blood on the floor. It was raining outside; riders passed in the mud, their ponies' hooves squelching as they trotted in the street. When dusk fell, Keegan roused himself and gathered his digits, wrapped them in a piece of cloth, got to his feet and quit the brothel.

The next morning, Keegan woke on the shoreline. He tore strips off his dress with his teeth and, using his teeth, rotated the cloth around his hand and folded it under itself when it was tight. He didn't have an easy time of it. He went to the general store to purchase the food and goods Reverend Brown had requested. He emptied the cigar box on the counter and the proprietor sorted and tallied the banknotes. The proprietor told Keegan that he still had about fifty percent to pay. Keegan offered the man his watch.

"I can't accept that," the grocer said. "On account—"

"On account of what?"

"On account that it's stolen property."

"It's my own."

The grocer turned to his son. "Go on, get Dick Cartwright." The grocer gave his son a nudge on the back of the shoulder and the boy ran out of the shop.

"On account of you possessing stolen goods and not having sufficient funds to settle your debt to me. I suggest you go on now," the grocer said, "before my boy returns with Dick Cartwright."

"I don't know Dick."

"You made each other's acquaintance at the pawnbroker's. He came to make peace."

Keegan snarled. "I'll be back."

"I admire a man who honours his debts," the grocer said. "You have yourself a good day."

Keegan kicked the door open, retrieved his horse and rode out of town, heading east.

It had been forty-five days with no sign of Beaudry or Keegan. Reverend Brown enlisted Bulah, Davey, Bleasdell and two other men and together they rode out at dusk, leaving Gussie and the reverend at the lumberman camp with the remaining ragtags. They passed the clown at the outskirts of camp. He bowed as they rode past. When the riders had reached a turn in the path, Davey looked back. The clown stood, his face slack and sad. He lifted a finger to his eye and slowly drew it down his cheek.

Halfway to the coast, they encountered Keegan riding alone. He wore an ill-fitting shredded dress and bloodied wraps on his hands. He was wild-looking and he reeked.

"Where's Beaudry?" Bulah said.

Keegan spat.

"Where is he?"

"Gone. North. Like the coward he always was."

Bulah nodded at his hands.

"A misunderstanding," Keegan said.

"Where's our money? Bulah said.

"Gone."

"With Beaudry?"

"No."

"Who then?"

"The whorehouse. Run by women. By the river."

Bulah considered his reply and was silent for a long while. "You best get back."

"Where you going?" Keegan said.

"To get our money."

NINETEEN

SMITH WOKE IN THE MORNING to birdsong. A raven floated high above, veered upward before it hung motionless, then glided off to his left. He closed his eyes and dozed for a while and when he woke again he reached for Lenora Bell. The blanket had not been used. He got up and saw that she was on the riverbank, doubled over on her knees, retching. "Are you okay?"

She wiped her mouth and coughed. She leaned over the river and took small sips and laved water over her face and neck. "Does it look like I'm okay?"

He placed a hand on her back but she shrugged him off. "You sure know how to carry a grudge."

She took another sip of water, sat back and tucked her legs beneath her.

"We need to get moving," he said.

Her face was pale but her eyes were bright.

He rubbed her back. "Can't we just put yesterday behind us and move on? I regret what I said to upset you." He continued to massage her back. "I don't like to see you faring so poorly."

Lenora Bell shook beneath Smith's hand. "I can't go on." She wiped her nose with her sleeve and coughed. "I feel like there's something horribly wrong with me."

"You need to put something in your stomach," Smith said. "You haven't eaten in a couple of days."

She shrugged off his hand and faced him. "I can't keep my food down. Why can't you understand that?"

Smith was silent.

"Aren't you going to say something?"

"What do you want me to say?"

She looked at him for a long moment and shook her head. "Nothing. Don't say nothing. I'd like you to take me back to town."

"We're two days out."

"I need to go back to town."

Smith stared across the river. A whitetail bounded into a stand of trees. "Why don't we just rest up here for another day? See how you feel tomorrow?"

"No. Now. I'll change my mind if we don't go now."

"What's the harm in that?"

"I'd like to return to town." She stood and brushed the dirt off her dress.

She marched in the direction from which they had come the day previous. Smith watched her for a few moments but she didn't stop or turn around. He caught up with her. "Fine," he said.

They loaded his horse, lit up on it and rode back the way they had travelled. When they reached the camp they had previously stayed at, Smith unsaddled his horse and turned it to pasture. He made a fire and brewed some coffee and fried up a sheet of deer flank and offered it to her. He cut a few pieces and tried to feed her but she waved him off. She got up, ran a few feet and gagged.

She spent the night in silence, alternating between bouts of nausea and refusing all attempts at reconciliation or touch by Smith. She slept beneath a tree where the horse was tethered, while Smith sat and kept watch from the fire.

In the morning, he brewed coffee and offered her a cup, which she took and managed a few sips. He ate a piece of meat he had cooked the night before and offered her a slice. She shook her head and put a hand to her mouth and turned away. "If you could be so kind as to keep that away from me. I'll eat when I'm hungry."

"We'll be in town by sundown." ·

"Oh, honey, I don't know why I'm so poorly. I feel better just resting. Can't we just stay another night?"

"I don't see what difference a day will make."

She touched his cheek. "You've been so kind to me. Just one more day?"

"Suit yourself. One more day."

TWENTY

BULAH, DAVEY AND THE OTHERS reached New Westminster late at night and found their way to the brothel. A young woman with faintly bruised eyes and a misshapen nose opened the door in a nightgown, holding a lit match before her.

"Are you the proprietor of this establishment?"

The woman tossed the match to the ground and retreated into the darkness without a word. She returned a few minutes later with an older woman. The older woman's hair was down and she, too, wore a nightgown. Her face was white with the light of the candle held in front of her. "Thank you, Sylvie." She rubbed her eyes. "How can I help you?"

"Do you know a man who goes by the name of Craig Keegan?" Bulah said.

The woman shook her head. "Is he a mean man?"

Bulah didn't respond.

"He might have been here three weeks ago, maybe longer," the woman said. "He tried to pawn his watch off on me to atone for his sins."

Bulah jabbed the barrel of her pistol against the woman's temple. Sylvie started to cry, but Bleasdell raised an open hand in front of her face and she quieted. Davey stood in the corner.

"In god's great name," the woman said, "what do you want?"

"My money," Bulah said.

"What money?"

"The money you stole from Craig Keegan."

"He had no money. He didn't even have clothes. He had nothing but a dead man's watch."

Bulah grabbed the woman's jaw and turned her face. There were deep lines across her forehead, a small scar to the side of her right eye, thin eyebrows. The candle shook in the woman's hand. Bulah pressed her pistol harder into her temple.

"I didn't take a coin from him."

"You're lying."

"Mother of god. I'm telling the truth. I had his fingers cut off for hurting my girls. He went to the grocer to settle a debt. Three weeks ago."

"You're lying."

"On my life, I tell you the truth."

Bulah nodded to Bleasdell and he took the stairs two at a time. She pulled up a chair, sat next to the woman and pointed her pistol at her. The candlelight flickered against the walls and Bleasdell's low voice reverberated throughout the house; it reached them along with the creak of the floorboards beneath the weight of his boots as he walked from room to room. Davey leaned against the wall. Bleasdell came down the stairs, shook his head and went out into the street.

The candle had burned down to a nub. Bulah slipped her pistol into her belt and the woman rubbed the spot where it had pressed against her head. "That man has no love in him," she said. "Anyone who meets him can see that. Yet, you believe his word instead a house of women who have suffered at his hand. Why is that?"

"He's one of ours," Bulah said.

The woman laughed quietly and smiled at Bulah and Davey. "That man is not, as you say, one of yours. What man put that notion in your head? He's got you all hoodwinked into making the journey here on his behalf. Nay, it's a wise woman that knows her own."

The woman knelt down and held out a hand. Sylvie took her hand and knelt beside her. Then the woman held out a hand for Bulah. "Pray with us."

Bulah studied the two women. They clasped their hands in front of their chests. Their fingernails had red half moons on them. Bulah put on her hat, nodded to Davey, and left the brothel. Davey followed but turned back at the door. The woman and Sylvie had their heads bowed and the woman's voice was low and soft. "Hear my prayer, O Lord, and let my cry come unto thee. Hide not thy face from me in the day when I am in trouble; incline thine ear unto me: in the day when I call answer me speedily."

The woman opened her eyes and Davey nodded; the woman continued. "For my days are consumed like smoke, and my bones are burned as a hearth. My heart is smitten, and withered like grass; so that I forget to eat my bread. By reason of the voice of my groaning my bones cleave to my skin."

"That's beautiful," Davey said.

The woman smiled at her.

Bulah called from the street.

"Take care of each other." Davey put on her hat, turned and went out, closing the door behind her.

———————

They stayed in town for three days. Bleasdell played poker and Bulah drank and stumbled around the taverns laughing among the men. Davey sat on the tavern steps looking beyond the buildings at the brown river, flat and silent.

At dawn on the third morning, Bulah staggered out of the tavern and tapped Davey awake on the shoulder. Davey stood. Bulah told her that the woman had been speaking the truth and that the redcoats were searching for Keegan.

"I know," Davey said. "She told us."

Bulah regarded Davey. "Well, now I know. For certain." Bulah wavered on her feet. "Saddle up."

"Bleasdell?" Davey said.

"Gone."

"Where?"

"California."

"The others?"

"Alaska."

Davey turned back to the street. A man was slumped over his horse.

"What did you tell them?"

"Nothing. It's their decision to make. Not mine," Bulah said.

"What about me?"

"I'd say the same thing."

"Would you come with me?"

She laughed, then stopped as she studied Davey.

"I'm just asking."

"I don't like what you're saying."

"You said you would."

Bulah nodded. "I did."

"Is the decision to go back ours or his?"

"Does it matter?"

"Yes."

"They're expecting us," Bulah said.

"Have I let you down yet?"

"No."

"What if I stay? Would you come with me?"

Bulah stopped smiling and shook her head. "He'd find us, sure as rain, no matter where we went."

Davey considered this. The street was quiet. The man sleeping on his horse shifted and then was still. "He's a man, like any other."

"He ain't like any other," Bulah said. "You've seen that. If we don't return he'll make it his life's mission to hunt us down."

"What about Bleasdell? The others?"

"He'll settle those debts in due time."

"He's just the one. We are two."

Bulah nodded. "Yes, we are two. We could leave now for Alaska or California or some other far-flung land. We could do that. But he'd have double the reason to chase us down. Even if he chose not to pursue us, then no matter where in this country, no matter where in this world we went, we'd have him right there chasing us down in our thoughts for the rest of our days. We'd always be looking over our shoulders. We'd never find peace from it. And what if we crossed paths with him? In that moment, we'd realize that our lives, all the turns and twists we made to avoid him, would make perfect sense, that our avoidance of him, in fact, led us directly to him. And there we'd be, face to face with the man who considered us betrayers. And then what? Do you think he would offer us forgiveness? Does that sound like freedom to you?"

"I don't see how things are any different when we're with him."

"A thing unseen holds more power than one seen."

"Nothing good ever came of you drinking," Davey said.

———————————

Bulah and Davey rode down the days and nights dozing in their saddles, each on their own horse with one pony in tow hauling a few supplies. On that broken valley bottom they met no other men and did not exchange more than a handful of words among themselves.

Two days out from their camp they encountered Deacon heading west by foot. He removed his hat and greeted them.

"Where are you headed?" Bulah said.

"Away. Home, maybe," Deacon said. "He's not the man I thought he was."

"No one is," Bulah said.

"You don't have to go back. You can come with me." Deacon looked from Bulah to Davey and back to Bulah again. "Are you sure?"

Bulah nodded.

He handed Davey the bible. "Remember the story of Jonah." He placed his hat back on. "Well then, may god be with you both. Take good care of one another."

Davey slipped the bible into her waistband and rode on in silence. She turned back once but Deacon was no longer in sight. They camped that night without a fire and sat alone in their thoughts. In the morning, they continued on until they reached the loggerman camp.

Benjamin Bowles asked where they were going and when they told him, he warned them that his men were furious with the reverend as he had not kept up his end of agreement to release all of the children and, instead, had held back one, a girl. "He's exhausted our patience," Bowles said. "You best head back from where you came from." He grimaced. "One of your men robbed the mail stagecoach that runs between here and Golden. He also stole a horse." He removed his hat and swept a kerchief across his forehead and placed his hat back on. "These are serious charges that carry serious consequences."

"I'll talk to him," Bulah said.

"I'm afraid that chicken has left the coop. For the sake of your lives, I encourage you to make tracks back to where you came from."

Davey turned her horse around, facing west.

Bulah nodded to her and rode toward camp.

Davey watched her for a moment and then swivelled her horse around to follow. Bowles shook his head.

The two women rode on. When they reached camp, they unloaded the ponies. The ragtags rifled through the goods until they located the whisky; they set to drinking immediately. Gussie sat next to two large mail sacks, slicing each envelope open and shaking it out on her lap. On the shoreline two dogs gnawed on a gutted deer. Upstream, the clown sat on a tree stump, his face expressionless as he stared at the horizon in the west.

"Are you sure?" Davey said.

"It's been a long journey."

Davey scowled at her. "I'll be camped over there." She pointed toward a lean-to at the edge of the brush where Bobby sat cleaning his rifle, away from the rest of the camp.

"Tomorrow. We'll head off first light. I give you my word." She offered her hand; Davey shook it.

Davey mounted her horse and rode on to join Bobby at the lean-to.

––––––––––

In the early-morning bluing light, the clown stood at the outskirts of the camp and looked upriver. A thin film of fog rose off the water. Trout nosed the surface silently for aphids. Two magpies chittered in the willows. A long line of men tramped toward the bridge. They clenched axes and lance-tooth cross-saws, five feet long, and thick lengths of rope; they stopped at the bridge, turned down the bank and shuffled down the dirt embankment, scuffing loose dirt into clouds until they reached the bottom and walked stealthily toward him. They seemed to float over the land in the stillness of the morning. As they drew near and the mist lifted, the lead man pointed an axe at the clown. Behind him and the other men, the sun rose over the peaks. The clown raised his palms at his waist and tilted his neck back. He closed his eyes; sunlight flushed over his eyelids and face. Deep inhale of a logger's breath. Creak of his hands tightening on a wooden handle. Heavy swing of the axe in the air. Shock of metal smashing through bone.

The loggermen raced through the camp in search of the girl who hadn't returned with the other children. They slashed open Gussie's tent. A logger grabbed her jaw and yanked her up. "Where is she?" he said.

Gussie swore and slapped at the man.

He held the axe above her. Gussie shook her head, her eyes half open. The man brought the axe down on her shoulder, which seemed to surprise her. The amount of blood was shocking as it sprayed across the tent's walls. She stared up at him and reached for her missing arm. The man swung the axe down on her other shoulder and then down again on her neck.

The loggers moved among the other tents in silence save for the swing of their axes and the dull smack of metal cleaving bone. Their axes and saws glistened among the bands of light where the sun now touched the higher ground and burned off the mist, the handles slick with blood.

Upon entering Bulah's tent they found her kneeling in prayer.

"Where is she?" one of the loggermen said.

"Please," Bulah said, "he's got her. It's always been him. Up there."

The loggers sneered.

"Please." Bulah began to weep. "It was always him."

One of the loggermen yanked her hair.

Bulah cried out. "Please, don't hurt my daughter."

A loggerman lifted his axe, brought it down on Bulah's chest, and split open her sternum. Bulah's lips moved soundlessly before she fell over on her side. The man had trouble removing the axe. He wriggled it until it popped loose and then followed the others.

The men climbed the hummock and tore through Reverend Brown's tent. It reeked of feces and damp animal fur. A small girl, covered in dirt, her hair matted with leaves and twigs, cried out when she saw the loggermen. The men slashed the walls of the tent. It fell down around them; they scanned the terrain below where the ragtags' camp was set up and they scanned the land to the east and to the north. On the horizon in the west, a small man loped, holding a cross with a figure affixed to it. A bear appeared to be chasing him. They ran up a short rise and then disappeared into the folds of the mountains.

––––––––––––

Three loggers advanced toward Bobby and Davey. The men were swinging axes and cross-saws; another held a handful of small blades, knives perhaps.

Bobby gripped her arm.

"Bulah," Davey said. "Come on." She raced toward the camp.

Bobby swore and chased after her.

They hurried downriver, ducking in and out of willows as knives whizzed through the brush, thudding into the tree trunks about them. They ran inland for a short while and skidded behind a fallen tree where they lay gasping for air.

"We're going to die," Bobby blubbered. He seized Davey's arm, crying brokenly.

"This way." She crawled along the ground until she reached Bulah's tent. Bobby scuttled toward her, sobbing. They entered the tent.

"Oh my god." Bobby crouched next to Davey. He bawled and slapped his face repeatedly. "Oh my god."

Davey raised Bulah by the shoulders and held her against her lap. Bulah's eyes were open but motionless. Davey removed her hat and leaned her ear against Bulah's nose.

"We need to go." Bobby gasped and spat out each word as if it took all his effort. He was crying unabashedly and placed a hand on Davey's back.

Davey's shoulders shook. She shrugged his hand off and kissed Bulah on the forehead. Wiped one eye with her thumb and the other eye with her index finger. Squeezed the sides of her eyes and shook her head from side to side, took a deep breath and pushed Bobby in the chest, which seemed to startle him. "You're all savages," she said. "Every trouble I've ever had is because of a man. He did this."

Bobby stopped hyperventilating and watched her silently.

"We need to bring her."

"I can't," Bobby said.

Davey glared at him.

Bobby cussed. He bent down, lifted Bulah and carried her over his shoulders, holding her arms across his chest. He started to weep again.

"Follow me," Davey said.

They scampered across the plain and headed for the cover of the woods. Near the river, the loggers had convened. They were covered in the rust of blood, but the mood turned ugly when two men began to argue with one another.

"This way." Davey sprinted toward the woods and Bobby plodded behind her. They paused behind a thicket of deadfall.

One of the loggers squinted at where Bobby and Davey crouched. He raised a knife in his right hand, took aim and hurled it at them as he stumbled toward them. The blade clattered off the disintegrated red rot at the base of the tree. He raised another knife and heaved it; it whirred through the air and stabbed the tree they crouched against.

"Now," Davey said.

They dashed inland, climbed a dusty bluff, descended the far side and reappeared again, scampering along the dirt and rotting scrub brush. The logger crested the bluff, aimed at them and swore when he released the knife. Davey turned and shouted out, grabbed at her shoulder. It felt cold and then hot, like she had been stung.

Bobby reached for her hand. "Come on," he said. They ran. After a while they could no longer see the loggerman.

Davey examined the knife in her shoulder. The blade was embedded to the wooden handle. She touched it and cried out. She tore at patches of lichen and packed the wound to staunch the bleeding. Bobby ripped off his right sleeve, wrapped it around the dressing and tucked the loose ends in. Davey winced.

"Are you all right?" Bobby said.

She nodded.

Bobby inspected the dressing on her shoulder. "Let me see."

"No."

"Don't be stubborn."

"Don't tell me what to do."

They journeyed north of the river along a narrow game trail and threaded the woods throughout the day, squinting against the sunlight when they entered an undersized clearing. The day blued into black; stars appeared overhead. The plumes of their breath rose above them and they rested against a tree where they shivered with their backs against one another before rising at dawn and labouring over the land. Davey's abdomen had tightened; she vomited, and twice she told Bobby to go on but he would not. They rested again.

"Let me see," Bobby said.

"There's nothing to see."

Bobby untied the dressing and repacked her wound and tore off his left sleeve and wrapped her shoulder carefully, avoiding the blade. "Let me take that out."

Davey shook her head.

They travelled a day and a night. The blistering green mural of the valley and blue sky shimmered before them. When they reached a camp set next to a creek, the sun floated low and red before them. A man in a white dalmatic knelt beside a small fire. They drew closer. Deacon's head was bowed and held both palms together as if in prayer or seeking forgiveness. He got up from his knees, made the sign of the cross and welcomed them.

Bobby set Bulah down.

"Are you okay?" Deacon said.

They leaned over the creek and scooped palmfuls of water into their mouths. Davey lowered her shoulder into the water and ran water over the knife and her wound. Blood marbled in the stream.

She drank from the creek until she had satisfied her thirst. When she stood, Deacon's eyes were wet.

"It's only us," Bobby said.

"May I?" Deacon examined the knife and then placed a hand on her forehead. "You're warm."

"I'm fine."

The air was still and fragrant of pine and grass, wet stones and creek water. Wolves howled at the yapping coyotes on the other side of the valley. Deacon lifted a stick from the fire and handed it to them. They took turns blowing on it and tearing the charred flesh of grouse meat from the skewer. Afterward, they drank again from the cold water that trilled over rocks in the dark.

Davey asked Deacon if he could build up the fire and he did as he was told until the fire burned hot. She went over to Bulah's body and motioned for Bobby to help and together they hauled her to the fire and laid her out on top of the flames.

"Would you like to say anything?" Deacon said.

Davey stared into the fire for a long time. She removed her hat and held it against her chest and the men did the same. "Being with her was like being with a porcupine. She was stubborn but she was the most loyal person I've known. She was my best—" Her voice caught and she paused.

Deacon placed a hand on her back.

"She was my best friend," Davey said. "I'll always remember what she did for me."

They were silent as the fire burned. Much later, they lay curled within their own bodies to keep warm and the animals up and down the valley quieted as if the world had agreed upon sleep.

BOOK
FOUR

1902

TWENTY-ONE

JACK SMITH AND LENORA BELL stayed in camp for ten nights, until she declared she was fit to travel. Her sickness had left as suddenly as it had appeared, and for the last two days under a blue sky, they resumed their relations at her insistence. After the first day, Jack Smith pleaded for respite but she would have none of it. She appeared hungry in a way he hadn't witnessed before, both in her appetite for him and for the deer or rabbit he provided after returning from a hunt.

They broke camp and continued westward, making up lost ground, travelling for long days. It took three days of riding before they arrived at the loggerman camp in the evening.

Smith dismounted from his horse. "Wait here." He walked around and noted the slashed tents dark with blood. He headed toward the sound of voices over a small rise and paused. Two loggermen were conferring with each other.

"What happened?" Smith said.

The men did not respond.

"Who did the killing?" Smith said.

One of the men held up a hand. "They brought this on themselves."

"Who?"

The man pointed west. "The man who's disguised as a holy man." His face remained expressionless. "That man has no god in him."

———————

Smith and Lenora Bell rose early and left the loggerman camp the next day. The morning warmed as they travelled in silence. Smith stopped and handed the reins to her and knelt down to study the ground. A rock splattered with blood, dark, nearly black. Smith touched it but it was dry. Other rocks covered in pebbled lichen had evidence of blood on them as well. He scanned the ground nearby. The bunchgrass to his left, up from the river, was crushed, as if the weight of a man had lain there. Smith looked ahead, squinting into the late-morning light, and looked back at Lenora Bell. Her face was drawn and grey, her eyes red. He offered his canteen and she took a long drink. He climbed back onto his horse and sat in front of her. She handed him the canteen. He took a quick swig and put it in his saddle, clucked to his horse and they continued on.

They rode down the morning with the sun overhead and wiped their faces with handkerchiefs that they wrung out and placed across their necks to keep cool. They followed the Stag and at midday they disembarked at a stand of willows where they drank from the cool water and splashed it over their faces and necks. Smith took off his boots and instructed her to do the same, but she sat down and stared at the river without replying. Smith unlaced her boots from the top grommets to the bottom and pulled off each one. He rolled down both of her stockings and set them on the rocks beside them. He soaked his handkerchief in the river and bathed her feet, massaging each toe, kneading the underside of her foot with his thumbs. She closed her eyes and leaned back with her hands clasped around her belly. When Smith was done he washed her stockings and wrung them out and laid them across the rocks to dry along with his own. He lay beside her. She put a hand on his and they rested in the shade of the willows, looking up at the sky through the branches.

They arose mid-afternoon. The day was silent except for the murmur of the river. They went on and by late afternoon the sun was in their eyes so they rode with their hats lowered. Smith's horse reared up. In front of them, a logger was hanging from the branch of a large fir. Smith turned to Lenora Bell. Her mouth was open but no sound came out except for a small, piercing cry, as if she was trying to inhale air and her lungs were too small to facilitate it.

The man hung from his garments. He was shirtless; the arms of his shirt were tied around his neck. His face was bloated and he had urinated himself. Flies buzzed around his open mouth and eyes. The base of the tree had long vertical claw marks that reached a height of about ten feet and there was bear scat on the ground. The logger's feet were missing. Torn and bloodied boots were scattered nearby; his legs had bled out at the shin bone.

"My god." Smith pulled Lenora Bell into his back. She leaned her face against him, rising and falling rapidly with each breath Smith took in and exhaled. Smith snapped the reins, kicked his horse and they continued on.

They hadn't been riding for long, following the path of large bear paws and those of another person, when they came upon a second logger lying on his back in the dirt, his hands pressed against his abdomen. The ground beneath him was dark with blood and he breathed hoarsely. He saw Smith and his eyes brightened for a moment; he spoke but Smith could not understand the man. Smith got down from his horse and knelt beside him. The man repeated the same phrase. Smith leaned in closer.

"Hair?" Smith said.

The man shook his head.

"Where?"

The man shook his head.

"Hair?" He turned to Lenora Bell. "What's he saying?"

"Bear."

The man nodded. He grabbed Smith with both hands and searched his face before repeating that word and another that Smith did not understand. He said the word again and again. "Devil." The man let out a rasping breath. Smith waited for the inhale but it did not come. He closed the man's eyes with the pads of his fingertips.

Smith and Lenora Bell made camp at dusk. He shot a rabbit, dressed and stuffed it with juniper berries and sage and roasted it. Lenora Bell ate little. Her colour had returned, but her movements were listless, as if she had lost all of her will and was merely moving from one spot to another. She sat in front of the fire with her forehead resting on her arms across her knees and wept. "I want to go home."

Smith let out a long breath.

"Please take me home."

Smith stared into the fire.

Lenora Bell raised her head. Her face was wet. "You will come to regret this."

"It was you who wanted, nay, insisted on coming with me," Smith said. "To the coast."

Lenora Bell stopped weeping when Smith said "coast" and wiped her face. "I've changed my mind."

Smith shook his head. "If I could get a silver coin for every time that has happened, I'd be able to buy a nice pony."

"I don't see any reason for you to insult me. Especially after what I've seen today."

"You made a decision to come with me. Do you remember? And here we are."

"I made the wrong decision."

"You didn't make the wrong decision," Smith said. "You made a decision for the wrong reasons. There's a difference."

"What's the difference?"

"One comes from here." Smith tapped his palm against his chest. "The other"—he raised his hands and gestured toward the land in front of them—"comes from there."

Lenora Bell looked out at the valley. "So, I'm being punished for both?"

"That's how it works."

"It ain't fair."

"Decisions are no trivial things."

"What if I decide to go back first thing in the morning?"

"That would be another decision for you to live with. As would my decision of whether to pursue you or keep moving on."

"So, we'd have different choices?"

"Maybe."

"And we'd each have to live with those?"

"Yes."

"And there's no way of knowing which is right?"

Smith nodded. "What's right for one might not be right for the other."

"Then how do people ever get along?"

Smith laughed. He jabbed a stick in the fire and refilled her cup. "What are you going to do?"

She sipped her coffee and stared at him for a long time. "Oh lord, if I knew that I wouldn't be discussing this, would I?"

TWENTY-TWO

DAY BROKE. Davey gathered two fistfuls of Bulah's ashes and placed them in a piece of cloth she tore from her shirttail. She placed it in the sack that hung from her waist.

In the pale light Bobby and Deacon studied two figures from the west trudging up the valley toward them.

"Why are they coming back?" Bobby said.

Deacon shook his head and nudged Davey. She sat up.

The reverend carried a cross with a body affixed to it. There was no head on the corpse tied to the cross but it was clear from the garments that the body belonged to the clown. Reverend Brown's cassock was filthy with the grime of the land; the bear was dressed in garments as if in a pageantry, a wedding or funeral perhaps. The strange duo lumbered on—Reverend Brown, a dark ghost like something rising from the ashes; the clown's headless corpse and the bear much darker.

"That man ain't from this world," Bobby said. "I seen him walk on water. I seen him climb a rope and vanish into the night sky. I seen him baptize the same bear he claimed he killed. He ain't one of us."

In a low, steady tone, Deacon quoted Jeremiah: "And I brought you into a plentiful country, to eat the fruit thereof and the goodness thereof; but when ye entered, ye defiled my land, and made mine heritage an abomination."

Reverend Brown and the bear halted before Davey, Deacon and Bobby. He jabbed the cross into the ground and took a length of rope that hung from the bear's neck and tied it to the cross. The cross was fashioned from two elk bones tied together with thin willow branches. At the top of the cross, where the clown's head ought to have been, a bird was nailed. A banknote was pinned above the bird, the letters INRI crudely hand-painted in blood.

"Good morning, brothers and sister. It's a good morning to be alive."

The bear stood beside the cross and raised its small dark eyes to Davey, Deacon and Bobby.

"It was the fire. I appreciate you sending me the signal." The reverend lifted his cedar crown and scratched his head. A pistol hung tied to the clown's hand. Reverend Brown removed it and smiled at the three of them. "Well, here we are. Reunited. Together, again."

No one spoke.

"Bobby," Reverend Brown said. "Can you sing something for us?"

Bobby didn't reply.

Reverend Brown rotated the pistol in his hand three times before he caught it by the handle.

Bobby spat and kicked at the lump of phlegm in the dirt.

Reverend Brown laughed. "Have I not treated you like a son? Have I not provided for and taken care of you? I brought you to our humble flock when you were but a small boy. You sang at our gatherings, I clothed and fed you, and now, as a man, you have a duty to honour my wish."

Bobby shifted from one foot to the other and looked to Deacon and to Davey.

Reverend Brown stopped twirling the pistol; the handle rested against the palm of his hand. "From one brother to another."

Bobby looked off toward the sun. The bear stood next to the cross sniffing the air. Bobby started to sing. His voice was rough, off key, and it cracked when he tried to hit a higher note. He started to weep.

"That's enough, brother."

Bobby lowered his head and continued to weep silently.

"Where's the others?" the reverend said.

Davey shifted her feet.

"Were they not in your custody?" Deacon said.

"Custody?" Reverend Brown said.

Deacon nodded. "You've asked Bobby to sing for you on account of providing for him. Were the others not always under your rule?"

"Rule?" The reverend looked at Bobby and turned to smile at Deacon again.

"That fire was for Bulah," Davey said.

The reverend studied Davey and then the firepit. He fell to his knees and grabbed a fistful of ashes. His shoulders shook for a moment. He stood and moved away from them, tossed the ashes in the air and watched them settle on the ground. When he turned around, his eyes were red. He wiped his hands on his cassock. "There's nothing left," he said.

Deacon glanced at Davey. She shifted her bow and nodded to Bobby and Deacon. "Let's move on."

Deacon and Davey turned to head west.

"Wait." The reverend pointed the pistol at Deacon. "You are nothing but a novice and yet you challenge my authority. I am a man who is grieving."

"It's a commandment," Deacon said.

Reverend Brown laughed. "A commandment written on stone tablets thousands of years ago by a fool with a beard. So we are told." He pointed the gun at Davey. "What's your life worth to you, lass?"

Davey didn't answer.

He nodded at the blade in her shoulder. "You're not long for this world anyway."

Davey remained silent.

"I'll spare your life but it will cost you another. Bobby? Deacon? You choose."

Davey shook her head. "I'll make no such choice."

"Your choice is your freedom."

"My choice is not to play your game."

Reverend Brown laughed. "Indeed." He spun the chamber and tossed the gun to Deacon. "What about you, my fellow brethren?"

Deacon held the gun and shifted it to his right hand. "For the life of the flesh is in the blood, and I have given it to you upon the altar to make an atonement for your souls: for it is the blood that maketh an atonement for the soul." He aimed the weapon at the reverend. His hand trembled; he pressed the trigger. The pistol clicked.

Reverend Brown laughed. "I knew you had it in you, thy novice man of god. Commandment be damned." He held out his hand and Deacon placed the gun on his palm. Reverend Brown lifted it, spun the revolver and emptied out a bullet onto the ground. "I knew it from the day we met."

"Come on," Davey said to Bobby. "Let's move on."

Bobby sat in the dirt and jabbed his fingers into the ground and dug out a clump of soil. He rocked himself back and forth, ran his fingers across it until his palm was empty. His trousers were damp at the groin. He grabbed another fistful and squeezed it into a black ball.

Davey slung the quiver over her shoulder and winced. She wiped her mouth with the back of her hand. "Are you sure?"

He stared down at the dirt in his hands. "He's been like a father to me."

Davey studied him for a moment and made her way across the brush. Grasshoppers and insects scattered in her wake and the scent of sage clung to her legs. A shot rang out.

Davey spun around, pulled an arrow from her quiver and notched it. Deacon held the side of his abdomen. Blood burbled through his fingertips.

Reverend Brown pointed his pistol at them. "You made your choice. Both of you."

Davey aimed her arrow at the reverend.

"That was my last bullet. Are you going to murder an unarmed man?" Reverend Brown said.

Deacon shook his head. "Leave it be, girl."

"Now you have another choice to make," the reverend said. "I counsel you to choose carefully."

She pulled the arrow and string back and held them steady. Reverend Brown no longer smiled. He appeared small in the sightline in front of her. "Choose wisely, lass."

Deacon held his hand against the wound. He walked around the bear, Bobby and Reverend Brown, placed a hand on Davey's shoulder and whispered into her ear. He told her there were no more bullets and that she was free to make her choice and if she chose to shoot the Reverend Brown, he would respect that choice as much as if she didn't shoot him. He told her she had her life in front of her and if she could foresee a life ahead with the weight of killing the reverend, then she should honour that. He removed his hand from her shoulder and stood next to her.

She kept her eyes on Reverend Brown and lowered the arrow. She glanced at Bobby. "Are you sure?"

He nodded.

She turned and Deacon followed.

"You won't survive the day out there." The reverend laughed behind them. "Enjoy the remaining hours of your lives."

Davey tore a length of fabric from her bedroll and tied it against Deacon's waist. Deacon pressed his hand against it and they set out across the valley. They did not turn around but kept a fixed course westerly. Bobby lifted his head as they receded into the valley. He dropped the dirt from his palms, wiped them against his legs and looked up again. After a while there was no one to see.

———————

Davey and Deacon travelled across the valley through swathes of blue-bunch wheatgrass and rough fescue, sage and willow. Crickets leapt against their legs. A rider slowly traversed the valley toward them. They stood while he rode up, and as his features came into view they recognized the rider as Keegan. He held the reins up with his pinky fingers and the bloodied stumps that were his hands. A pistol lay in his lap.

"These trials are but a test," Deacon said.

"That so?" Keegan looked at Davey's shoulder and at Deacon's bloodied hands pressed against his stomach. He dropped the reins and rested the nubs of his hands on the pommel of his saddle.

"Bobby's back there," Davey said, "with him and that bear."

Keegan looked east across the valley. "How far?"

"You won't miss them," Deacon said.

"The whores gave this to me." He held up the pistol with one small finger and lifted his reins with the other pinky and spat. "I can't shoot if my life depended on it." He rode on, stopped and twisted around in his saddle. "I'd appreciate it if you could say a prayer for me."

"Prayer only works if you believe in it." Deacon cleared his throat.

Keegan studied Deacon and raised his bandaged hands. "It's easy to believe in a time of need, isn't it?"

"The timing of it doesn't matter to the lord. The intent does."

Keegan turned and rode on, slumped over in his saddle, the palms on both of his hands facing upward. Davey and Deacon kept watch on him until he blurred into the landscape, well advanced down valley, before they continued their course.

TWENTY-THREE

THE NEXT DAY, Smith and Lenora Bell rode beneath a sky stitched with thin clouds. It was warm and muggy and swarms of gnats and blackflies rose up with each step the pony took. Lenora Bell waved her hand in front of her face and after a while she tired of this and rested her face against Smith's back.

They rode along the valley bottom and chased the tracks that they picked up along the river. They rode farther and encountered another man hanging from a tree branch, turning in the breeze. He was younger than the other men, his abdomen had been clawed open, the entrails spilling out severed and black. At the base of the tree, *Traitor* was carved into the trunk. Smith continued to ride. As they passed the man, Smith felt Lenora Bell's face lift and then press deeper into his back. "That's one of his followers."

Smith nodded.

The wisps of clouds burned off late morning, and when they rode out into the open the sun beat down on them mercilessly. They stopped in a shaded draw, shed their clothes and waded into the river. Afterward they lay on the sand to warm and dry themselves.

"Oh honey, I'm so hungry I could eat the bark off a tree," Lenora Bell said.

Smith raised himself on his elbows and turned to her. "You haven't kept anything down for days."

"Oh lord, it feels like a lifetime."

Smith pulled on his boots, grabbed his rifle and marched off into the woods. After a while a shot boomed out and Smith came striding back, clutching his rifle in his left hand as he dragged a small deer by the hind leg with his right. He butchered it quickly, cut off two large pieces near the belly, and after he started a fire he laid these steaks to the side of the flames where they grilled slowly.

"I do love a man who knows his way around a fire," Lenora Bell said. "'Specially one dressed in his finest."

Smith stood and raised his hands to his shoulders and moved them down either side of his body in an elaborate gesture, palms facing upward. "I don't know what's come over you, and I don't want to know. But I'm glad you're back." He stepped toward her, his privates swelling.

Lenora Bell smiled. "Slow down, honey. I need to eat something first."

Smith sighed and lifted a stick, jammed it into the steaks and flipped them.

They started out again late in the afternoon. The air was still and dry, the sky washed out with light. Lenora Bell pointed at birds that flew overhead and asked Smith what species they were.

"I don't know," he said. "Birds."

She slapped him on the back. "Can't you at least pretend that you know?"

"What would the point in that be?"

"You're a strange one, Jack Smith. I'd known that the day we met."

A murder of crows squawked ahead over a stand of trees. "Crows." Smith pointed at them. "Hallelujah, those are crows."

Lenora Bell laughed.

They rode toward the trees and the crows leapt up from their branches and screeched at them. Smith stopped the pony and placed his palm over Lenora Bell's face. "Close your eyes."

Lenora Bell tried to shake his hand free.

"I mean it. Close them, now."

She grabbed his wrist and lifted his hand from her face. "Why?"

"Just do it."

Lenora Bell looked past Smith and screamed. The crows flew off. Smith winced and covered his ears.

A man was lashed to a tree in front of them. He was naked, his throat had been garrotted from ear to ear; blood covered his chest and privates and legs and pooled at his feet. Flies all around. There were open sores over his face and neck and shoulders. His hands were bandaged stumps with only a small finger left on each. *Traitor* was carved in the tree trunk above the man's head.

"Oh. My. God."

Smith turned to her.

"It's him."

Smith studied her face. She pointed at the man. "It's him. Oh lord, it's him."

A crow swooped in and sat on the man's shoulder and pecked at his face. The man's eyes opened and his lips moved.

Lenora Bell shrieked and the crow flew off. The man lifted his eyes toward them.

Smith got down from his horse and instructed her to wait, but she climbed down and rushed to the man. She tore the hem of her dress and used the fabric as a tourniquet and wrapped it around Keegan's neck. Her hand trembled when she placed it against his cheek. "Oh honey, who did this to you?"

Keegan smiled slightly.

Lenora Bell told Smith to fetch his canteen. Smith did as he was instructed, came back and handed it to her. She opened the stopper and tipped some water into Keegan's mouth. Keegan gagged. The bleeding from his throat recommenced, soaking through the tourniquet.

"Oh honey," Lenora Bell said.

Smith put a hand on her shoulder.

Keegan glanced at Smith's uniform. "Where's your gun?"

Smith didn't respond.

"Hush," Lenora Bell said.

"Who did this?" Smith said.

"Your gun," Keegan said.

Lenora Bell turned to Smith. He twisted the left end of his moustache and shook his head.

"There's no one who would find fault in you," Lenora Bell said.

Smith shook his head. "I would."

"Have mercy on him."

Smith shook his head again. "It's a capital crime. I won't do it."

Keegan sputtered, "Your gun. Get it."

"I give you my word. Please," Lenora Bell said.

"You don't know what you're asking of me," Smith said.

"I'll do it myself then."

"I'll have to arrest you."

Lenora Bell turned to Keegan. His lips were dry and chapped. He muttered gibberish. She opened the canteen and spilled some water on a kerchief and put it against Keegan's mouth. He sucked the cloth. She dampened the cloth and gave it back to him. "Does that help?"

Keegan lifted his eyes but did not acknowledge her question.

"We can't just leave him like this," Lenora Bell said.

Smith took her by the shoulders and turned her away from Keegan. He spoke low in her ear. "There's nothing we can do for him."

Lenora Bell shook her head.

"You best say your goodbyes," Smith said.

Her eyes welled up. She shrugged Smith's hands off from her shoulders and turned to Keegan. She placed her hand against his cheek and stroked him. She leaned in and spoke to Keegan and when she was done she looked into his face. Keegan's eyes opened and searched hers. She pressed against him so he could place his small finger against her belly. She put her hand over his finger. "It's true. Every word of it."

Keegan tried to smile but it looked more like a scowl. Lenora Bell kissed him on the cheek and said something again low in his ear. She kissed him one more time, wiped her tears, turned and walked toward Smith's horse. She held Smith's rifle in both hands at her waist, raised it, pressed on the lever and a shot boomed out.

"What are you doing?" Smith said.

The crows squawked. She shot the rifle again and then one more time, each shot barrelling past Smith, before he grabbed the gun from her. She gave it up without struggle. "You'd rather see a man suffer to keep your conscience clean."

"I'd rather do the right thing," he said. "You can't do that for me."

Keegan's chest had three holes blasted in it; his head was bowed as if in prayer and he no longer breathed.

"Well, come on," she said. "Shouldn't we hit the trail before it gets cold?"

"Just so we're clear, you're a felon now."

"What were you when you were paying for my services?"

Smith walked back to his horse, slipped his rifle into his saddle, pulled himself up. "I was a damn fool." He nudged his horse forward.

TWENTY-FOUR

DAVEY AND DEACON took to the high country where they rode out of the valley, past a shallow alkaline lake encased in a thin mist rising off the milky water, light cutting through the pines surrounding it. In the early evening they descended to Christina Lake, and stopped at a stream feeding into the northern end of the lake. A moose had perished here and the two of them made their way among its yellowed bones and carcass with its rags of tattered hide and they knelt upstream to drink from the low water.

They stole up from the creek and set off across the beach that rimmed the southern end of the lake and then scrambled up shallow hummocks protruding like calluses from a weary and worn land. They were well advanced on the side of the mountain that abutted the lake and looked back at the pleated waters where a night fire flickered in the wind at the edge of the shoreline.

The moon rose, wolves bawled in the night and then stopped and the land was silent, and then the wolves began howling again. A wind lifted off the lake and Davey and Deacon lay down with their backs pressed against one another. They refrained from making a fire and shivered throughout the night, their hands clamped tight in their armpits as they laid on the barren ground in small coils, their noses pressed into their knees. When the sun rose, Deacon sat up in his bloodied rags and rocked himself back and forth. The two of them stood and fixed their course and before they headed west, they looked back to where the sun was up and the land was lit bright. They searched the horizon.

"There," Deacon said.

"Where?"

"Over there."

"I don't see anything."

Deacon studied the land. "He's there, I know it."

Davey placed her palm on Deacon's back. "We can't keep looking back."

He nodded. They limped together across the land.

A wind blew down from the north. The valley below was green and scrubby and absolute from the river carving through it. Monstrous mountains towered above them. They moved on, two small beings insignificant against the vast canvas of the world. Two single grains of sand. Or errant bird feathers. Falling leaves. Scrabbling ants. An immense world all around them. There were upturned rocks left by sheep that had traversed the mountainside in steep narrow pitches, sending shale scurrying down in plumes of rock dust hundreds of feet below. In the afternoon, the terrain rose before them in vertical pitches offset by wide gulches they could not traverse. They retraced their steps for an hour to find a creek bed of runoff that descended and from this they drank and bathed their wounds. Deacon breathed in heavy rasps as they laboured along. They chased the creek down the slope and reached the valley floor.

———

They headed north and reached an abandoned cabin late the following day. They stayed in the trees and waited out the night and in the morning there was still no sign of anyone. Davey winced as she stood. She checked her wound; blood seeped lightly through the dressing. Deacon lay curled into himself on the ground, breathing heavily. His face was pale and his forehead damp. She offered him a hand and helped him to his feet. They walked the treeline around the cabin and there was a long meadow and a small lake at the end. Here they cleansed their wounds and dried themselves in the sunlight and at night they went into the woods and spent a fireless night sleeping upright, back-to-back with a view of the cabin. After a while, Deacon lay down. Davey listened to him breathe. She studied the cabin for a long time and then lowered herself next to him, pressing her body against his, wrapping her arms around him. His chest rose and fell as she held him close. Deacon woke her babbling in a fever dream. "Take me home ... I've never spoken to god and he's never spoken to me. That's the truth. This is as good a place to die in ... god's beauty is all about ... perhaps that's the way he's speaking to us all ... I want to go home." He mumbled and became quiet. Birdsong woke them in the morning. Tufts of wiry grass frozen in the meadow. They rinsed their wounds again, dressed them and then they moved on.

The country to the west was rolling and grassy, and beyond, the mountains ran as far as their eyes could see. They stayed north three days, cleansing their wounds in creeks and sleeping in the woods at night. They made no fire and they dug small holes to bury their excrement and they swept the trail behind them with the branches of soft hemlock needles.

They changed their course and headed southwest. For several days, the country was white with frost in the morning and then it was warmer as they fixed their course westerly. In the patch of open ground before them, low on the slope, sweeping up toward the treeline where immense firs swayed in the breeze, a sea of fireweed burst up in waves of green and pink mourning, the spray overburdening the ground it covered, a live wreath over a wreath of land.

They drank from the cold river, flushed their wounds and ate blackberries and salmonberries by the fistful. They saw signs of bears—vicious claw marks scraped on tree trunks, piles of dung, diggings—and they changed their course slightly, heading north or south for a stretch before turning westward again. One day, during a long period of silence, they stopped on a rise studying the river ahead, wide and brown and placid, splintering off into estuaries.

Davey turned to Deacon. "Which way?"

"You know best."

They kept to the left of one of the estuaries, following the path where the shoed horses before them had scarred the rock and manure rose up in clumps. The sun fell and the land transformed into a cold, wide plank of green and brown and blue. They set up a fireless camp and slept shivering against one another among crying owls and the scent of juniper while the stars swarmed in the bottomless night.

"This has never been my place," Deacon said.

"How do you know?"

"Just do. Everyone recognizes it."

"Where's yours?"

"Out east, across the country."

Davey nodded.

"You could come with me," Deacon said.

Davey was silent.

"Consider it," Deacon said.

"What if it ain't my place?"

"People make places their own."

"But not you?"

Deacon shook his head. "I tried but I'd be a fool to keep trying anymore. This land is too formidable."

In the days ahead, they came out of the mountains and rode onto a wide valley bottom chasing the river. Men in wooden paddlewheelers slapped past them, the chopped wake muddied and boiling. They circumvented New Westminster and journeyed past camps where men floated along in scows and eulachon were smoked over blue alder fires.

They passed stacks of duck potatoes, women and girls pulling arrow-shaped leaves from them and tossing them onto a pile.

They were both in poor shape when they eventually entered a fishing village clustered along a scrim of land that met the Georgia Strait. They shivered and alternated between cold and hot sweats as they passed bunkhouses of Chinese and Japanese and Coast Salish peoples and heard tongues speaking in languages they could make no sense of. They passed a brightly lit cannery clanging in the night and the pungent smell of ripe fish hit them and they covered their mouths and noses with a cloth. They staggered through the mud streets, past the houses of rough-hewn boards and crude planks in their rows, across the gravel strand of the beach where the cannery blinked in the night like an immense ship.

Stripped logs lay polished and damp along the shore. The gravel gave way to sand. Sandpipers stood on stick legs and seagulls flew overhead or perched on logs. Davey leaned down and picked up a flat seashell and ran her hands over the smooth interior and noted the indigo and pearl colour. Her teeth chattered. She placed it in her pocket and looked out over the water, her arms wrapped around herself. The sun smashed on the hammered disc of the sea in the west. Otters slipped through the water silently and down shore waves struck the shoreline. Deacon stared out upon the darkening world around them. His fever broke; he no longer shivered or sweat.

"If this isn't a sight to reaffirm one's faith."

"It's so pretty," Davey said, "it hurts my eyes."

They looked out over the water before Deacon spoke again.

"Let's find a doctor and something to eat."

"I want to wait here and just watch it."

"Are you sure?"

Davey nodded.

"I'll be back in a while." He headed into the village.

Davey sat on a log, shivering. Gulls hovered over the water. She inhaled the briny damp air. She reached into her pocket and rubbed her forefinger and thumb against the shell. The light faded. Her teeth chattered and she hugged herself. She stood and paced back and forth. Stars fell across the sky and dropped into the Strait and she made out movements on the water but could not identify what she saw. She shivered and sniffed her shoulder and began to weep. A figure advanced toward her along the shoreline. She wiped her eyes. It was Deacon. He held a plate of fish.

"How are you managing?" he said.

She nodded.

"You look poorly. Take this." He offered her the plate of fish.

"Don't be fooled by how I look." She refused his offer of food.

He lifted his shirt to show her his clean dressing. "The doctor declared me lucky. It was only a flesh wound."

Davey nodded.

"Will you let me take you to him?"

"I'll be fine."

"You've always been your own person," he said. "I've long admired that in you, but that needs attending to." He looked out over the water. A gull glided above the surface before landing on the shoreline. "Have you thought about my offer?"

She picked up a palmful of sand and tossed it into the water. "It wouldn't be my home."

He nodded. "A train leaves in twenty minutes."

"I'll manage," she said. "You're fortunate to have a home to return to."

"Are you sure?"

"Yes."

"If I don't go straightaway, I might never go."

She nodded.

"Can I take you to the doctor?"

Davey shook her head. "I want to stay for a while. It's so pretty, it stings my eyes."

Deacon looked at the black water and nodded. "When I see something beautiful, I sometimes feel if I were to blink it would all vanish."

Davey nodded.

He instructed her on the location of the doctor who would tend to her and then removed his hat, jammed it beneath his armpit and wiped his eye. "I've always been fond of you. You have been blessed in your short life. You saved my life. I'll never take that for granted. You are like a daughter to me. I know no other finer person." He held out his arms; she walked into them. He embraced her and held her close, her face against his neck. She breathed in deeply and clenched him tighter. She pulled away and they studied each other, their eyes damp. "You're shivering. Do you want me to stay with you longer?" he said.

"I'll be fine. You should go home."

Deacon placed a hand against her cheek and smiled. "Please see the doctor. Can you promise me that?"

"Yes," Davey whispered.

Deacon put his hat on, nodded, and walked along the shoreline. Low waves loped out of the night and splashed along the beach. Davey walked on the hard-packed sand toward the water, stopped at the edge and leaned down to place her hands in. The water was cold and she laved palmfuls over her face and inhaled the strange, briny smell. She tasted it and spat it out.

Stars burned above. The dull clamour of unrecognizable tongues, the shrill whistle of the cannery, a gull that soared overhead. Deacon stood with his head down. His shoulders shook. He lifted his head and strode into the village.

Davey looked up at the sky and traced its contour to where it met the water on the horizon. She shivered uncontrollably and wiped the damp from her forehead. Closed her eyes. Low murmur of waves along the shoreline. Clanging of metal in town behind her. She opened her eyes, looked up and struggled to draw the constellations. Her teeth chattered. She was dizzy from the effort. Closed her eyes again and felt the ground shift beneath her, held out her hands before she dropped to the sand and lay in a small heap against the shoreline. Darkness swarmed all around her, perforated with fish rising and starlight streaking in a swollen black sea.

TWENTY-FIVE

LENORA BELL HAD TAKEN TO not speaking with Jack Smith again as they rode on and made camp. She lay on the ground next to the fire that Smith had built, moaning inconsolably. She cried when Smith placed a hand on her shoulder and shook violently when he tried to soothe her by rubbing her neck. She squirmed and slapped Smith when he grabbed her wrists and handcuffed them to his own, and in this manner they spent a sleepless night watching the low embers of the fire fizzle out, manacled together.

Smith uncuffed her in the morning. She rubbed her wrists and avoided looking at him. He handed her a cup of coffee, which she accepted and sipped quietly. They rode out early and within an hour they had picked up the trail. They found blood-spattered rocks and lichen, bear scat, boot and bear prints, slaughtered birds, and they passed an area of blowdown where they stopped. Smith descended from his horse and studied the ground and slash but the trail had vanished. He walked back some steps from where they had come and then forward, past Lenora Bell sitting on his horse. He removed his hat, stared up into the trees and ran his hands over his head.

Lenora Bell sighed. "What?"

"It's like they've disappeared without a trace."

"Now what?"

He scanned the land in front of him to the west. "We keep going."

He slipped his hat on, walked back to the horse and mounted it. He turned to Lenora Bell. "You okay?"

"What do you think?"

"I don't know. That's why I'm asking."

"I'll be fine."

"Do you need a rest?"

She shook her head.

"You sure?"

"Sure as sure is."

By late afternoon they reached a small lake and bathed and rested for the day before setting out again. They rode down the daylight and camped on the banks of the river and the following day the river had widened into a silent formidable swath that cut through the land heading westward.

"We go left," Smith said.

"Why? Why not right?"

"Because everyone goes right."

"That makes no sense," Lenora Bell said.

In the days ahead, they picked up a trail of blood here and there and they saw bear prints and those of a man's boots, but they saw no other person until they rode past the Katzie camp. Lenora Bell's mood improved as they neared the coast, and by the time they reached a fishing village at land's edge, darkness had settled on the land; she held Smith tightly and kissed the back of his neck as they rode. When they disembarked from their horse, she ran toward the ocean squealing like a young girl and high-stepping in the water. Smith watched her from the shore. He noted a small clump farther down along the shoreline and squinted to see it better. When Lenora Bell returned, her boots squelched in the sand and her face was flushed, her eyes bright.

"Oh honey, thank you. Thank you. Thank you." She kissed Smith on the face and jumped up on him and tilted her face back and laughed. "I'm so happy right now. So very happy."

"I'm happy you're happy."

"Twirl me faster," she said. "Faster."

"How do I know this will last? How do you even know?"

"I just do."

"How?"

"Twirl me faster. Please. Faster."

Smith turned away from the shoreline and did as he was instructed, spinning her while she leaned away from him, her hands outstretched over her head, laughing, the wind in her hair across her face, the waves at her feet.

"I'm dizzy with happiness, so very happy," she said. "You're going to be the father of my child. A father. Imagine that. We're going to be a family."

BOOK
FIVE

1902—1927

TWENTY-SIX

DAVEY WOKE UP in the sand shivering, her mouth parched and the pain in her shoulder stinging fierce across her chest and down her arm. She hugged herself, her teeth chattered uncontrollably. She laid her face down across her arms. In that delirium, Reverend Brown held a long knife and sliced through pages of the holy book, one at a time, dropping the thin strands over Davey's body.

Someone pulled Davey up beneath both arms and another grabbed her by the ankles and she felt herself lifted and carried through the darkness. The man carrying her by the armpits wore a scarlet jacket with brass buttons and he had a waxy moustache. His face was creased with concern. There was a murmur of voices. Davey made out Cepheus and Orion, tracing the stars across the fabric of the world above and then all was dark.

In that fever dream Reverend Brown hovered over her, his filthy hand clamped over her mouth and nose. She fought to breathe and couldn't draw in air and gasped, choked and cried out with a whimper that startled her.

Davey shivered violently and winced as she was carted along the shoreline up over stacks of driftwood, along a double-wide plank that served as a walkway. The boards bent beneath the boots of the men that carried her. She encountered sounds before the origins of those sounds emerged from the darkness. Prostitutes laughing and calling out to men; the whistle of the cannery signalling the end of shift; Chinese butchers slicing up fat-bellied fish on a steel countertop, their knives singing as they carved out the innards and pushed them to the side in deft strokes.

A small voice, that of a woman, informed the men that the doctor was out on a call at the cannery and when this news was received, the man in the red coat murmured something in reply. They went down the planks, stopped, passed through a doorway. There was a jangling of keys and then Davey felt herself laid out on a cot that creaked beneath her. The redcoat placed a blanket over her and assured her that he would fetch the doctor as soon as he returned and then he left. A woman's voice and then all was silent and dark.

Water lapped somewhere beyond the wooden walls of the room. Davey trembled. She wrapped a palm around the knife and moved it slightly. She cried out and rested her hand against her wound; her hand was sticky with blood.

"You're awake," Lenora Bell said. "I knew you wouldn't leave us."

Davey propped herself up on the cot against the back corner of the room. Lenora Bell swirled before her. Davey closed her eyes and fell into a fitful sleep. In that fever dream Reverend Brown hovered over her, smiling, his hair smoothed down and shining with pomade, and he smelled of talc. He told her he had rescued her as an infant and welcomed her to his flock, provided her with food and faith, protected her all these years, that he gave her a sense of purpose, a reason to live when there was none, and he told her that the land eats itself, that it's ravenous and can't get enough of those who inhabit it, that it gorges on the men and women who trample over it, trying to tame it, that the land belongs to no one and no one is spared this truth. The world has a long memory and could vouchsafe for him for he had claimed her when her father had discarded her, for he was the only constant presence in her life, never demanding anything of her and that she, in return, had shown her gratitude by abandoning him and the family he had brought her up in. That her wilful desertion was an act of defiance, her life was nothing but one long-drawn-out breath of deceit.

———————

Jack Smith returned with a young doctor and nurse who appeared to be his wife. The three of them stood before Davey. Lenora Bell held a damp cloth to Davey's forehead and stroked her face. Davey was curled up on the cot, shivering uncontrollably.

"You need help," Jack Smith said.

The doctor said something and Smith turned to Davey. "Do you want to die in this room?"

"Leave her be," Lenora Bell said. "She needs her rest."

Jack Smith asked about the bible against Davey's waistband. He told her that anyone with a bible is never alone, that god's voice is in the printed words of the book, aspirational, the truth of the past, present and future. When we read the book, we give our eyes to him. And he in return will bend his ear. Smith cleared his throat. "It's a conversation. That's what most people don't understand. It goes both ways."

"Do you believe that?" Davey said.

"Be ye doers of the word, and not hearers only, deceiving your own selves."

"Do you believe in anything you're saying?"

Smith frowned. "The words are a comfort. That much I know."

"Go away." She turned and faced the wall.

Lenora Bell scowled at Smith and returned the cloth to Davey's forehead.

———————

In that fever dream Reverend Brown told Davey that she came from violence, an unholy transgression, and in that violence, she was stripped of everything before she could claim it and no history, no people, nothing tethered her to any other; she was nobody and she would perish without leaving a trace on the earth to mark her brief transient passage; she would die as she was born: alone, with no people, a nonentity, an inconsequence that would hold no recollection in the world's memory except her abandonment.

———————

Davey's fever broke when Smith appeared alone the next morning. He opened the door and handed her another jug of water and a piece of bread and something that smelled briny, the meat of which lay in oil on the plate. Davey sniffed at it, lifted a corner of the meat and set the plate down. She drank from the jug and tore the bread into pieces and ate each piece slowly. She offered a piece of bread to Lenora Bell and handed her the jug.

Smith pulled out a piece of paper and unfolded it and read it out loud. He read about the battlefield she was born on, the harm she suffered at the hands of the reverend. He read about the widow and the train robbery. The loggerman camp, the revivals, the thievery. He read that she had met her father at the mine in Morrissey, but couldn't confirm the truth because he died before she could speak to him. He detailed her trip across the mountains to the coast. When he was finished, Smith placed his hat on, folded the paper and handed it to her.

"Where did you get this from?" Davey said.

"A holy man who called himself your friend. He gave it to the doctor before he boarded a train east." Smith cleared his throat. "He said you'd be stubborn and refuse help from anyone who offered it. That you were the finest soul he had ever encountered. And he said that you should remember what he told you about Jonah. To not let anyone take your grace."

Davey started to weep.

"Hush, girl," Lenora Bell said. "That's all in the past."

Jack Smith held out a kerchief. "I'm truly sorry," he said, "that you've never had a chance to live the life of a young girl."

Davey wiped her eyes with her fingertips. "I don't need your help."

Smith returned the kerchief to his pocket. "I think we both know that's not true."

In the afternoon, Jack Smith returned with the doctor and his wife.

The doctor asked Davey if he could examine her wound. Davey didn't reply. He turned to Lenora Bell who nodded. The doctor cut open Davey's shirt with scissors and removed the dressing on her shoulder and inspected the blackened wound. He sniffed it and pressed on it lightly. "Thank god there's no smell. Do you have any pain?"

She didn't answer.

He pressed the wound with his thumb, careful to avoid touching the blade, removed a device from his coat pocket and pressed its cold flat metal against Davey's chest and listened in one ear. He told her to keep still and listened intently. He moved the stethoscope lower, below her rib cage.

Davey grabbed his hand.

The doctor held the stethoscope against her abdomen and listened for a long moment.

"It's all right. He's just checking on your heart," Lenora Bell said.

"My heart's up here." She tapped her chest.

"You have two heartbeats. Yours"—the doctor pressed the stethoscope against her chest—"and this little one's." He slid the stethoscope down to her abdomen. "Two. No doubt about it."

He removed the stethoscope and placed the ear tips in her ears. He slid the stethoscope to her abdomen and let it rest. Davey's face tightened. She pulled the tips from her ears and tossed the stethoscope against the wall. She reached for the sack around her waist and held it in her palm.

Colours, sand, stone, water, the names of birds, honeycombed sky stretched out overhead, a world like a dream, the names of things one believed to be true, all of it more fragile as a result, here or gone, in front of her, behind her, beating steady all along, breath of god, a cookfire reduced to embers, trying to preserve its heat, but weakened to wink out forever, leaving no trace save for a skiff of grey ash, which, too, would be carried off into the wind and scattered unseen over the land she had once trod, the land she had once called home. Dust.

The doctor said it was urgent that he perform the surgery to remove the knife and advance the delivery of the baby.

"Are you sure?" Lenora Bell said.

The doctor nodded.

"Can you give her some time to consider this?" Lenora Bell said.

"Of course."

Lenora Bell told Davey she should have some time alone and that if she needed her, to summon her and she would come straightaway. She left with the doctor, his wife and Smith.

Davey turned away, wiped at her eyes and stared at the wall.

Smith returned in the evening and handed her a lump of banknotes.

Davey looked at the money and gave it back to him.

"You're responsible for another life," Smith said. "You can no longer make decisions for yourself."

"I don't need your advice or money."

Smith sighed. "You're blessed," he said. "That's the responsibility you must carry for yourself and the little one for the rest of your days. Here, take it. I won't accept no this time."

He removed his hat and ran his hand through his hair. "I'm going to be a father. Lennie's convinced it's going to be a boy." He cleared his throat and lowered his voice. "The child isn't mine. But I'll care for him as if he is. How could I not? I can only pray that he's got half the fight that you have." He placed his hat on his head. "I give my word that I will find the man who did this to you."

Davey studied him for a long moment. "And do what?"

"That's my job." Smith placed his hat on his head. "Can you walk with me to the doctor's?"

———————

Children chased one another, laughing. One child fell on the board-walk and stood; his mother brushed dirt from the child's face before he raced off to join his friends. Davey turned away from the children and let Smith lead her by the elbow through the village to the doctor's office.

Smith knocked and when the door opened, Davey held the banknotes and offered them to the doctor's wife. The doctor came from the rear of the premises and studied Davey. "Please, put your money away." He turned to Smith and bowed slightly. Smith told him to send for him or Lenora Bell if they needed anything.

"I'll hold you in my prayers," Smith said to Davey, and then left.

Davey entered the room. The doctor's wife stood near the door.

The doctor nodded at her bow and arrow. "I'm going to need for you to leave that with me. For safekeeping."

Davey shook her head.

"It's okay. It will be here for you when you are discharged."

Davey removed the quiver and handed it to the doctor and then she handed him the bow.

He nodded. "Please go with Fumiko. She will bathe you. If you require anything, ask."

Fumiko led Davey to a small room in the rear of the premises that held a solitary bed and a wide wooden barrel with steam rising from it. Fumiko nodded and went behind a shoji screen. Davey slipped into the warm water and lay there with the water against her neck. Fumiko came out from behind the screen and gestured for Davey to rise out of the barrel. Davey stood. Fumiko motioned for her to remove her trousers and when Davey had pulled them down, she stepped out of them in the barrel and the trousers floated up. Fumiko fished them out of the bath and placed them on the floor. Davey had difficulty removing her shirt and turned to the doctor's wife. Fumiko nodded and pulled the fabric of the shirt toward her, away from the knife; she tore a large hole in it and lifted it slowly over Davey's head. She added it to the pile of clothes on the floor, which plumped wet and left pools of water around them. Fumiko then gestured toward the sack on her waist and Davey untied it and handed it to her and after Fumiko placed the sack down with her garments, Davey slid into the barrel. Fumiko held out a bar of soap and a dark pumice stone. Davey shook her head. The woman left the soap and stone on the edge of the barrel and went behind the screen. Davey soaked in the barrel until her skin grew goose pimples and then soaped and scrubbed herself. The water turned grey and cooled. Fumiko returned holding two buckets of steaming water. She poured them into the barrel and stirred the water with a large wooden gourd. She left again and returned with a several cloths and set them down on the floor and went behind the screen. Davey stepped out and towelled herself dry. She wrapped a clean cloth around her body, picked up the sack and stood on the damp floor.

Fumiko returned and led Davey to a soft mattress in the room adjacent. Davey laid down and Fumiko drew a thin cotton blanket up to her chin and laid out a heavier wool blanket on top, then left the room. Davey held the sack close to her. Children played somewhere outside. A dog barked. Laughter. When Fumiko returned, Davey was still awake. Fumiko placed a warm palm on Davey's forehead and brushed her hair back from her face. She reached for a cloth and wiped Davey's forehead and face, and carefully cleaned her wound.

She grabbed another clean cloth, tipped the contents of a brown bottle against it and held it up to Davey's nose and said, "Breathe deeply. Count to ten."

Davey did as she was told.

In that narcotised state she saw herself operated on: she hovered over her bed where her body was stretched out and watched the doctor and his wife work in silence, an observer to all that occurred to her corporeal self. The doctor gently pulled on the knife, paused and looked at Davey and then Fumiko before teasing it out slowly, and Fumiko staunched the wound with white cloths. The blood seeped through and they cleaned the wound and staunched it again, and stitched it. They turned to Davey's abdomen. The doctor passed a small blade across her belly and sliced her open and pulled a tangle of bloodied limbs from her body and lifted it up in the light that shined in the room. The doctor wiped mucus from the silent infant's mouth and nostrils and the infant began to cry and the doctor's and Fumiko's eyes were moist above their mouth masks. The doctor held up the infant, its male sex a nub in a blotched red corpus, and handed it to Fumiko who placed it on Davey's chest and the infant curled against Davey, and she looked at his closed eyes and wrapped her arms around him and held him close, kissed the damp down of his elongated head, inhaling the scent of the gummy white vernix coating his skin, and she kissed him again and rested her lips against his head breathing in his amniotic musk, his body tight, his hands clenched and elbows and hips and legs flexed against her body, his toes curled pink, taking in and releasing his breath rapidly, and she held him back to study his puffy face, the flattened ears and nose, and she wiped the blood and sticky white from it and the infant opened his eyes, crossed and bluish-grey, and she stared into them and smiled and kissed his forehead, taking in his scent in deep breaths. Fumiko placed her hands over Davey's, picked the infant up and left the room. Davey tried to cry out, but no sound issued forth and then all went black. She woke to the surgeon passing long strands of catgut through her abdomen with a needle and when she woke again she was alone, the room dark, a faint voice floated in from afar, and then all went black.

In that narcotised dream Will looked down at her and his eyes were dark but gentle and he reached for her hand and then he was no longer there but Deacon stood before her whispering the story of Jonah and then Bulah appeared, her face soft and cleanly scrubbed and her eyes, too, were wet and then she was no longer there and then Reverend Brown smiled down at her and spoke in a low voice, words she could not make out but the intention was etched in his facial scar and then he was no longer there but another man was and this other man she could never see in his entirety but his coat was blood-red with shiny gold buttons and epaulettes and he smiled down at her and then all was black again.

A vendor hawking wares in the street. Dogs barking. A child crying. The slam of a door. Davey opened her eyes. Her shoulder and abdomen were wrapped in gauze, blood leeching through, and her arm rested against her chest in a sling. Her mouth was dry and her lips stuck together. She ran her tongue over them, tried to muster moisture where none was to be had. Fumiko came with a small pail of water. She dunked a sponge in the bucket and pressed it against Davey's lips and Davey sucked on it. She held a few strands of her hair and inhaled the scent of her infant.

"I want to see my boy." Davey's voice was hoarse and sounded far away.

Fumiko left the room.

The doctor entered and told her she had been brave and strong and that this pain would pass and that she'd be on her own in due time.

"Where's my boy?"

The surgeon considered Davey's question. "I'm afraid I'm not at liberty to discuss that with you."

"Is he here?"

He shook his head.

Davey lifted herself off the bed, grabbed the doctor by his collar and pulled him close. "Where is he?"

He tried to pull himself free.

"Who took my boy?"

"A holy man."

Davey fell back to the bed and cried out; the pain in her abdomen was sharp, radiating throughout her body.

"I'm sorry. He gave me no choice. He threatened Fumiko's life."

"What kind of holy man threatens another person's life?" She turned her head and stared at the wall. "He's not a servant of god. He's a murderer and a thief."

That evening she lay her hair down over her shoulders and rested her face against it, breathing deeply. She rose and held a hand against the pain in her abdomen. Picked up the banknotes Jack Smith had left her and stuffed them into her sling. She went through the streets and paid for a cot in a bunkhouse by the week and spent her days prostrate in the musty damp, running her fingertips over the nubbled tracks of sutures across her belly. After a week she held the tip of her knife over a flame, wiped the blade and methodically sliced and yanked out the strips of catgut from her shoulder. She cleaned away the pinpricks of blood and then pulled the sutures from her stomach. Rested her palm on her wound. It was raised and corrugated with small bumps of hard, gnarled flesh. She held her hair up to her nose. The smell of the infant was faint. It was there and then it wasn't. She went out and walked along the riverfront where she found Lenora Bell waddling up the boardwalk toward the brothel. Her stomach extended beyond her dress, as if she were concealing a basket of bread. When Davey asked about Jack Smith, Lenora Bell told her she hadn't seen or heard from him in a few days. "That man can't make up his mind on a thing any more than a scared rabbit darting about in a meadow."

"He's a good man," Davey said. "They seem to be in short supply anywhere I've been."

Lenora Bell massaged her stomach. "Being good ain't a destination. It's every step along the way."

"I am grateful for all that you and he have done for me." Davey tipped her hat and walked to the village. Lenora Bell held her belly, her face wet in the dark night.

───────────

Davey searched the village for her son and asked every man, woman and child she encountered whether they had seen the reverend. She described him, the scar on his face, his hair, his cassock, but no one had seen the man or her infant.

That autumn, Davey found another cot in a larger bunkhouse down the boardwalk from the cannery, she and forty men from countries she had never known existed. Every day she stood on the shoreline for hours. She saw white-headed eagles soaring with wingspans that dwarfed all lesser birds, and the gulls that shrieked underneath were more like swallows. She saw snow geese blanche the sky in long V-shaped pearl strands, chattering raucously on the shoreline slick with soft pellets of their green slime droppings.

In November, she passed Fumiko in the street who inquired after her health. Fumiko pointed to the bible against Davey's waistband and asked what her favourite passage was and Davey replied that the book had been gifted to her and she only knew one passage. She repeated the words from memory: "People who worship worthless idols forfeit the grace that could be theirs." Fumiko smiled and asked where she was staying.

The next night and every night at the same time, by dim candlelight, Fumiko came to Davey's bunkhouse and taught her the letters of the alphabet and the direction the lines of text flowed. She was gentle in her instruction and generous in her praise and soon Davey learned to decipher the words and pronounce each one in a halting tongue, practising into the late hours of the night when she was alone.

Throughout the winter Davey worked shifts in the cannery, mopping up slop and dumping buckets of fish entrails at the shoreline. She worked side by side with an old woman and at the end of shift on a dark, rainy day, the old woman offered Davey a small knife. She told Davey that she had heard about a redcoat who had been garrotted near the cannery, that no man had been charged with the murder. She said that a woman needed to take care of her own being if the men were unable to follow the law.

Davey left the bunkhouse each day at first light to work and when she was done work, she spent her time searching for her son. Every night she returned to the bunkhouse late when the other men were sleeping. One night, a large man waited for her at the entrance, grabbed her by the neck and showed her to the rear of the premises where there was no light. He threw her to the ground and lowered himself to his knees. Davey raised her knife and bludgeoned him in the shoulder and thigh, then rolled away and left him cussing in the dark. She quit the bunkhouse that night to sleep beneath the dock where boats creaked in the harbour and vermin skittered and squealed over the sand and algae-slicked logs.

The next day, she stopped at the doctor's office and asked for her belongings. He returned a few minutes later and held her bow and quiver.

"Where will you go?" he said.

"Have you seen my boy?"

The doctor shook his head.

"Where did that man take my boy?"

"I'm sorry," the doctor said. "I know as little as you do."

Davey told him it was all right, that she understood the choice he had made. She thanked him for the care he had given her.

"There are not many men or women made like you," the doctor said. "I won't ever forget you." He dug his hands into his pockets and handed her a small stack of banknotes. "Take this. The redcoat wanted you to have it when you returned."

"The redcoat?"

The doctor nodded. "He said for you to take every precaution wherever you go."

Davey instructed him to give the money to Fumiko and left.

———————

In the spring, she went to the livery, bought a horse and tack and trotted out of the village, eastward. She rode through the summer and fall, moving from one camp to another, inquiring about her boy, staying for weeks at a time before moving on. She found work with outfitters and stayed on with them long enough to know it when it was time to leave and carry on alone. In winter, she fashioned webbed snowshoes from crudely carved cedar branches strung with the sinew of rabbits and deer that she had shot. She led her pony and traversed the snowy landscape while avalanches thundered down the sides of mountains, leaving a hoary cloak on the firs whose limbs already bent beneath the weight of snow. Over the years, in the camps where she temporarily settled and from other outfitters she intermittently encountered while criss-crossing the country, she learned that a revolution had begun in Mexico and Halley's Comet had been observed photographically for the first time and the RMS *Titanic* had sunk. An archduke and his wife were assassinated and a worldwide war had begun. She met outfitters who told her the war had ended and that influenza had wiped out millions, and in those uncertain times she heard from incredulous men that there were talking picture shows, but did not meet a man who had seen one.

In a quiet patch of forest in eastern Quebec, she crossed paths with a man sitting on the ground against a maple tree with a rifle facing him, the barrel up against the underside of his chin. His feet were splayed in front of him with a rope on the toe of his left boot affixed to the trigger. The man shuffled his feet but the rope kept slipping from the boot and he lay in the dirt weeping. In northern Ontario, she came across another man sitting on a decrepit horse beneath a tree in the woods. The man had tied a noose over his neck and looped the rope over a tree branch above him. She came upon him as he was beating his horse but the horse wouldn't budge. Davey rode up and cut the rope without a word and carried on. On the prairies, a level plain of land that stretched to all four corners of the world, an immense boulder rested, a solitary die on a croupier's velvet tabletop, forgotten by its bettor. Twelve or fifteen feet tall, smooth as the hide on her pony. The top was flat and wide; a deep trench surrounded the rock where thousands of buffalo hoofprints scored the ground as the animals had rubbed their bristly, shaggy sides against the boulder, now worn smooth from the chafing, a chunk of polished stone. Several rows of the dead lay on the top of this rock beyond the reach of the wolves and prey. The remains of a small child had fallen and lay at the base of the boulder, wrapped in an old blanket like a discarded doll.

TWENTY-SEVEN

IN MAY 1927, when she was forty years old, Davey was hired on the west coast to guide a small party through the wilderness. They set out on the trail east from Steveston on a warm day. The group made good time along the valley bottom and they camped near a river swollen from the runoff. Davey lay against a tree upstream from the party. Late in the evening the trail boss crept up behind her, but she was awake and pointed her bow at him, the string drawn with an arrow notched.

"Thought you might need some tending to," the trail boss said.

"You ain't had a single good thought yet," she said.

He slipped back into the darkness and returned to the others. She lay awake until just before daybreak, loaded her horse and set off on her own.

She stayed to the high country and followed the river eastward and travelled during the days and had fireless camps at night high up and away from the river.

On the outskirts of a village she passed a tent that was erected, yellow candlelight illumining its canvas walls. A small procession of pilgrims trundled past, led by two boys and one girl. The boys held a cross between them and the girl followed, singing in a sweet voice. A procession of villagers trailed the children and six men carried a long, wooden box. They entered the tent. Davey rode on.

Davey spent the night beneath a wind-scrubbed tree. At dawn she stood facing east where the light broke and then she saddled her horse and moved on. By mid-morning black clouds darkened the horizon and thin fingers of lightning jabbed the land. In the distance, smoke gathered in thick columns.

The heat of the day reverberated off the granite around her. The smoke was thicker now and Davey tasted charcoal and creosote with each breath. She coughed; her lungs were parched. Her eyes stung as she squinted into the distance. Grey ash fell lazily from above. Ravens flew against the leaden sky, the sound of their wings flapping through particulate. Her horse began to toss its head and soon it would not go and stood frothing and breathing heavily. Davey climbed down. The clouds were upon her, the wind had picked up and the land before her was scorched and smoking from where the lightning had torched a path of blackened debris. She ripped a piece of cloth from her shirt-tails, covered her nose and mouth. The smoke grew thicker. Her throat was raw, her eyes watered, her cough constant. She found a draw with a small stream and leaned into it for relief. Led the horse under the shade of the rock wall, hobbled it and moved along the rock, down the slope. Removed a blanket from her saddle, placed it over the pony's face, and the two of them spent the night wheezing and coughing.

In the morning the smoke had thinned but she rode with her face covered. The land was charred and hissed, branchless trees burned like broken spears. She came across a lone homestead. The small shack had been decimated by the fire and burned weakly. She circled the property, rode to a depression where smoke rose from the ground and climbed down from her pony. The well was shallow and smouldering, and in the boiling water lay a woman, a man and their small son, curled among each other. Davey studied them for a sign of movement but they were badly scalded and blistered and did not breathe. She tested the water, placing her palm just above the surface, but it was too hot to remove the bodies. Alone, by the smoking home reduced to ash, a young girl knelt in a faded long dress with her eyes fixed upon Davey.

Davey crossed the scorched land and stood before the girl. She was very young. Dirt had collected in the folds of her clothing; her face was blackened with soot, as if the land had scrubbed itself into her. Davey knelt on one knee. "Are you all right?"

The girl stared at her.

"Is there anyone else?"

The girl shook her head.

Davey opened her canteen and offered it to her. The girl reached out with her small, grimy hands, tipped it back and drank until the water spilled over her mouth and chin. She coughed and wiped her face. Davey nodded and she drank again.

Davey told her she had come from the coast and that she was headed back to the place of her birth and that she had a son that had been taken from her and that she had spent her life searching for him, that it comforted her to know he was in the world somewhere and she hoped he was doing good, for the world needed more good men. She told the girl that the world needed many more good people, for she believed that the good could outnumber those that were not and that the world could be a worthy place for one to live in. "I can still smell him sometimes," Davey said, lifting a palmful of hair and dropping it on her shoulder.

Davey touched the girl's arm; the girl shook her head. Davey withdrew her hand and the girl seized it and pulled herself into Davey's chest and held herself tightly there, breathing fast and shallow, her body shedding ash and soot against Davey's garments. She pulled away and looked into Davey's eyes for a long moment before thrusting herself against Davey's chest. Davey held her close and rocked her gently. "What's your name?"

The girl didn't respond.

"Can I call you Grace?"

The girl's breathing quieted. She nodded against Davey's chest. "It's a pleasure to make your acquaintance, Grace."

––––––––––

In the early autumn Davey rode onto the Tobacco Plains with Grace clinging to her waist from behind. Grace had not spoken and Davey had accepted the silence of the land and the girl's breathing against her as a comfort.

They crossed the shallow waters of St. Mary's and then the Kootenay on a cold morning. The sky was blue and larch needles rained gold all around them as they rode through a forest dappled in colour. At dusk they came upon two old men sitting next to a low fire. A pot hung from a tripod over the flames. They were dressed in filthy garments and from a few yards away, they reeked of woodsmoke, carrion and liquor. One of the men stood when they approached and waved at Davey and Grace. The other man had his head down, sharpening his knife against a whetstone, spitting on it and sliding his knife over the stone. The man who stood grinned. He had no teeth.

"Evening," he said. "Some coffee?"

Davey declined his offer.

The other man paused from sharpening his knife and raised his head. "There's plenty enough to share between the four of us."

The man without teeth grabbed two cups from his bedroll and scooped coffee out of the pot and handed the cups to Davey. She took them and held one out to Grace but the girl shook her head. The old man laughed. Davey handed him one of the cups and kept the other for herself.

"Where you headed?" the old man asked.

"Nowhere special," Davey said.

The other man lifted his head, spat on the whetstone, and ran his knife over it. He told them of how the land here was once blackened with coal deposits as far as the eye could see. He spoke of how the forests were once thick with trees and that any clearings or meadows were natural occurrences and he spoke of the fish in the rivers, so many fish that climbed and wriggled over one another, the water teeming with them, flashing like white bands of treasure.

He spoke of the massacre here and how a man who had posed as a man of god had reneged on his promise to the loggermen camped nearby, that his perversions and heinous crimes against their children resulted in the gruesome deaths of his followers. He spoke of a man named Will who built the mine near Bull Head and how he was the origin of all troubles that plagued the area. All good people, he said, caught up in the abominable actions of one man. He paused from working his knife on the stone. "What kind of world exists where god allows this?" He glanced at Grace, lowered his head and swept his hand over his eyes. "God's children did this." He shook his head and stared into the fire. "They ain't men of god. They're nothing but thieves and cowards." He resumed sharpening his knife.

Davey asked if he had met Deacon. The old man considered her question. "There's a man over in Bull Head"—he thumbed eastward— "preaching to beat the band. Maybe that's your man?"

"Is he a good man?"

The old man chuckled low. "I suppose it depends on your definition of good. I've only heard stories. It's hard to know what to believe. Never met the man myself."

The other man jabbed a stick in the fire and jostled the logs. Orange sparks rose in the dark sky and faded.

"Tell you the truth," the old man said. "I don't want to meet a man whose reputation precedes him. Ain't no man can live up to that."

He pointed his knife at the bridge that spanned the river where the loggerman operation had once resided. "First, the bison. Then gold. And coal." He was silent a long while. "Now all they're hauling out of here is timber and animal pelts, killing every animal that ever walked, swam or flew. Getting the trees down as fast as they can and cartin' all of it elsewhere. Ain't going to be nothing and nobody left but the men who brought this on themselves. And then what?"

Davey and Grace parted ways from the old men and rode for three days in a country as familiar as Davey's hand. The land appeared rusted, the trees large and viridian green, haunted by crows and whisky jacks and coyotes that yelped. Grace fell asleep and jostled against Davey's back. In the distance a sporadic stream of cars trickled to the northeast, gleaming like humped metal beasts.

The next day, Davey held out her bow and arrow and told Grace that Bulah had gifted them to her because Bulah had never carried any arms herself but that she wanted Davey to be able to protect herself if she couldn't do so. "Would you like to learn how to use this?"

Grace nodded gravely.

Davey told her to hold up the bow and close her right eye. Grace did as she was instructed. Davey asked her to open her right eye and close her left. "Which one can you see better with?"

The girl pointed to her right eye.

"Hold the bow in your left hand and stand like this." Davey encouraged her to take a stance with her left foot in front of her right and bend her knees slightly.

Grace did as she was told. Davey showed her how to put her legs two feet apart and square her hips. She handed the girl an arrow. "Point your bow toward the ground and nock your arrow."

Grace clicked the nock at the end of the arrow into the bowstring.

"Raise it and take aim on that tree. Good. Relax your grip on the bow. Keep your shoulders soft. Draw the string and arrow back and slow your breath. Take your time. That's it. On the exhale, release the arrow."

The arrow shot through the air and landed in the dirt beyond the tree. The girl turned to Davey and smiled. Davey laughed. She handed Grace another arrow. "You'll hit that tree before we head out today."

An hour later, Davey and Grace rode northeast in a splatter of sunlight and circumvented Bull Head in the night. They rode north of the road that cut through the valley. Car lights flashed and faded south of them. The valley appeared wider but after a while, when the stars came out and the moon rose, Davey noted the valley was the same but that the flanks of the mountains had large bare patches. They rode the night down and headed over the Pass into Alberta. In the late afternoon they entered Crowsnest and stopped at a lake where they made camp. Their fire twisted and turned in the wind, whipping off the lake, and the embers scattered into the air with the stars. Davey and Grace moved around the fire, for the wind changed and it seemed as if wherever they moved the smoke from the coals caused them to cough and their eyes to tear up.

"I forgot how horrible this wind was," Davey said. "Gets up inside you and rattles your bones."

Grace wore Davey's coat and a blanket around her shoulders and still she shivered despite Davey holding her close. She pointed to the sack on Davey's waist. Davey told her the story of Bulah, of how she saved Davey's life from her first breath and how she protected her until the last day of her own life. Grace reached for the sack and held it in her small palm.

"All those memories, a life reduced to ashes. It's heavier than you think, isn't it?" Davey said.

In the morning Davey told Grace they would leave on account of the wind and they travelled back in the direction they had come from the day previous. They rode down the day and crossed at the Pass, staying high above Summit Lake and carrying on until they reached the bottom of the valley they had passed through the night before in the dark. The sun was still up but the wind had petered out and by twilight they walked side by side with their horse through Hosmer. In the long red dusk, random headlights from cars headed west along a black belt of road cradled on the low valley bottom before them. Grace motioned that she was tired and hungry.

They entered Bull Head at dark and walked to the side of the road as more cars passed; shop fronts were lit and there were people strolling along the roads. Grace's eyes were bright and she smiled at the sights of town. Women and men walked arm in arm. Children sprinted after each other. Roasted meat and scorched sugar on the air. Bright lights over the church grounds farther ahead. Cars moved slowly up the street, windows rolled down. They were filled with people and these people smiled and pointed out the sights to one another and sometimes they called out to Davey and Grace, and when Davey lifted her head, they laughed and continued on.

Davey and Grace passed a stall before the lamplit stables and the horse nickered and snuffled shyly at the hocks of other animals standing there. They went on. Lean dogs crossed before them. Fiddle music floated into the street and Grace clapped her hands and giggled.

Davey smiled. "You like music?"

Grace nodded her head and clapped again.

Near the western edge of town, they led their horse to a lamppost, tied it there and stepped up the low wooden stairs into the dim light that fell from the doorway. Davey stopped at the desk and asked the clerk for a room. He was an old bald man with tufts of thin white hair on the side of his head and he wore a patch over his right eye. The clerk placed his hands on the counter and raised himself on one leg. He regarded Davey and Grace as if they were antecedents in costume from a time long past. "You all here for the Chautauqua?" he rasped.

"The what?" Davey said.

The old clerk stopped writing in his ledger and stared at her. He cleared his throat and spat in a spittoon that he hauled up from beneath the counter.

Davey pulled a banknote from her pocket and laid it on the desktop.

He took the money and held it to the light before he slid it into a drawer and closed it. He handed her a key and pointed with the spittoon to the stairs. "Second door on the right. Number seven."

Davey led Grace up the staircase, unlocked the door and closed it behind them. Piano music and the voices of men floated up from the floorboards. They surveyed the room. Grace ran to the cot and jumped up and down on it.

Davey laughed. She handed her the bow and arrow and told her to stay put and shoot anyone who tried to come through the door and that she'd return soon with something to eat.

She went down the stairs, passed through the lobby and exited the building. There were drunks everywhere. A man slumped over at the side of the street cradling a bottle in his lap. One man stood urinating against the *Free Press* building. There were drunk men in pairs or threes, lying in the dirt between buildings. An old man rattled a tin cup he thrust at any passerby. A crowd stood in front of a small cage. An emaciated grizzly bear with dull eyes looked out. It appeared crushed by its surrounds, as if it could inhale deeply and that very act alone would suffice in snapping the prison in which it was held. "Someone should just put it out of its misery," a man said. Davey went back into the hotel, into the tavern.

The light was dim and tobacco smoke curled upward toward the oil lamp sconces on the walls. There was every manner of naked women with ribbons in their hair and rouge-painted faces sashaying between the tables, their bottoms and bellies and breasts bright red with welts from the men who slapped and pinched them.

Two boys and a young girl stood terrified in front of the patrons. A large cross leaned against the wall behind them. The younger boy grimaced as he moved his weight from foot to foot. A bald man clapped sharply, twice, and a short, stocky man weaved throughout the crowd hugging an accordion. Someone played the spoons. Men shouted and swore and spat onto the floor where their phlegm curled up like slugs in the sawdust. The bald man clapped twice again, but the younger boy stood in place, squeezing his privates. He looked as if he was trying for all he could not to cry. His face was twisted in a grimace. He shifted his weight from foot to foot. The bald man glared at him. The boy's trousers bloomed dark with urine. His eyes were damp; his lips trembled. The bald man clapped twice and the younger boy grabbed the cross from the wall and walked around the tavern holding it against his shoulder while the older boy followed behind him, his hands on the younger boy's shoulders as if he were marching him forward. The boy fell to his knees. A prostitute rushed over, wiped his face and helped him to his feet. The boy continued around the bar and fell a second time. Another prostitute helped him up. He stumbled around the bar and fell to his knees a third time. He lowered his head and said, "Father, help me." The older boy helped raise him up and both boys continued to circle the bar until the bald man clapped twice. They stopped. The younger boy slid the base of the cross into a bucket so it could stand on its own. Both boys fell to their knees and bowed before it several times. The bald man clapped twice and the girl stepped forward and sang an aria in a halting voice. "And I saw another mighty angel come down from heaven, clothed with a cloud: and a rainbow was upon his head, and his face was as it were the sun, and his feet as pillars of fire." The older boy reached for a burlap sack to the right of the stage and emptied its contents onto the stage. Both boys grabbed fistfuls of leaves, threw them at the cross and prostrated themselves while the girl sang on, "Hosanna! Hosanna! Hosanna!"

Davey made her way through the crowd to the bar. There were several boys working. One wiped down the tables, one swept the floor, another emptied spittoons.

"I ain't got all day, miss," the barman said.

"Some food."

"I've heard it called many things, miss, but that"—the barman laughed—"is something I've never heard from a lady." He set up a glass, uncorked a bottle, and poured two fingers' worth. "Five cents."

She pushed the glass toward him. "I need some food for me and my little one."

The barman shook his head. "We might have some flank steak and potatoes, maybe some beans."

"I'll take two portions of whatever you got." Davey dug into her pocket and held up a coin to ascertain its worth and slid the coin to the man.

"That'll cover the drink. Fifteen cents for the food."

Davey pulled a few more coins from her pocket and laid them on the bar top and pushed them toward the barman. "One for your trouble."

The barman scooped up the coins and left the whisky glass as it was poured. He called a boy who was wiping the tables, relayed Davey's order and the boy scampered off.

A man laughed in the corner of the tavern. He wore a black cassock with a bolo tie hanging on the outside of it. He held a fan of cards and studied them before removing two and tossing them onto the table, motioning for two more. These he picked up and slid into the ones he held in his hand. He tipped back a cedar crown and smiled. Two long scars formed a cross on his face. The others at the table spread their cards on the tabletop and he slapped his cards down, laughed and wrapped his arms around the banknotes, pulling them toward him, stacking them into neat piles.

"How long for the food?" Davey asked.

"Takes the time it takes," the barman said.

Davey handed him another coin. "I'd be grateful if you could hurry it along."

The barman tapped the coin on the bar top. He waved to the boy waiting by the kitchen.

"I won't be needing this."

The barman studied her for a moment. He lifted the glass. "To your eccentric noble nature." He knocked back the shot and cleared the bar top in front of her.

The young boy ran up holding two plates covered with faded red gingham towels.

She took a plate in each hand and turned to leave. The barman shook his head as he towelled a glass dry. An accordion groaned and the young girl singing arias hit a high note that rose above the rabble in the bar and held the note for a long while so that Davey held her breath before the girl's voice fell. The two boys were still prostrating themselves and tossing leaves at the base of the cross.

Davey made her way through the crowd carrying the plates. In the foyer a naked woman gyrated on a bearded man, he pinched at her pink flesh with hands blackened with soot from the coalfields. Davey walked up the stairs and stopped at a room with the door ajar. An older woman had taken off her drawers and peeled off her red stockings while examining herself in the mirror. Flesh sagged from her body; her stomach and breasts were etched with stretch marks. A lamp sat on the table and the room glowed. "Do you think I'm pretty?" the woman asked the man. She brushed her hair and smiled at Davey in the mirror, a crooked, sad smile.

Davey recognized her as Lenora Bell. "Do you want some assistance?"

"Assistance?" Lenora Bell regarded Davey through her reflection in the mirror. "Help is what people offer to make themselves feel better."

"You once saved my life," Davey said. "I'm forever indebted to you."

The man grunted for her to come to bed. Lenora Bell laid her stockings over the back of a chair and turned around in a slow pirouette, stopping with her back to Davey. Skin sagged loose from her shoulder blades and gathered in a plump pouch on her hips and spilled down into her buttocks. She brushed back her hair with her hands and let it fall down her back and brushed it out again.

Davey continued down the hall until she reached her room. Lenora Bell came out into the hallway holding a candle. She ran a hand through her hair. The man, shirtless, his belly drooping over the rim of his unbuttoned trousers, came up behind Lenora Bell and grabbed her wasted breasts, hanging like two socks, and kneaded them roughly.

"How's your boy?" Davey said.

Lenora Bell's lower lip trembled.

"He told me. The redcoat," Davey said.

Lenora Bell wiped her eyes. "That was a long time ago. Like it was all a dream."

The man raised his head from snuffling on her neck. "I'll be coming for you next. You stay put, you hear?" He pulled Lenora Bell into the room and kicked the door shut.

Davey listened to the squeak of the bed as the man laid down and called for Lenora Bell and a moment later, a slap and the sound of Lenora Bell's voice, crying out. Davey set down the plates to open the door. She picked them up and entered her room. Grace held the bow pulled back with an arrow aimed at Davey. When she realized it was Davey, she set the bow down. Davey closed the door with her boot heel.

After they had eaten, Davey told Grace that they needed to leave straightaway, that they would spend the night outside of town and continue their way westward and stay in the next town.

Grace pointed to the leather sack hanging off Davey's waist. Davey untied it, opened it and took out a bloodied piece of fabric, a finger's width of black hair tied together with a piece of twine, a soiled handkerchief with WF stencilled into a corner, the deposition Deacon had given to secure her freedom, Bulah's ashes, and a palmful of dirt. She laid these out on the floor. Grace glanced back and forth at the items and searched Davey's face.

"It's been a long while since I've seen these." Davey smiled and wiped at her eyes. She held up the fabric. "This was from my mother's sleeve."

Grace held the fabric and turned it over in her hands and set it down.

"This is my mother's hair." Davey held it up to her nose and inhaled. She handed it to Grace.

Grace took the hair and smelled it and made a face.

"It smells musty, doesn't it?"

Grace nodded and set the hair down.

"This was my father's. It was found on my mother's body."

Grace didn't reach for the handkerchief but nodded slowly.

"These are the ashes of the woman who was my guardian for fourteen years."

Grace felt the weight of the cloth and returned it to Davey.

"This is a testament from a dear, holy man who saved my life."

Grace held the sheet of paper and studied it line by line, and when she was done reading, she returned it to Davey with a solemn expression on her face.

Davey picked up the dirt and spread it in her palm and held her palm out to Grace. "This is the earth from where my mother took her last breath."

Grace put a fingertip into the dirt and levelled it in Davey's palm.

Davey held the dirt out and nodded to the sleeve, the handkerchief, deposition, Bulah's ashes and the hair on the floor. "Bulah was afraid that I would forget who I was as a child, so she kept a memory sack for me and filled it with small things that she knew would help define who I was, where I came from and who my people were. Things

I could look back on and think, *I remember*, even though I have no recollection of my childhood at all."

Davey paused and nodded at the sheet of paper. "I added that and this." She reached into the sack and held up three pieces of cloth. "These are from your people."

Grace's eyes were wet. She curled into Davey's chest and sobbed. Davey rested her chin on top of Grace's head.

"I bet she was a fine woman," Davey said. "I bet your mother was a fine woman." Davey kissed the top of Grace's head and put the dirt back into the sack. She picked up the hair, handkerchief, and sleeve and put those back into the sack, then the deposition, Bulah's ashes, and the three pieces of cloth. She tied the top tight.

Grace pointed to her waist.

"You sure?" Davey said.

Grace nodded.

Davey tied the sack to Grace's waist. They gathered their belongings, descended the stairs, passed through the lobby. The proprietor glanced up at them as they exited the hotel, then he returned to reading the newspaper spread out before him.

The air was cold, stars winked over the quiet earth: the land was covered in darkness, men were shut in their wall tents or stumbling forth from the saloon, laying in rancid-smelling brothels and on church pews, or out in the open, beneath a burnished sky where the stars scuffled overhead, each man with some form of light, and the dead, all those who had perished up and down the valley, awakened to sit in their dirt tombs, praying about the life they had lived and the life they were not afforded to live. Davey stood, the great night swimming around her, in her, night on top of night. Those lights below, above, and that cold in the darkness, that thin icicle of a moon in the sky—they didn't belong to one night alone, they were infinite; and she considered the nights of

Bulah, the nights of Deacon, the nights of her mother, the nights of her father, the nights of her grandfather, and the nights of a family she had never known, each naked in their own dignity, defenceless, humiliated as only the living can know when night falls upon them. But did that make her any less of a woman than one who had known her people, or one who had not, or one whom the dead claimed as their own?

Davey and Grace went down the walk boards. Grace pointed up at the sky rippling with waves of colour that changed from moment to moment, undulating in streaks.

"Head straight over there, toward the river," Davey said. "I'll be along in a second."

Grace shook her head. Davey held her shoulders. "I won't be long." She ushered her ahead. Grace walked forward and looked back to see Davey encouraging her to continue on. When Grace was no longer looking back, Davey strode to the cage where the grizzly bear sat.

She unclasped the cage and swung open the door. "Go on," she said. "Go home."

The bear backed into the corner of the cage and grunted.

Men shot their guns into the air. The sound of drumming rose from way off. Three men urinated off the walk boards into the mud of the street.

Davey rattled the side of the cage and the bear grunted again. She shook the cage and slapped the bars. The bear lunged forward, barrelled down the street and continued to the end, where it slowed and then limped into the woods.

On the riverbank, Davey and Grace stared at the stars, the sounds of town muffled behind them. The sky pulsed with incandescent flares of green, gold and red on the horizon. Grace leaned against Davey.

"It's as if there are others, sitting around a fire, warm, content," Davey said. "I wonder if there's others out there."

Grace let out a small giggle and ran along the shore, picked up pebbles and flung them into the water. Across the river a fire flickered. Davey peered into the darkness and made out the face of a man and a woman. Smoke rose from the fire. The scent of fish grilling. Grace cried out behind her.

Davey turned. Reverend Brown stood with his hand on Grace's shoulder. She tried to run toward Davey but the reverend's grip held her in place. She wriggled in his clutch and whimpered. His grey, kinked hair spiralled through the crown above his head. The scar that crossed his faced was a deep purple and appeared larger than Davey had remembered. She detected pipe smoke on his breath.

"Well, well, well. Here we are again," he said. "Reunited."

Davey stepped away from the river, glanced back at the fire and turned to the reverend. "Let her be."

"You had no authority to let Lazarus escape. He was bound to me. I was bound to him."

"Let the girl go."

"You must cleanse yourself of your sins, of your origins. Of your actions. A long chain of bloody events that you have continued from your father. You have never wiped the stain of your birth, the curse you have promulgated." He held out his hand.

"Leave her be."

"Consequences, lass, consequences."

"That so-called curse is a lie. Everything you've ever uttered is a lie. Where's my boy?"

Reverend Brown smiled. "If it is a lie, then all of these men and women have no reason to be here. And yet they are indeed here."

"I'm asking a simple question."

"The real question is, why are you here?" He swept his arms outward. "You've come home. We've all been drawn to this place like metal to magnet. You and I shared the experience of what happened many years ago. We're bound by history, bound by place, bound by people.

And now bound by the transgression you've just committed in letting Lazarus go." He smiled, his teeth shining.

"Tell me where my boy is."

"Or what?" Reverend Brown chuckled. "Indeed, or what? The land nor any man will do as you wish. All those men in the saloon cannot cut down enough trees. They cannot dig enough coal. They cannot pan for enough gold. They cannot own enough of the very land that breaks them every day. These men are little more than husks of themselves, hardly fit to house the human spirit at all."

"Where's my boy?"

"Our boy. Note the distinction. You don't hold sole proprietor rights. Our boy. A man seeks his own home," he said. "Each man's providence is only as large as the world he inhabits, all that he has seen."

"You've never made any sense."

Reverend Brown smiled benignly. "It's elemental, lass. All of it. The water, the fire, the sticks that fuel it, the stars that burn overhead. All witnesses. All a mystery."

A fish flashed in the dark above the water, landed. Another fish broke the surface.

He smiled and offered his hand. "Come."

Across the river, the young man and woman rose and made their way to their tent. The man held the canvas flap open for the woman, who lowered her head and entered. He looked out across the river at Davey, waved and called out, "Good evening." He looked as if he was in his early twenties. He pointed up at the flickering lights. "Beautiful night, isn't it?" He studied the sky for a moment and then entered the tent and closed the flap. The fire had dwindled but twisted in the night breeze.

Davey faced Reverend Brown. "Leave her be. You can have me. You have my word."

Reverend Brown smiled. "It's not your decision to make. Let the girl decide." He held the girl by both wrists, turned her to face him and crouched down. "What do you want?"

Grace shook her head.

"Speak, girl."

She shook her head.

"How can anyone, least of all yourself, know what you think if you don't speak?"

Grace wriggled against the reverend's grip. He pulled her closer, turned her and laid his palm across her chest. He smiled at Davey.

Davey lifted her bow, drew an arrow and notched it. "Leave her be."

"You'll not do it, lass. It's all a false pretense. We both know that." He removed his hand and nudged Grace forward. She ran to Davey and held her. Davey asked if she was all right and Grace nodded. She asked again and Grace nodded. "Go on back to the hotel. I won't be long, you hear?"

Grace shook her head and clung to Davey's waist. Behind them in town, men shouted and cheered at something; gunshot ripped through the air. She covered her ears.

"Can you hold these for me?" Davey handed her the bow, arrow and quiver. "Go on, I'll be right behind you."

Grace shook her head.

"I'll get you a piece of pie if you go on now." Davey nodded toward town. "Go." Grace wandered a few feet away along the shoreline. To the north, the sky pulsed and flared in waves of green, white and pink. The quarter moon was up and shone on the shoals downriver.

Davey turned to Reverend Brown.

He smiled and offered his hand. "A man, or woman, is only as good as their word."

"I don't owe you anything."

"Reneging on your word." Reverend Brown grabbed her and seized her wrist. "You're still as predictable as a child."

"Let go of me."

Reverend Brown laughed. "You gave your word." He pulled her toward the river and entered it, stumbling on the slick rocks. Water seeped through Davey's boots. Her feet sought purchase on the river rock and her legs trembled. The fish continued to jump and flash around them in the moonlight. Reverend Brown stumbled twice, fell against Davey and righted himself. Davey's knees buckled against the current in the shallows.

"One more step," Reverend Brown said.

The current in the middle of the river moved swiftly. Here, the water ran over her waist and it was much stronger. She spread her feet apart to brace herself. "Where's my boy?"

"Fall back, lass."

"Where is he?" Davey removed her hat and placed it against her chest.

"Our boy is out there making a place for himself. Somewhere."

"You abandoned him."

Reverend Brown smiled. "We're all orphans, utterly alone, aren't we?" He held her hand and placed his other hand on the middle of her back. "Now, fall back."

She faltered and leaned into his hand. He tottered, the current rushing against his waist, dragging him. He shifted his feet. "You should have protected him," Davey said. She turned to Grace on the shoreline. Her face was troubled. Davey mouthed, "It's okay." Grace shook her head. Davey repeated her words, nodded and dropped backward into Reverend Brown's hand. She looked up into the scar that split his face into four sections, each separate, each that contributed to the whole. Cold water against her back, then her head and into her ears. Reverend Brown spoke. She studied his lips but could not discern what he was saying. He stopped and smiled again. Her hair swirled in the river. The sky flared green and white and red and the current tugged at them. Reverend Brown hauled her up. Two ducks flew low over them and landed on the river upstream. He said something, a cuss perhaps. He struggled to gain footing in the river and tried to let go of her but Davey jerked him closer. The current tore them downstream. He thrashed in the water beside her. Davey gripped his hand, flailed and tried to raise her mouth and nose above the water but Reverend Brown held her tight as he sought purchase with his feet. She dug her nails into his wrist. They both rose above the surface.

"You should have done everything in your power to protect him," Davey gasped, spitting out water.

He pushed her face down into the water but she held him fiercely. "Who's going to protect the girl when I'm done with you?" he said.

They thrashed against one another, drifting downstream. Grace hurried along the bank, hair lit by the glow of the sky, eyes ablaze, knees lifting. Water rushed into Davey's mouth and ears. Aurora borealis shimmered above her. She struggled to lift herself but Reverend Brown's weight drew her down. She punched him, wriggled and rose above the water, coughing. Grace's mouth was open, her eyes terrified.

Davey flailed and was pulled under again, then shot her head above the water, gasping, spitting, sucking at the air.

"Momma!" Grace screamed.

Reverend Brown wrapped his arms around Davey as he tried to rise to the surface. She twisted against him but he clutched her tight. Grace sprinted, framed against the dark land the large lit sky, waved her arms to the couple across the river. "My momma, my momma!" The man stood outside his tent and called to Grace. The woman crawled out of the tent and pointed to Davey and the reverend thrashing in the water. A bend in the river. The sky flared red and green and yellow and white, an incandescent pulse.

Davey gripped Reverend Brown's arms tighter and seized him as he flailed against her. A wash of water flooded her lungs, the world around her slowed.

Across the river, the young man leapt into the water and swam toward the bend, but there was no sign of them. He circled and waded toward Grace, drew near the bank where she stood crying. Grace turned and sprinted toward the hotel. The young man and the woman called after her.

Grace bursts through the doors and rushes into the tavern. The older boy has joined the accordionist and he keeps the measure of the music with a pair of spoons, which he claps between his knees while the boy in soiled pants sings off key, hands cupped over his privates. Men play cards at round tables, tobacco smoke blues the air above them.

Two women laugh with the bartender. Grace runs to them and stops. She pants, forehead sweating, and leans over her knees to catch her breath. She lifts her face, her eyes wet and terrified.

The women smile.

"Well, what is it? State your claim," the bartender says. "Speak, child."

The door to the tavern swings open. The young man from the river, drenched, water dripping onto the floor. He runs to her. Grace turns to the barman.

"Quit playing games, child. Speak or forever hold your peace," he says.

An old loggerman bellows, raises his hands above the keyboard and the bar is quiet for a brief instant. He grins and slams his hands down and begins to play the piano. Men and women hoot and holler, laughing like there will be no tomorrow. Floorboards rise and fall under stomping boots. The loggerman nods to the boy who sings a new aria that has no rhythm or pitch, but he sings as if his life depends on it. The loggerman starts slow and steady and then increases his time, bows to the accordionist who keeps pace, bows to the older boy playing the spoons, bows to the whores seeking out any man in want of company. And he bows to Lenora Bell descending the stairs, each step in time with the music. She holds a garish feathered hat to her head, passes beneath the lamps where a man grabs and swings her about, and then she tosses her hat across the tavern and turns around the room. The piano tinkles, the accordion heaves, the spoons clatter, lights blur, the boy's voice sings. The hat floats through the air and is caught by the barman. Lenora Bell's head tips back in a full-throated laugh.

Grace shifts the quiver on her shoulder and opens her mouth. The barman listens carefully, flings the hat to the ground, nods his head, and yells instructions to several men, who rush out of the tavern and race to the river. The young man reaches Grace and tells her that they will help find her mother, that she is safe. Grace nods, her hands protecting the small sack around her waist.

Around and around Lenora Bell turns, swinging from anonymous man to anonymous man, each one laughing and clapping his hands, reaching for her, she who is spinning and spinning, hurtling around the room. In the water, past the river's bend, Davey yanks the reverend down in one final heave, his cassock in her fists, away from the surface, away from Grace, and all goes dark, the world falls silent, and water, water, and forever dark, silent, forever silent, amen.

ACKNOWLEDGMENTS

I am profoundly indebted to my wife, Nancy Lee, for her support, wise counsel and the vast space she provided for me to quietly work on this book over the years. One of the many benefits in sharing a life with an extraordinary woman/writer/teacher and life artist whom I deeply admire is that patience and silence and relentless inquiry are vital to unlocking the myriad problems that multiply, rather than diminish, when writing a book. This novel is for her.

Heartfelt thanks to Brian Lam, my Canadian editor and publisher, and Francis Geffard, my French editor and publisher, for their unwavering belief and support in me and in my work.

Thank you to the amazing team at Arsenal Pulp Press: Robert Ballantyne, Alison Strobel, Linda Pruessen, Catharine Chen, Jazmin Welch, Cynara Geissler and Jaiden Dembo. They do their work with such care, respect and generosity. It's a privilege to be part of their creative community.

For invaluable assistance, I am grateful to: Adam Honsinger, Nancy Lee, Denise Ryan and Calvin Wharton—rigorous, perceptive readers. My squad, the indomitable Lyin' Bastards: Sally Breen, Dina Del Bucchia, Keri Korteling, Nancy Lee, Judy McFarlane, Denise Ryan and Carol Shaben for their challenging questions, astute observations and unflagging encouragement. Dave Gaertner for an early sensitivity read and thought-provoking conversation. Marita Dachsel, Jennica Harper, Laisha Rosnau for weighing in on the cover. Alivia Maric for her infinite wisdom and ways of seeing.

Thank you to the UBC School of Creative Writing, and a special shout-out to my students for inspiring me to be more alert as a writer and teacher through their bold, creative risks, thoughtful questions and infectious enthusiasm.

Although this a work of fiction where many liberties have been taken, some of the texts and sources that provided historical perspectives include: *Backtracking* (with the Fernie & District Historical Society); the colourful anecdotes and stories of Sydney Hutcheson; *A World Apart: The Crowsnest Communities of Alberta and British Columbia*, edited by Wayne Norton and Tom Langford; *Crowsnest: An Illustrated History and Guide to the Crowsnest Pass* by John Brian Dawson; *Crowsnest and Its People* by the Crowsnest Pass Historical Society; the Holy Bible, King James Version; *The Complete Signet Classic Shakespeare*, edited by Sylvan Barnet; the Gulf of Georgia Cannery; the Steveston Historical Society; the Fernie Museum and their helpful staff. A special thank-you to the incredible staff at the Ktunaxa Interpretive Centre at the St. Eugene Mission. Any errors or artistic liberties that remain, are, of course, my own.

A final note of gratitude to my family and their forebears who immigrated to Canada in the early 1900s to set up their lives in southwestern Alberta, a rugged, unforgiving landscape that tested their resolve and spirit and from which they built their own lives. I've always been riveted by their tragic and often comedic stories, stories that never grew tiresome for they, like good family yarns, gathered additional details over the decades as they passed from generation to generation, giving shape and meaning to each of us.